14.53

BRIAN WIPRUD

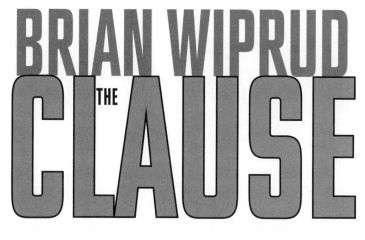

THE CLAUSE

FIVE ENEMIES, ONE MAN, ZERO OPTIONS

MIDNIGHT INK
WOODBURY, MINNESOTA

FIRST EDITION
First Printing, 2012

Book design by Donna Burch
Cover design by Kevin R. Brown
Cover art: Motorbike: iStockphoto.com/narvikk
    Dark alleyway: iStockphoto.com/Denis Jr. Tangney
    Mafia: iStockphoto.com/Nebojsa Bobic
    Somebody in the city: iStockphoto.com/tunart
    Man in black leather jacket: iStockphoto.com/Michelle Gibson
    Ruthless: iStockphoto.com/Chris Schmidt
Cover illustration: Steven McAfee
Editing by Brett Fechheimer
Interior image—Eagle: iStockphoto.com/PixelEmbargo

Midnight Ink, an imprint of Llewellyn Worldwide Ltd.

Library of Congress Cataloging-in-Publication Data
Wiprud, Brian M.
 The clause / Brian Wiprud. — 1st ed.
  p. cm.
 ISBN 978-0-7387-3416-3
1. Jewel thieves—Fiction. 2. Veterans—Fiction. I. Title.
 PS3623.I73C57 2012
 813'.6—dc23

       2012015225

Midnight Ink
Llewellyn Worldwide Ltd.
2143 Wooddale Drive
Woodbury, MN 55125-2989
www.midnightinkbooks.com

Printed in the United States of America

DEDICATION

For Joanne

ACKNOWLEDGMENTS

Special thanks to Terri Bischoff and the fine graphics team at Midnight Ink for indulging the intricacies of this novel; Alex Glass, my intrepid literary agent; Sean Daily, my persevering film agent; my first readers, Skip, Chris, Ted, Liz, and Kerry—you were a huge help. And, as ever, special thanks to Helen Hills for copy-editing the first draft.

ONE

My hand was pressed to Trudy's breast. I felt her heart faltering, tripping, stumbling. My heart was galloping ahead of hers, like it was trying to pull her heart along, keep it in the race.

I'd given up trying to stop the bleeding; all I could do was will her to stay alive.

If only for a few more minutes. Or seconds. And then my life would be over, too, at least as I'd known it.

A hospital? That wasn't part of *The Clause*, what you signed onto without signing anything when you enlisted in this business. It was the pact; that was the way it was. If you got compromised on an operation, that was pretty much it: you'd been compromised and were a liability to the team. You didn't expect your partner to do anything except maybe watch you die or kill the bastard that shot you. At the hospital was heat, questions, and no answers that would keep you out of prison or contain the collateral damage. There was the temptation to leave an injured party where the cops could deliver him to the hospital and maybe save his life. It happened now and again. But alive or dead, the injured party was a link to the rest of the crew and the operation. Cops and reporters would figure out who the patient is and find out who that person knows, and next thing they know the crew is arrested and being questioned and it hits the evening news. If you took an injured party to the hospital, you risked bringing heat down on everybody. You didn't let mistakes or bad luck multiply like that; it only spread it around. That was what The Clause was all about: limiting liability. Everybody is expendable.

I could feel Trudy's heart squeezing for all it was worth, about to burst, trying to make what little blood might have still been in those adorable curves keep making those laps in the veins, keep life's race going. Then her heart would pause.

One Mississippi, two Mississippi…

It was as if it was taking a breather. It couldn't keep up but would stumble a few beats more. I put Trudy's hand on my chest.

"Feel it, sugar, keep going."

She gasped, tiny bubbles of blood on her lips. Her big browns opened and focused on mine. Yellow street light through the SUV's back window cast deep shadows on her face.

"Damn," she whispered.

"I know, I know, I know."

"We got it?"

"Don't you remember?"

"We got it?"

"We got it, and there was a lot, a whole lot. We could go away to the beach house for a while. I don't even know who did this to you, it's completely nuts."

Trudy's lips twisted into a half-smile. Her eyes were clear and bright with tears that ran down her cheeks. "I'm sorry, Gill."

"I know, sugar, I know, I know. *I'm sorry.* It's not your fault."

Her heart tightened like a fist. Then I felt it slowly loosen its grip, like a reluctant hand dropping a flower onto a grave.

Trudy's lips parted, exhaling. I looked deep into the canyon of those big browns and the shadow of forever filled them, never again to warm with a sunrise. The eyes were no longer eyes. They didn't see.

"*Trudy!*"

The blood gurgled in her throat. Her whole body became heavier. I put my lips to her forehead and inhaled the last of her, along with a tangy whiff of acidic reality. She was dead.

This was the deal, this was the pact, this was the way it was. This was the risk, the price you knew you might one day pay and not realize it was too much, that none of it was worth it.

But she was also my love. The Clause makes no special provisions for that. Except maybe that love was my mistake.

I knew in that instant that my life from then on would be filled with regret, for all the things I might and might not have done.

Yet in the yellow shadows of the SUV, I felt my soul get lighter, like Trudy's was pulling mine along with her. My soul wanted to go, too. It didn't want to stay here without her, to stay in a world of regret, to stay and be alone. My heart actually skipped a beat, like it was considering calling it quits and letting my soul go with hers. My chest ached from my spirit struggling to escape.

My mind stepped in—it wasn't going to give up that easy. It told my body that we were staying, that we had to stay, that I had to follow policy. Why? Because following policy is what I did, that's how an operation doesn't go south, that's how Trudy and I got this far and always got the gems free and clear. I had to be smart, I had to have a clear head. I knew what I had to do.

Since her bad luck was contained and didn't compromise the operation, I felt like it was mine to use. I was going to aim Trudy's bad luck at the people who needlessly took her life, and mine. We never hurt anybody by lifting sparks. Boosting jewelry for us was stealing into dark places at night and slipping out without anybody seeing us. There was no smash-and-grab and no gunplay.

Then out of nowhere: this.

Trudy dead in my arms.

I wanted to explode into a jillion pieces, to scream and shatter the dark sky, to thunder and crack the earth, to pull my own heart out of my chest and rain. And rain and rain and rain, the gutters swollen with my agony, my anguish, my regret.

I trembled in the yellow light of the SUV, Trudy's lifeless, flat eyes looking at mine.

Releasing her body, I felt like I'd been embracing a sack of mulch, like it had never even been alive. The inside of the SUV filled with an organic, tinny smell like lawn fertilizer, and the windows were steaming up. Maybe it was from my sweat, her blood, the smell of death. My shirt and pants were warm with Trudy's blood. I couldn't drive like that, much less spread it all over the SUV. If I got pulled over, there'd be no explaining it away.

Self-preservation and policy began to edge out my regret, rage, and self-pity.

I stripped off my shirt and used the back of it to wipe the blood from my chest, neck, and face. I slipped out of my pants and draped them and the shirt over the body. Then I rolled over the seat into the rear passenger seats, next to our black knapsacks.

There was a compartment under the seat, and inside was a change of clothes. Believe me, in this business, you have to have lots of spare sets of clothing around. You get dirty, you get sweaty, and witnesses ID you by your clothes more than anything else. Out came the pack of clothes, in went the knapsack, the ones with the sparks and our tools.

Dressed in a Hawaiian shirt, shorts, and sneakers, I climbed into the driver's seat, keys still in the ignition. I put the windows down to air out the SUV. Sultry summer washed over me, the smell of grass, trees, and cooling asphalt.

I was parked on a side street in West New York, and drove to Boulevard East, a busy two-lane that runs along the edge of a cliff called the Palisades across the Hudson River from Manhattan. At the stop sign I watched as two townies raced by with their lights rolling, no sirens. I knew where they were headed, toward the Grand Excelsior condos, toward where Trudy got unlucky.

I made a left, in the opposite direction, midtown Manhattan shimmering in the summer heat a half-mile below and to my right. On my left were a jumble of three-story row houses and plain brick apartment buildings. About a mile up, I made a right turn, down one of the few steep roads that leads down the cliff. At the bottom of the cliff is River Road, a four-lane commercial with strip malls, townhouses, high-rises, and lousy Italian restaurants. River Road took me to a small, dark side street next to the pollution control plant. I killed my lights and swung into the gated entrance to the plant, careful to position the SUV in front of a row of metal plates, but also to block the view of any possible cameras pointed my way from the plant. Cameras are everywhere these days. Someone in a passing car could see what I was doing if he looked carefully into the shadows, so my idea was to work fast.

With a tire iron, I pried open one of the steel hatches in the driveway and heaved it up until it leaned against the bumper of the SUV. Below in the darkness was the gush of water and the roar of the grinders, their carbide teeth meshing. This was the spot where raw sewage came into the plant, and it was the grinders that removed solids, made them into slurry, and took them out of the sewage before treatment. I opened the SUV's back and pulled my bloody shirt and pants off of the body, tossing them into the grinding chamber. Hands under the body's armpits, I lifted the torso. It didn't look a lot like Trudy anymore, and it helped not to think of it that way. Trudy was gone. This was no more Trudy than her clothes; it was just something she wore when she was alive.

Then I made the mistake of taking a last look at her face, remembering the time we actually talked about this moment. That was almost like a joke, but we talked about what if one of us were the injured party, what we would do with the body, how we would follow policy. And we came up with this. I never in a jillion years thought that it might happen, that it would be me dropping her into the grinder.

"Fucket, sugar, I am so sorry. I love you, baby." I started to cry then. I just couldn't keep it bottled up anymore. I pulled, stepped aside, and heard her thud on the pavement and then pitch down into the manhole: *splash*. The pavement shuddered as the grinders ate her. I pulled out the bloody splash mat from the back of the SUV and dropped that down into the grinders, too, before closing the back of the SUV and the steel hatch.

Life really sucks sometimes.

For me it was never worse.

TWO

Driving north on River Road, I was numb. I rubbed my face with my shirt to wipe away the tears. I thought maybe I should have stepped into Outback Steakhouse at the mall, to be seen in a public place, to establish some kind of alibi in case I needed it. That was too much; I just couldn't risk drawing attention to myself by suddenly bawling. I wasn't in complete control and had to make sure I didn't let Trudy die because of The Clause only to get caught doing something stupid. Lying low until daylight was more important than an alibi so I could check out the SUV and make sure there was no blood, inspect the sparks, and then stash the take in one of the lockers. Like having lots of sets of clothes around, it was good to have various stashes. Going home was not a good option. If you don't have a solid alibi, it's best that nobody sees you and can verify your comings and goings to conflict with your story. Sometimes it's better to have been nowhere than somewhere.

As you drive north on River Road through Edgewater, you come to an older part of the coast, a part that wasn't a giant real estate scheme, just a place to live since back when. There's a park next to the river with ball fields and crappy little houses across from them. Yeah, there are a couple high-priced townhouse developments, but when those are gone the road starts to go up and away from the river. On the left you pass a steakhouse called River Palm, the kind of place where the governor and TV anchors are seen, followed by a little bar called Rusty Kale's, the kind of place with a shamrock in the window where the governor and TV anchors would never be seen. On the right, between the road and the river, is a forest crisscrossed with twisty little cracked roads linking a jumble of houses, some nice, some not. Back in there I rented a wood garage I called "the barn." It used to be part of a house until the house fell down and only the garage was left. A neighbor bought the land where the house used to be and kept it wooded so he wouldn't have to look at the neighbors. But he rented me the barn, and the way it was in the thick woods of August, nobody could really see me come and go.

The SUV safely parked inside, I swung the wood barn doors closed. I pulled a lamp string and a shaded bulb popped on, swinging overhead.

Out came the knapsacks and onto the workbench they went. I pulled the string to another lamp. I had done this a jillion times. It was an old routine, but mostly back when I worked solo. Funny, how suddenly I was solo again, and I was right back doing what I used to do. I guess sometimes patterns help a guy do what needs doing when life sucks that bad.

Like old times, I opened the cabinet and found the bottle of Old Crow with the glass over the top. Next to it was half a pack of Winston Lights. I'd smoked the first half of the pack five years back, before Trudy. Inside the pack was a black lighter, black because white lighters were bad luck. Every kid knew that back in the day.

I blew the dust off the bottle, wiped the glass with my shirttail, and dropped a couple fingers of bourbon into it. The cigarettes were dry and crunchy when I rolled one between my thumb and forefinger, and when I matched one it eagerly glowed red, crackling softly.

I took the bourbon down in two quick slugs, and shuddered, exhaling smoke.

The SUV's engine ticking and cooling behind me, I closed my eyes and ran through those last moments with Trudy. How many times would I have to do that? How often before I stopped having to relive her death? They say grieving is a necessary process. I say grieving is self-pity and regret. It's masochism, like beating yourself up as a guilty pleasure. When someone dies, you don't cry for that person, you cry for yourself, partly because you miss the person, but mostly because you looked death in the face and oblivion has you scared. Real scared. There's a grinder in all of our futures.

There would be a lot of sleepless nights, and the best I could do was keep my head straight, stay on policy, and know that once Trudy was compromised there was nothing anybody could do, and Trudy was cool with that. I was sure of that.

I opened my eyes, wiped the tears off my face, and dropped in a few more fingers of Old Crow but set the glass aside. Out of habit, it was time to do a little inventory.

The roll of cash from the sock drawer totaled eight thousand four hundred and twenty dollars. That would come in handy.

I slid Trudy's knapsack toward me, unzipped it, and dumped the contents onto the bench.

In a dark apartment, a burglar doesn't spend a lot of time looking at what he lifts. Especially not in this apartment, because there were a lot of sparks in the safe. I could tell by the weight and the sound of it that it was quality. But on the bench before me were some really nice pieces. I plugged a jeweler's loupe into my eye.

Too nice.

Too nice?

Yeah, like a four-carat ruby pendant in a filigree platinum setting. A gold necklace set with maybe thirty one-carat lemon-and-lime diamonds. A red diamond rose broach that filled my palm. A cabochon emerald ring the size of the end of my thumb. Marquis blue ruby earrings, matching aqua sapphire teardrop earrings and pendant, and an elaborate tanzanite necklace that must have weighed two pounds.

All of it marked Britany-Swindol. That's a high-end international jeweler, appointment only, and you have to be both rich and famous. They turn away mobsters. They can afford to. Harry Winston is almost as good as Britany-Swindol.

My knapsack contained the pedestrian Tiffany, Cartier, and Mikimoto stuff that was easy to fence for a high return. It was the kind of stuff I sold to jewelry stores, which in turn sold to rich slobs I might one day take it back from. It was the stuff from the jewelry box. I knew because the sack had the Patek Philippe watch in it, the one from the dresser.

I took a slug of bourbon.

The apartment we targeted was not the kind of place where the super-rich and famous lived, not the kind of place you expected to find Britany-Swindol, probably because the local gentry had never even heard of anything nicer than Bulgari. A pile of Britany-Swindol the size of a turkey platter at the Grand Excelsior was almost like finding the Hope Diamond at Zales.

This was all wrong, but it clicked somehow, because Trudy getting killed was all wrong, too. They shot her without any warning, when she was unarmed.

The safe and its pile was the reason the goons showed up. That's where we tripped the alarm. Had we set off an alarm somewhere else in the apartment, they would have been there sooner. And something told me they wouldn't have been willing to use deadly force if they were a legit security outfit.

I drained my glass but froze when the glass was halfway to the table.

The Britany-Swindol heist.

It was a Macau couture-store smash-and-grab heist back in June by the Serbian mob.

I suddenly understood.

THREE

My day job brought me to the Grand Excelsior to fix screens. That's right, I was "The Screen Man." It said so on the side of my white van. I made house calls servicing the high-rise buildings along Boulevard East, the ones on top of the cliff called the Palisades across the Hudson from Manhattan. I knew most of the supers of those buildings, and bought them Johnnie Walker Blue for Christmas so I would get called in to fix the tenants' torn or bent screens. Some of these high-rises were more exclusive than others, and the Excelsior happened to be one with rich slobs on every floor. By slobs I mean new money—self-made men with a string of hardware stores or in construction or car dealerships. They need to show everybody that they're rich, so they throw their money around on things of value, namely their cars, their suits, their wives, and their wives' flashy couture jewelry.

You could give me a ring of keys to Martha's Vineyard mansions, and I'd hand it right back. The people who are used to being rich buy paintings and art because good taste in their circle is valued over cash and flash. I wouldn't know what to do with a hot Picasso. Frankly, I think I'd be too afraid to get caught with it and burn it. The great thing about jewelry is that most of it isn't unique; there's more than one of a kind and they aren't numbered or anything, not the Fifth Avenue stuff. It's also small, easy to fence and re-sell.

I was talking to the Excelsior's super, Mikos, back in May. We were in the lobby next to the mailboxes, making chit chat, when this hot brunette with collagen lips and unnaturally high cheekbones walked through the front door. She pointed her tits at Mikos and held out her fluffy, little rat dog. Her accent sounded Slavic, and she said, "Please to hold Brane."

Mikos took the dog, his eyes on her cleavage. That's where my eyes were, too, but not on her tits. My focus was the Tiffany "Jazz" diamond and platinum necklace set. Her finger sported a big rock there, too, but I couldn't make out the brand. On her ears were Tiffany drop pendant earrings. About fifty grand retail was in just the necklace and earrings.

The brunette opened a mailbox, pulled out a pile of fliers, took her dog, and went toward the elevators, her butt squeezed tight into a white skirt.

I jerked a thumb at her. "Whossat?"

"Idi Raykovic, on eleven, hot stuff."

That was her, that was the one Roberto told me about, and that's why I was snooping around. Roberto came to me with targets now and again.

"I'd do her screens for free. She mobbed up with the Russians?" That was pertinent. You ripped off the Russians, and you had to be extra careful. Roberto never told me those kinds of details. That stuff I had to figure out for myself.

"Nah. Macedonian, I think. Her husband is Serbian. One of these Gold Coast developers."

I didn't think anything of that at the time. Sure, Serbians could be rat-bastards, but it didn't necessarily follow that they were part of a ruthless international gem-theft ring.

I noted Idi's mailbox number: 11M.

From there the operation was pretty simple. Google her name at that address, find out more about her, get the phone number, check out her Facebook page, watch the place to see when she went out, and check on exactly how spark-worthy she was. I spied different baubles, too, not a lot of repeats. Her husband, Tito the real estate developer, took her out every Saturday night like clockwork. So after months of surveillance either by me or Trudy or both of us, we waited by the garage and watched Tito guide his Jag up the boulevard, the silhouette of Idi's giant teased hair next to him.

There was a functional pay phone across the street, and we used it to ring their apartment. No answer. Nobody home.

We climbed over a low wall at the edge of the cliff and around the side of the swimming-pool enclosure on a rocky ledge. Just where the ledge gave out, I boosted Trudy to the top of the wall. On the other side there was a dark stairwell that led down into the pool's pump room. She surveyed the surroundings, then gave me a hand up. We both wore the super-grip gloves, great for climbing walls and ropes. At the bottom of the stairwell, we both pulled pry bars from our packs and in unison levered the lock away from the jamb and pushed in.

Through a connecting basement room, we made our way to a stairwell. In a high-rise like that, the stairwells were only used as fire exits, except maybe now and again by security or maintenance. Up we went, to the eleventh floor.

Part of what took us so long to initiate this operation was that Roberto said we had to wait until he gave us the go-ahead. Timing was critical, and he figured July sometime. The other part was that we were waiting for an apartment near 11M to open up—either above, below, next to, something. Tito and Idi had an alarm pad next to their door and a very serious-looking armor-plated lock, so we had no intention of going in that way. Normally we would have just come down onto their terrace from the roof on ropes, but the building was twenty-four floors high. It wasn't that we were scared; heights stopped bothering me a long time back when I was a window washer in Manhattan. It was just that we would be exposed to too many windows on the way down. We'd be seen.

A vacancy did come up in July, number 11K, two over at the corner and perfectly positioned across from the stairwell. A real estate agent let us in the first time, and we noted the code the agent poked into the lockbox on the door handle. Inside was the key. After telling the front desk that we were there to see the apartment again, we used the lockbox key to bring two planks, thick and wide, and put them in the closet. Anybody else who visited the apartment would think the planks were spare shelves. Those would be our bridges from one balcony to the next. As it happened, 11L next door was being renovated and so was empty. All we had to do was go from one terrace to the next, over a three-foot gap, to find ourselves on the terrace of 11M.

Almost nobody ever locks their terrace doors that high up. They think that being high up gives them security, and it does, keeps teenagers and riffraff from stealing their laptops. Even still, I had a lot of experience with sliding terrace doors, and they were dead easy compared to actual locks, which take way too much time to pick even if you had a talent for that sort of thing, which I didn't.

So that night we let ourselves into 11K, got our bridges from the closet, and crawled across 11L's terrace to 11M's terrace. They had a wide view of Manhattan's glowing mountain of light, which glittered on the river. Of course, those views were available to most people who live in the high-rises on the Gold Coast, and even some who lived in the jumble of townhouses, apartments, and pier developments down below. The views are part of the point of living there.

Technically, the Gold Coast is what the realtors call the west bank of the Hudson River—New Jersey—across from Manhattan, from Bayonne in the south to Fort Lee in the north. Developers created a housing market to lure cramped Manhattan dwellers with spacious apartments complete with fireplaces, decks, views, and parking. The more dots on the map labeled "gold," the better for real estate agents.

Locals, on the other hand, think anything south of the Lincoln Tunnel is a different state. If you live on the Palisades, the Gold Coast is only the towns bracketed by the Lincoln Tunnel and George Washington Bridge: Weehawken, West New York, Guttenberg, North Bergen, Edgewater, and Fort Lee. Six towns straddling the Palisade cliffs.

All of the Gold Coast was laid out below us and to the horizon north and south as we crawled across our bridges to 11M. The terrace's sliding doors were locked, with a broom handle lying in the channel. A helpful piece of burglary equipment is a set of spring steel strips bent and curved into various shapes. Different shapes can be slid between windows or through door jambs to manipulate locks. Trudy used her pry bar to lift the sliding door off its track so that I could insert a piece of spring steel and lift the broom handle out of the door channel. Another piece of spring steel at the handle flicked open the latch. I slid the door open.

Brane the dog came trotting into the living room, growling, about to make a huge fuss. We made nice sounds, tossed him a slumburger, and retreated back to the balcony for fifteen long minutes. When we peeked back in, the burger laced with sleep-aid capsules had done its magic—Brane was curled up on the couch. His eyes were half open, but he clearly was in no mood to make a fuss.

Almost nobody with alarms actually sets them. Why? Probably because they're lazy, or because the alarms keep going off by accident—the sensors can freak when the wind blows hard or when the window frames expand in summer. Motion detectors were not an option for Tito and Idi because the dog would set them off. Anybody with cats or dogs is an easier target for that reason.

Almost nobody hides their jewelry, unless you think a jewelry box on a dressing table is a good hiding spot. Diode lamp in my teeth, I looted Idi's box while Trudy went in to check the walk-in closet.

Trudy sang: "Found it."

If there is a combination safe, it is usually in the closet with the rest of the woman's clothes. This time it was pretty clever. You lifted a shelf and it was hinged, folding up a panel that covered the safe.

We're not safe-crackers, but you don't have to be one, because safes are left mostly unlocked. If it is locked, just take the whole thing. We're not talking about a half-ton safe here. Wall safes are about the size of a toaster oven, and a lot of times you can just pry the whole thing out of the wall or out of the floor. Then it's just a matter of hauling it back to the garage and power-sawing it in half like a melon.

This safe was locked.

Here comes another "almost never." Even when people do lock their safe, they usually don't spin the dial beyond the last click, which is what you have to do to scramble the combination. I think people are afraid that they will forget the combination and so just turn the dial partway away from the last number. Either that or they are too lazy to spin the dial a couple times. And those that do lock the safe often write the combination on the wall somewhere nearby. Laughable.

Trudy gently turned the dial counterclockwise with one hand, the other vibrating the tumbler bolt.

"Bingo," she sang, and the safe door opened.

I know, this all sounds easy, but Tito's place was actually a *difficult* job. The fact of the matter is that people usually don't think anybody is going to rob them because nobody ever has, even though they took the trouble to install security devices, and unless they're paranoid or obsessive-compulsive, people generally make the least effort possible. I think it might be sort of like people who buy gym memberships and never go to the gym.

Tito and Idi were security geniuses compared to most. Hidden the way it was, the safe's concealment indicated that some serious thought had been put into the possibility of actual thieves looking for it. Most closet safes are right behind a curtain of clothes on hangers.

Trudy slung her sack under the safe door and shoveled the contents of the safe into her bag, closed the safe door, turned the knob several times, and lowered the tricky shelf. "You hear all those sparks? The safe was loaded. Let's scramble."

"Not yet. Sock drawer," I said pointing to the bedroom.

I always looked forward to this part of an operation. A sock drawer sums up how little people think about where they hide stuff, and how they think exactly the same.

Top right-hand drawer of the dresser is usually the sock drawer for a man. It is in this place that mankind—after making atomic bombs, moon landings, and artificial hearts—cleverly believes that a crook will never think to look for valuables. Okay, sometimes it's the underwear drawer.

Tito had a roll of cash in with his socks, and I shoved that down into my knapsack.

There was a glint on top of the dresser, and I pointed my diode on it.

"Patek Philippe. Nice." I put his watch in my sack.

"You done already?"

"After you."

We wiped up where the hamburger had been on the carpet, used the spring steel to relock the door and roll the broom handle back into place, and went back across our planks to 11K's terrace, taking the bridges with us.

From 11K's terrace we saw lights come on in 11M. We could hear several people enter, males, and they spoke urgently.

Trudy looked at me. "Fucket! That safe must've been bugged."

Back in 11K, we stashed the boards and removed our black T-shirts and gloves, tossing them into the bathroom sink cabinet. We had spares in the front pouch of our sacks, wrinkle-free casual plaid shirts that make a person look a lot less like a burglar.

We listened at the front door. No voices. It would take them a while to open the safe because we scrambled the combination. We stepped out into the hallway.

To our left was a very serious-looking young man in a shiny suit and spiked hair, standing guard in front of 11M.

I smiled at him. Trudy smiled at him.

"You got your glasses, sugar?"

Trudy was holding her sack like it was a purse, in the crook of her elbow. "I didn't forget this time."

We walked the hallway, hearts in our ears. Going down the same stairs we came up was impossible because that goon would have seen us, and using anything but the elevator would seem suspicious. At the same time, using the elevators was dangerous— they all have cameras in them and it was too easy to get trapped. Not that I hadn't used elevators in a jam, and walked right out the front lobby, but it was better to exit in a way that maximized the escape alternatives, especially with goons in tow. So we walked past the elevators and into the other stairwell at the opposite side of the building. Faster than any elevator, we bounded down to the first floor and then to the basement.

Just outside the door to the basement was a sign pointing right that said *POOL*.

Around we went. Walking fast. Didn't see anybody. We could smell the chlorine.

Nobody was poolside because the lifeguard was off duty and the pool was officially closed, submersed lights off.

We crept next to the building, under the cameras, until we reached the wall that separated us from the sidewalk. I boosted Trudy halfway up, and she took a peek around the corner toward the lobby.

"Clear."

Moments later we were walking north along the sidewalk toward our mountain bikes chained to a lamppost.

I know, sounds stupid, but bicycles are tactically ideal for making a transition from the operation to the getaway car. No license plates, for one. For two, mountain bikes go places cop cars can't and where people on foot can't keep up.

We had them unlocked and were about to pedal away when we heard a shout behind us. There was no looking back, just moving forward: escape.

There was a pop.

Even Trudy didn't realize she was compromised until we got to the SUV.

I've already been through what happened next.

A jillion times.

ALL WARFARE IS BASED ON DECEPTION. WHEN ABLE TO ATTACK, WE MUST SEEM UNABLE. WHEN USING OUR FORCES, WE MUST SEEM INACTIVE. WHEN WE ARE NEAR, WE MUST SEEM FAR. WHEN FAR, WE MUST SEEM NEAR. BAIT THE ENEMY, PRETEND YOU ARE WEAK, THEN CRUSH HIM. IF THE ENEMY IS READY, BE READY FOR HIM. IF YOUR ENEMY IS IN SUPERIOR STRENGTH, EVADE HIM. IF THE OPPONENT IS IRRITABLE, IRRITATE HIM. FAKE WEAKNESS TO MAKE HIM RECKLESS. IF HE RESTS, GIVE HIM NO REST. IF HIS FORCES ARE UNIFIED, DIVIDE THEM. ATTACK YOUR OPPONENT WHEN HE IS UNPREPARED, AND APPEAR WHERE YOU ARE LEAST EXPECTED.

—*Sun Tzu*, The Art of War

FOUR

In the barn that night, I realized that I'd stolen from a syndicate.

And not just any syndicate.

The Serbians.

The Britany-Swindol heist? They drove a stolen dump truck into the front of the Britany-Swindol store, machine-gunned the staff and display cases, looted, and left in a getaway car. They'd done likewise in other cities like London, Tokyo, Milan, and Monaco. Now and again the heat caught up with them, put one or two in jail. Those captured never fingered anybody, and often as not these guys were such hard cases that they escaped in a burst of unexpected violence. Some fugitives were killed in their escapes, though largely due to their thinking they could survive a swim across the English Channel, a thousand-foot dive off a cliff into the Mediterranean, or win at chicken between a Fiat and a bullet train.

I'll try to put this as politely as I can: there were no greater scumbags in organized crime than these Serbs, known to many as The Kurac. Or simply Kurac, which always sounded to me like some sort of skin disease. *Kurac* was a common Serbian expletive. It translated to *cock*, and even though I think this gang of thieves was labeled *Kurac* by others as an insult, they seemed to like the name. *Kurac* was swagger and badass.

I'm not an expert on Balkan history, but the word on the street was that these guys were the nasties left over from the Serb wars. A lot of them were no more than kids at the time, but they survived through not caring about anything except money, except taking. I mean *nothing*. Kill their mother, kill their sister, kill them, throw them in prison—they just don't care. To escape capture, they will jump from buildings, gouge eyes, set children on fire—anything to keep out on the street and make money. To them, being a badass is essential to survival and their sense of purpose. If they die? They all have come so close so many times and seen so many atrocities that they don't fear death. *They expect it.* Death comes when it comes, and they figure you might as well die robbing rather than being robbed. And no matter what anybody does to them—interrogate, torture, set their hair on fire—the only answer they'll give is "*Fock you!*"

So the pile of jewelry in front of me was Trudy's death sentence. It was also even money that it would be mine, too.

The Serbs were on the street that very second, breaking the fingers of anybody they thought might know who took their stuff. Any hoods they found, even if the crook wasn't the guy who did it, they'd castrate the poor schmuck, rip his tongue out, and let him bleed to death hanging from one foot just on the off-chance it was the guy who ripped them off. I knew enough people that I had to operate on the assumption that they were out there narrowing down a list that I was on.

Trudy's and my phones were in the sacks. I found them and turned them off. There was no knowing whether the Kurac had the ability to get AT&T or Verizon or whatever to triangulate and ping our phones. I had to assume that the Kurac's friends in the Russian mob had telephone company people or cops on their payroll that could push the buttons to ping our phones.

I filled my glass with Old Crow and held the amber liquid to the lamp. Be nice if I could have just given it all back. The local Cubans, the Italians to the south, they would let me do that if I groveled and paid a penalty. Russian mob not so much, could go either way, but would be worth a try.

The Serbs? Giving the sparks back would only make them laugh harder as they made me watch them feed my legs into a wood chipper.

My mission was pretty clear. I had to stay alive and take out the shitbags—if nothing else, for Trudy. If they killed me, her death would mean nothing. I couldn't let that happen.

My plan for that night was to hook a motorcycle battery to a charger, finish the Old Crow, roll out a sleeping bag, and finish as much grieving as possible. By morning, there would be no more crying, no more drinking, no more night's sleep. If I didn't keep moving and stay at least a step or two in front of those Serb freaks, I was a dead man.

At best I had a couple days.

FIVE

DCSNet 6000 Warrant Database
Transcript Cell Phone Track and Trace
Peerless IP Network / Redhook Translation
Target: Dragan Spikic
Date: Sunday, August 8, 2010
Time: 142–147 EDT

SPIKIC: TALK TO ME, VUGOVIC.
VUGOVIC: ONE THIEF WAS SHOT.
SPIKIC: AND?
VUGOVIC: WE DON'T HAVE THEM YET.
SPIKIC: YET?
VUGOVIC: WE WILL GET THEM.

SPIKIC: I KNOW YOU WILL. THERE'S [UNINTELLIGIBLE]. HOW DID THIS HAPPEN?

VUGOVIC: BURGLARS. THEY CAME IN ACROSS BALCONIES.

VUGOVIC: WHO ELSE KNEW THE GEMS WERE THERE OTHER THAN US? PERHAPS THEY ARE INVOLVED.

SPIKIC: TITO RAYKOVIC.

VUGOVIC: PERHAPS HIS WIFE. IT COULD BE A COINCIDENCE.

SPIKIC: COINCIDENCE? ARE YOU FAMILIAR WITH THE STORY OF THE COBBLER WHOSE SHOP WAS HELD UP THE NIGHT BE-FORE HIS DAUGHTER'S WEDDING?

VUGOVIC: TELL ME.

SPIKIC: THE COBBLER HAD THE DOWRY WITH HIM READY FOR THE NEXT DAY. SO WHEN THE BANDITS SHOWED UP AND PUT A GUN TO HIS HEAD, WHAT DO YOU THINK HE SAID?

VUGOVIC: WHAT?

SPIKIC: HE SAID, "IF YOU TAKE MY MONEY I WILL SHOOT MY SON-IN-LAW IN THE FACE AND HAVE HIS MOTHER RAPED BY FERAL RAMS."

VUGOVIC: WHY DID HE SAY THAT?

SPIKIC: TO MAKE THE BRIGANDS LEAVE, WHICH THEY DID, WITH-OUT THE MONEY. YOU SEE, WHO ELSE BUT HIS IN-LAWS WOULD KNOW THE AMOUNT OF THE DOWRY AND WHERE TO GET IT? EVEN A SIMPLE SERB COBBLER KNEW THERE ARE NO SUCH THINGS AS COINCIDENCE. YOU ARE NOT NATIVE TO OUR HOMETOWN. THEY HAVE A SPECIAL WISDOM. HAVE YOU CHECKED THE HOSPITALS?

VUGOVIC: WE HAVE OUR FINGERS TO THEIR TEMPLES, AND ARE INVESTIGATING UNSCRUPULOUS DOCTORS.

SPIKIC: WHAT ABOUT THE CUBANS? THAT'S THEIR VILLAGE. WAKE THE CORPORATION.

VUGOVIC: THEY WON'T TALK TO US UNTIL TOMORROW.

SPIKIC: WHY?

VUGOVIC: ROBERTO LIKES HIS SLEEP.

SPIKIC: AND THEY CALL THEMSELVES CROOKS. PATHETIC, LAZY SPICS. FIRST THING IN THE MORNING I WANT THEM ON THIS.

VUGOVIC: WE'LL MEET THEM AS SOON AS WE CAN GET THE SPICS OUT OF BED. WHAT IS THEIR INCENTIVE?

SPIKIC: PEACE, MUTUAL RESPECT, WE'RE NOT GIVING THEM A DIME. WE KNOW THE RUSSIANS IN PATERSON AND TRENTON. HAVE THEM PUT IN THE GOOD WORD FOR US. ANY OTHER INFORMERS?

VUGOVIC: THIS IS NOT OUR TURF.

SPIKIC: THAT SOUNDS LIKE A WEASEL IN YOUR ASS, AN EXCUSE.

VUGOVIC: IT'S A REASON. WE WOULD SHAKE THE TREE FOR AP-PLES, BUT THERE ARE NO BRANCHES.

SPIKIC: I'M TOLD THEY RODE AWAY ON BICYCLES?

VUGOVIC: YES. THEY WENT DOWN THE HILL. WE FOLLOWED AND FOUND BLOOD, BUT COULD NOT TRACE WHERE THEY WENT.

SPIKIC: GET THE RUSSIAN PHONE PEOPLE TO TRACE ANY CALLS THEY MIGHT MAKE TO ROBERTO. THESE BURGLARS MUST WORK FOR HIM. THEY ARE OPERATING ON HIS TURF. THEY WILL LIKELY CALL THE CORPORATION FOR HELP. THEY WILL SEEK HELP FOR THE INJURED ONE.

VUGOVIC: IT WAS A WOMAN.

SPIKIC: A WOMAN?

VUGOVIC: YES, IT WAS A WOMAN AND A MAN, AND IT WAS THE WOMAN THAT BOBO SHOT.

SPIKIC: IS BOBO THE HOMOSEXUAL WHO USES THAT SWISS PIS-TOL? GIVE BOBO A BOWLEGGED BOY WHORE, GOOD WORK. THE WOMAN THEY WILL SEEK HELP FOR. AMERICAN CROOKS ARE NOT PROFESSIONAL. THEY DON'T KNOW HOW THESE THINGS SHOULD WORK, SHE SHOULD HAVE BEEN ELIMI-NATED AS A LIABILITY. BUT THEY DON'T DO THAT HERE. LIKE THE SPICS THEY ARE WEAK AND SYMPATHETIC, BOATS THAT FOUNDER WITH TOO MUCH GRAIN. I AM SURE OF IT.

VUGOVIC: THE POLICE HAVE BEEN A HEADACHE. THEY ARRESTED BOBO FOR CARRYING AN UNLICENSED HANDGUN. WE HAVE

BAILED HIM OUT. THE POLICE OF COURSE ARE INCOMPETENT AND DID NOT SEE THE BLOOD. WE HAVE TOLD THEM WE ARE A SECURITY AGENCY TO PROTECT THE ASSETS OF OUR CLIENTS SO THE COMPANY WE HAVE INSTALLED HERE AS A COVER IS WORKING WELL.

SPIKIC: WHAT OF TITO?

VUGOVIC: HE IS UPSET. I THINK HE IS MORE WORRIED THAT THE LITTLE GLASS WENT MISSING FROM HIS CARE THAN ABOUT HIS WIFE'S MISSING JUNK. PERHAPS HE HAS ALREADY SURMISED THAT YOU MAY SUSPECT HIM.

SPIKIC: SEND ME HIS WIFE—THAT WHORE, IDI. I WILL RAPE HER AND FIND OUT WHAT SHE KNOWS. EITHER SHE WILL KNOW HE DID IT OR SHE WILL DIVULGE TO ME HER DEVIOUS PLOT TO ROB US.

VUGOVIC: SHE HAS A DOG.

SPIKIC: BRING THE DOG TOO.

VUGOVIC: WHEN?

SPIKIC: WHEN DO YOU THINK? NOW, BEFORE THEIR STUPID BURGLARS CAN GET FAR.

VUGOVIC: WHAT DO I TELL TITO?

SPIKIC: MUST I EXPLAIN EVERYTHING TO YOU? I DON'T CARE WHAT YOU TELL HIM. SAY I WILL FUCK HER ASS LIKE A DONKEY IF YOU WANT.

VUGOVIC: AS YOU SAY. I WILL BRING HER WITHIN THE HOUR.

SPIKIC: VUGO, GET THAT GLASS, DO YOU HEAR ME? THE JEWS HAVE ARRANGED THE MONEY.

VUGOVIC: I'LL GET IT. WHATEVER IT TAKES.

SPIKIC: GOOD BOY. NOW GO BE A STIFF DICK AND FIND THOSE BURGLARS.

VUGOVIC: FAREWELL.

SPIKIC: GOOD HUNTING.

END

SIX

I woke up thinking about a movie I once saw. In a hospital.

It was a Western, and railroad barons had sent out goons to murder a farmer and his family rather than pay for the farmer's land. The assassins sported long coats worn by a local outlaw gang so that they could lay blame for the murders that way. The youngest son of the farmer was left unharmed so he could witness those long coats. The outlaw gang didn't like being blamed for the murder, and began to investigate who did do it. Out of nowhere came a loner with a harmonica and a vendetta against the head railroad goon. When the loner was a child, the same goons had left him alive as a witness. In a sort of mysterious way, this loner helps guide the outlaws to confront the goons, in turn making an opportunity for the loner to settle his score and escape.

Some instant coffee in a hot pot from the cabinet got me going. I tried smoking another Winston, but a stale cigarette just wasn't doing it for me.

I inspected the back of the SUV with a black light and found light blood smears. The black light I kept around to check out certain kinds of gems, but I knew black lights could also make blood and semen glow. Even though the Serbs saw us escape on bikes, they didn't see the black SUV, which are common enough. Still, the vehicle was a link to me. Technically, it belonged to Trudy, it was in her name. The Serbs would get our names soon enough, probably through intimidation or torture in combination with a process of elimination. Somebody would talk, somebody would give them a list of local crooks, and in no time they'd be on my doorstep. While I was at the barn they'd be out looking for our vehicles and searching our apartments.

I used Trudy's cell phone to ring Roberto.

"'Allo?"

"Tomás, this is Gill. I need to see Roberto."

"He still sleep."

"It's important."

"Yes, we hear."

"Is it safe to see Roberto?"

One Mississippi, two Mississippi …

"You are one of our locals. Roberto has respect for friendship and loyalty."

"Can I meet him at Sabor, outside, eight thirty?"

"He will be there. Be careful. They are looking very hard for you all night."

"Serbs, right?"

"El Kurac."

"*Gracias*, Tomás."

In a plastic container I found a pair of black cargo pants, the ones with lots of zippered and hook-and-loop pockets. There was also a heavy denim canvas shirt with large pockets. I put them both on, along with a pair of running shoes. The eight thousand dollars went in the pockets of the cargo pants.

A first-aid kit had large sterile pads and gauze, and I used those to wipe up blood smears from the back of the SUV. While I did that I noticed a brassy glint in the corner, almost shoved under the corner of the carpeting. It was a slug, a bullet, but no casing, sticky with blood. I blinked. This must have fallen out of Trudy's clothes when I tore open her shirt. Maybe it hit the metal buckle on her knapsack as it went through her and stopped. The slug had traveled some distance before it hit her so was slowed some anyway. Odd: it wasn't badly deformed. In fact, it appeared to be a special application bullet, the type used to penetrate metal and glass, not just slaughter. A chill ran up my spine. Of course. The Clause at work. The bullet gave me all the more reason to survive.

I tucked the bullet in my pocket and gathered up the bloody bandages and put them in a pile next to the sleeping bag laid out on the workbench, along with several bottles of over-the-counter painkillers and anti-inflammatories. I set Trudy's cell phone next to the pills and left it on.

Most people don't realize how intrusive cell phones can be. The FBI can virtually listen in on any call and read any text message—not just in real time, but after the fact, because all calls are stored for a short time. Certain phones, even when off, can be turned on and made into listening devices. Then there's pinging. Providers like Verizon can send signals to a cell phone from different towers and time the delay to triangulate and locate the phone.

Federal and to some degree local officials are the only ones who are supposed to be able to have access to these systems. *Supposed*. I wasn't betting my life on *supposed*.

In my situation, I could have looked at cell phones as a liability. Instead, I intended to use them as a tool. I left that phone on because I wanted to see if the Corporation would take her number and ping it, or pass it along to the Kurac. I wanted them to find the garage and the bandages to think Trudy was alive. Why? I could use that, too. They wouldn't understand my motivations or be able to accurately predict my moves. They would waste a lot of time wondering where she was and how I would take care of her.

Idi's sparks I wrapped in paper towels and stuffed into a couple Band-Aid boxes. The Britany-Swindol treasure I wrapped individually in toilet paper and put into a large plastic socket wrench set box. All that I placed on the bench next to my burglar tools: a pair of binoculars, some climbing rope and hardware, my spring steel kit, and compact bolt cutters.

I fished our passports out of the knapsacks. We never did an operation without those handy. You never knew when you might need to blow town and country. When I saw my passport, part of me was scared and wanted to run. That option was more complicated than it sounds. With that much merchandise in my luggage the scanners would detect it. Of course, I could have stashed it and come back, but I needed a lot of cash to run. A lot of those sparks needed to be liquidated so I had the ability to get out.

I had a mission and I had the home-field advantage. Wherever I landed on unfamiliar turf, the Kurac would have the advantage hunting me down. Dealing with them on my home turf gave me an edge.

Trudy wouldn't have wanted to lose, especially when she forfeited her life. That raised the stakes. Winning against the Kurac would be for Trudy, and killing the person who had her shot was my mission.

Maybe then I could live with myself for having to let her die.

I used an X-Acto to cut the photo out of her passport. Her butchered passport I then burned in an empty paint can. My passport with her photo went into a zippered pocket next to a wad of bills.

In the corner of the garage was a white sheet. Under it was my motor bike. Nothing fancy, just an old Honda Nighthawk 750. I cleaned off the spark plugs, checked the ignition, filled the gas tank, sprayed out the carburetor with Gunk. The charger on the workbench said the battery was full.

The Honda was cranky, and spewed smoke when I finally got it to kick over. It still had plates but the registration had lapsed, and it wasn't insured. That was the least of my problems. On the back of the bike was a saddle bag. I unhitched it and loaded it with the sparks and burglary tools.

Fitting a shielded black helmet on my head, I goosed the sputtering Honda out of the garage and closed the doors. I took a last look at the barn—many a glass of Old Crow had been quietly toasted there after an operation, the sparks spread out on the workbench before me.

I turned left at River Road. The sun shone, the birds tweeted, and a canopy of dark green locusts jostled above in a river breeze. It could have been a really nice day. Like the time I took Trudy on our fourth date. She was on the back, her chin on my shoulder, her arms clasped tight around my waist. We went on a picnic up the Palisades, at Bear Mountain, and tried to make love in the tall grass by a stream, just like in a movie, except we got covered in ticks. Believe it or not we had a big laugh over that. The memory was so strong, it was almost impossible to believe that her vibrant little body had been shredded by the grinders. That Trudy's mind was gone, never to tease or laugh or plot or scheme again. You just never know when what you have will be taken away. All of it.

I stopped at a deli for a fresh pack of Winstons. It wasn't like I really cared about my health anymore. It was possibly the last pack of cigarettes I'd ever get to smoke anyway. At an ATM I drained my checking account—there wasn't much there anyway, almost a thousand, just a balance I keep in there to cover my bills, and I'd just paid rent. I put that cash with the eight thousand four hundred and twenty dollars I nabbed from Tito.

A winding drive along the top or the bottom of the two-hundred-foot-tall Palisades was a quick tour of the Gold Coast's first four towns, which had only a couple miles of Hudson River frontage. While there was an ethnic mix in those towns atop the cliff, there was a large portion of Hispanics, and Cubans formed the cultural backbone, in small part through their mob called the Corporation. It was run originally by a patriot who was in the Bay of Pigs invasion and was rumored to still have ties with the CIA. While the Corporation operated gambling operations and cathouses, it also owned a piece of just about any business that mattered in West New York, as well as concessions at the airports. But as Roberto would say: "Yes, but it's either me or the banks, so what's the difference?"

Roberto had made strong pacts with the Italians to the south and the Russians to the north. He knew how to play rough, but also knew it didn't pay to fight turf wars. There was enough for everybody so long as nobody got greedy.

Sabor wasn't open that early on a Sunday, but it didn't mean that staff wasn't there prepping for brunch, or that the owners wouldn't accommodate Roberto if he wanted them to be open, if only for him.

Roberto's vintage baby-blue Lincoln Continental was in the parking lot next to the three-story brick restaurant, an Italianate iron balcony on the second floor, a patio facing River Road on the ground floor.

Helmet under my arm, I approached the bodyguard, Ramón, standing next to the patio. "*Hola!*"

Ramón adjusted his jacket, a cream suit draped over a black shirt and snakeskin loafers. "You stepped in it this time, amigo."

He waved me past to the patio, where Roberto sat at a café table in a striped bathrobe. Thick white hair and mustache framed piercing black eyes and a large cigar. His huge hands were on either side of an espresso. Behind him was the main dining room, and he was framed by open French doors with flowing gauzy curtains. A samba played softy from within.

Roberto's bullet-hole eyes slid my way. "This consultation will have to be short. Sit."

I sat, but not before digging into my pocket and placing the palm-sized red diamond rose broach before him.

He leaned forward to look more closely at it, then at me. His hand slid a napkin over the broach, and he put it in his robe pocket. "Why was there shooting?"

"This was one of those operations with unforeseen consequences, Roberto. I didn't know the Serbs had gems stored there. You must have known, though. That's why you wanted us to wait."

Roberto huffed, his eyes in the distance. "I thought you knew how to play this game. Don't expect me to tell you everything. I don't even tell myself everything."

"It just would have helped to know, and it might have averted the gunplay."

He cocked his head at me. "Are you blaming me for your inability to escape these asses, the Kurac?"

"No. Things went bad, that's all. I come to you now out of friendship, as a business associate, not looking for handouts."

"Dead men don't need friends. You know the Corporation cannot involve itself in this blunder, you know that, don't you? If they even knew we were consulting like this, all hell would break loose."

"I'm not looking for any direct help, Roberto, just a little exchange of information. First, we wanted to tell you that we're sorry this happened. It was a miscalculation, we didn't mean for our operation to interfere with the day-to-day operations of the Corporation."

"The Kurac have called a conference this morning to have the Corporation help locate you."

"Yet you have consulted with me in confidence, and for that I am grateful."

"Everybody hates the Kurac. They are lousy businessmen and have no manners. How bad is Trudy?"

"I've done what I can. She needs a cat doctor."

Cat doctors were medical professionals other than doctors who would treat gunshot wounds on the sly. Usually they were veterinarians. It was easier for vets to fly under the radar for that sort of work.

Roberto puffed a large cloud of smoke.

I lit up a Winston as a waitress set an espresso in front of me.

"Call Felix Ramirez on Bergenline Avenue. He is an associate; you can use me as a reference. Tell him you are a cousin. You better do it fast, though, and I'm doing this more for Trudy than for you. She deserves better."

"We're partners. We deserve each other and expect nothing more."

"You two should have gotten out of this business years ago, once you bought the beach house."

"I know that now."

"The Clause makes no provisions for love. Yet you two seem destined for each other. There's an old saying: 'Two like hearts don't find each other, they seek each other.'"

"Destiny is a crock. It's all a roll of the dice."

Roberto's eyes twinkled. "Is that so?"

"But you can influence how the future turns out through knowing the odds. For instance, can you tell me what the Serbs have on us?"

"They know Trudy is injured. My sources tell me they suspect Tito Raykovic was involved with planning your operation. That confusion will delay them some. They were up all night bothering Ramón and roughing up punks looking for information, trying to meet me in the middle of the night. They are making noises about getting the Russians involved, and I cannot have them doing business in my town. Can I tell the Kurac you plan to cut and run?"

"Yes, but I have to take care of Trudy and put together a bank-roll all in a few hours."

Roberto held his cigar away from his face and examined the ash.

"And after the few hours? Where will you relocate?"

"Our Long Beach Island house. It's out near the lighthouse, out in the wide open where I can see any bad guys coming. I'll be able to get Trudy well before we move off for good. She needs to be able to get on a plane."

Roberto's eyes moved from the ash to me, and squinted. "I see."

"I've ditched the phones, the apartments, and the cars, so they can forget that. I figure it will take them some time to find the beach house. It isn't exactly the only one on the island with a red door."

The information I was giving him was intended for the Serbs—I knew and he knew he had to give them something, if not me. I figured I might as well feed the Kurac what I wanted them to know. The red door? I didn't like the idea of the Kurac torturing innocent real estate agents or delivery boys, so I thought I'd help them locate it on their own.

"That is a lot of jumping around while Trudy is left alone. If they find her ..." He shifted uncomfortably in his chair. "You know what getting caught means? If they find Trudy? I heard a story. It was about how a Kurac had a collision with his car and that of a Frenchman. I think this was in Rome. An argument followed, but the police showed and broke it up. The Kurac used the police report to track the Frenchman. Not to France, but to the Seychelles, a small island somewhere off Africa. He found the Frenchman and butchered him. And I mean, butchered, like a goat, and packed him into the refrigerator. He was caught at the airport trying to leave the country. When questioned by the police, the Kurac said it was a joke. He was tried, but before he could be sentenced, he stabbed a guard to death with a pencil in the eye and escaped. Even on that island, they never did find him."

"If they're that relentless, then I might as well fight them here on home turf. It is tactically unwise to concede defeat even in the face of the shifting odds. Odds, by their very nature, can be shifted back in your favor as easily as they went out of your favor."

"So you aren't really cutting and running? You're not abandoning the mission?"

"Not the way you're thinking about it, no. These Serbs: how will I know them?"

"They drive Audis, wear shiny suits and white wifebeaters, Porsche sunglasses, thick messy hair. They prefer machine pistols, and sloppy Serb and Italian pistols. M70s are their favorite. What's your endgame, how will you close out this operation?"

"It all depends on Trudy and how much time I have." I dropped my smoke into my untouched espresso and stood. "Thanks for everything, Roberto, I'll miss you."

He nodded. "Farewell, Gill. Drop me a postcard if you make it. No need to write anything, just a postcard."

I tried to smile, walked past Ramón's scowl, got on my Nighthawk, and left.

SEVEN

I NEEDED TO GET set up with phones. Bergen County had blue laws preventing most retail sales on Sundays, which meant I had to head to Newport Plaza in Hudson County to the south, in Jersey City, right next to the Holland Tunnel. At a phone store there I bought three prepaid phones, all of them without privacy screening. Prepaids pose a problem even for the FBI. I wasn't exactly sure of the technical reasons, only that it was difficult to listen to the calls or track the calling history. Just the same, I intended to take every precaution possible.

And not just with phones. At Best Buy I picked up a three-hundred-dollar "secure" flash drive loaded with a private and en-crypted browser. This puppy was military-grade—they use them in Afghanistan. Anybody attempts to crack the password and the drive wipes itself clean of all data, self-destructing. If I needed to go online at a library or anywhere else, this puppy would do all the processing through a virtual private network. The data of where I went online and what I wrote would come with me, and not be on the machine.

Leaning against my bike in the parking lot, I used Phone #1 to call Felix.

A male voice: "Bergenline Veterinary. How may I help you?"

"I need to speak with Felix."

"Who is calling?"

"His cousin, it's important."

"To hold, please."

A Hispanic male voice came on. "Yes?"

"Roberto sent me. I need a house call for a sick cat."

There was a pause. "When?"

"Hour?"

"Where?"

"Go to the Edgewater marina, and I'll call you there."

He gave me his cell number and hung up. I put the number into the phone's speed dial, then turned Phone #1 off and clicked out the battery. With Phone #2 I called Teddy, a jeweler. I got a machine.

"This is Astoria Fine Jewelers. Our hours are Monday through Saturday, nine to six. If you wish, leave a message. We look forward to servicing your needs."

"Teddy, this is Gill. I'm hoping you're there today. Please give me a call back at …"

"Hallo? Gill?"

"Hi, Teddy, good to find you there."

"You have quality sparks to show me? Because I don't care about silver, or crap stones."

He hadn't heard about last night's operation, which was good. He would have mentioned it if he had. "It's all Fifth Avenue, Teddy."

"I can't meet you today, though, I am only here briefly. I have my niece's wedding at three."

"I can be there within two hours."

"I don't want to rush."

"There's no choice."

"Er … so this is a rush? What's going on? Is there heat?"

"No heat, just circumstances. I either bring Fifth Avenue to you or someone else. Now."

"Who else?"

"There are others."

"You and Trudy always come to me, that's why I give you the best price."

"Not the best price, a fair price."

"A fair price is the best price, my friend."

"Can I come or not?"

"Hm, I don't like to be rushed."

"I hope you have cash on hand."

"Is there a lot?"

"There could be."

"Er, yes, come."

"See you." I had to get to Teddy fast—he'd be making calls to find out what happened last night, and I didn't want him to have a chance to sell me out to the Kurac.

Phone #2: off and battery out.

I fired up the bike and drove to a gym in north Hoboken. It was in a refurbished brick factory space. I had a membership there, but only used it for the locker, bathroom, and showers when I needed to clean up after an operation. In the locker I kept a toiletry kit, change of clothes, and tennis gear. From the clutter at the bottom of the locker I pulled two tubes of tennis balls. I found some privacy in a bathroom stall, and sat on the toilet with the tennis ball tubes. They were slit, and inside each ball was a stash of sparks that I wrapped in toilet paper and transferred into the pockets of my cargo pants. On my way out I dumped the empty tennis balls into the trash.

I snapped in the battery on Phone #2 and dialed.

"Whitestone Jewelry."

"Steve there?"

"Who's calling?"

"Renaldo, I'm his cousin."

"Gill, how are you, nice day out there, isn't it? Ack, but here I am, stuck in the store on a Sunday. It's a crime. There was a time when I used to go to mass on Sundays, but with the economy who can afford God? As a jeweler I have to compete with Jews who are open on Sundays. If God wanted me in church, he would have made the Sabbath the same for everybody, you know what I'm saying?"

"Can I come over?"

"You mean right now?"

"In three hours or so."

"Usually we wait until closing."

"This can't wait."

"Oooh, that doesn't sound good."

"There's no heat, but I have a schedule."

"Please tell me you have something nice for a change. You know I always try to do my best, but with the economy and the competition—I'm a businessman struggling to survive."

"It's Fifth Avenue. You want it, or do I take it to someone else?"

"Gill, please, who else are you going to deal with? I'm the most fair guy you're going to find, you know that. You always come to me, we're friends. How is lovely Trudy?"

"She's fine. So is it a date?"

"Call me from the parking lot. We can go over the sparks in my Hummer."

"See you." Phone #2: off and battery out.

If you sell sparks in smaller quantities you get a better price, and I knew Teddy and Steve wouldn't have the cash on hand to take the whole lot off my hands. So I needed several of my resources. Like they say, don't shit where you eat. I cultivated several jewelers away from home base, east across the Hudson River in New York City, all more or less on a loop around Queens and the Bronx with a straight shot on I-95 back across the GW Bridge and the Gold Coast. If I used a jeweler on the west bank of the Hudson, say in Fort Lee, they'd likely already have heard about the operation, possibly from the police. Most midsized jewelers will buy the Fifth Avenue stuff, and never ask where it came from—the brand name stuff has a high re-sell value. There are so many of these midsized stores in the New York City area that nobody checks up on what they buy and from where. Who is to say I didn't buy the lot at an estate sale? Who is to say my mother or wife didn't die and leave them to me?

After Teddy I'd call Doc Huang at East Trading Jewelers in Flushing for a third stop. Liquidating my entire stash wouldn't be possible—besides, I wasn't sure I wanted to. Sparks can be a good hedge against inflation, and frankly a Cartier diamond necklace is more compact than ten thousand dollars cash. Just the same, big wads of cash would go a long way toward completing the operation of staying alive.

45

EIGHT

DCSNet 6000 Warrant Database
Transcript Cell Phone Track and Trace
Peerless IP Network / Redhook Translation
Target: Dragan Spikic
Date: Sunday, August 8, 2010
Time: 955–1002 EDT

SPIKIC: TALK TO ME.

VUGOVIC: HE MET WITH THE SPICS.

SPIKIC: AND THOSE CUNT-CRUST CUBANS DIDN'T CALL US?

VUGOVIC: HE'S ONE OF THEIRS, MORE OR LESS.

SPIKIC: SOON TO BE LESS. I WANT ROBERTO'S BALLS, YOU HEAR ME?

VUGOVIC: NOT NECESSARY. WE TURNED A SPIC ON THE INSIDE, ROBERTO'S NUMBER TWO, RAMÓN, GAVE US A NAME: GILL UNDERWOOD. THE GIRL THEY ONLY KNOW AS TRUDY. BUT WE GOT HER CELL PHONE NUMBER. THE RUSSIANS ARE WORKING ON THE NUMBER NOW. IF IT'S ON WE SHOULD HAVE A FIX ON HER. WE WENT TO HIS APARTMENT. NOBODY HAS BEEN THERE, BUT WE HAVE A MAN ON IT.

SPIKIC: THE GIRL, HOW BADLY DID SHE GET IT?

VUGOVIC: THIS MAN, GILL, IS LOOKING FOR A CAT DOCTOR FOR HER. WE GOT THE NAME OF THE CAT DOCTOR FROM RAMÓN. THIS VET'S NAME IS FELIX, AND WE'RE WITH HIM NOW AT THE EDGEWATER MARINA. GILL IS SUPPOSED TO CALL HIM HERE OR MEET HIM TO TAKE HIM TO TRUDY.

SPIKIC: STAY WELL BACK. THIS SON OF A ROACH NAMED UNDERWOOD IS PROBABLY WATCHING TO SEE IF HE HAS COMPANY.

VUGOVIC: WE SHOULD HAVE THIS COMPLETED IN AN HOUR.

SPIKIC: MAKE HIM SUFFER LIKE A LEGLESS DOG IN BARBED WIRE.

VUGOVIC: THE BOYS WERE SUGGESTING WE MAKE HIM EAT HIS OWN TESTICLES WHILE HIS COCK WATCHES FROM A SAFE DISTANCE.

SPIKIC: [LAUGHTER] VERY WELL, CALL AS SOON AS YOU HAVE THE LITTLE GLASS. THE JEWS ARE WAITING.

VUGOVIC: WHAT OF THAT WHORE IDI RAYKOVIC?

SPIKIC: SHE WAS A GOOD FUCK.

VUGOVIC: AND WHAT ABOUT TITO—DID THEY ARRANGE FOR THIS MAN GILL TO STEAL FROM US?

SPIKIC: IF TITO DID, THE BITCH DOESN'T KNOW ABOUT IT. I'M GETTING SOFT, VUGO—I SPARED THE WHORE'S DOG.

VUGOVIC: [LAUGHTER] IT WOULD ONLY HAVE MADE A MESS ANYWAY. MY OPINION IS THAT TITO IS NOT CLEVER OR BRAVE ENOUGH TO HAVE ARRANGED THIS. THE MASTURBATING

LONG-HAIRED SMALL RODENT WAS SO FRIGHTENED HE WAS WEEPING AND WETTING HIS PANTS.

SPIKIC: [LAUGHTER] BRING ME GOOD NEWS AND WE'LL BE NECK DEEP IN RUSSIAN WHORES AND SMALL MELONS BY TO-MORROW MORNING.

VUGOVIC: SOON.

SPIKIC: GOOD HUNTING.

END

NINE

FROM THE EMBANKMENT ABOVE the barn next to a boulder, I kept my binoculars trained on the road below. Sure enough a red Miata appeared. I gave Felix directions over Phone #1, the same phone I used to call him the first time. But I hadn't even called him yet when the Kurac goons showed themselves in the woods, slipping from tree to tree as they drew near to my stash of Old Crow, bloody bandages, and the SUV. Like I figured, they'd found the garage through a fix on Trudy's phone, the one I left on in the barn. They'd made someone talk. It wouldn't have been Roberto; he wouldn't have compromised the mission. But one of his men may have sold me out. Or maybe Ramón sold me out without Roberto knowing—he never liked me. Since I'd called Roberto on Trudy's phone first thing that morning, Ramón had that number, either through caller ID or through phone records from the Kurac's sources through the Russians at the phone company or the police.

It was grim to watch the Serbs in muscle shirts and track pants close in, knowing what they would have done to me had I actually been in the barn. At the same time it was good to know my caution was paying off. When you're in a tight spot, it's better to know who you can't trust than who you can. It was also good to know that I could use the Corporation if I wanted to leak misinformation, like the details I gave to Roberto about the beach house.

As instructed, Felix stopped his red Miata in front of the garage doors and beeped his horn twice.

The goons began moving in, and when I didn't come out the way I said I would, about eight of them stormed the place. Felix sped away.

Another car came down the drive.

An Audi.

Two got out. One was another soldier. The other wore a shiny suit, six-foot and in his fifties. The pale, pocked face told me it had been a hard five decades. He had brown hair streaked white in a short ponytail, shaved close at the sides, and he walked chest out.

That was the guy I was up against. No doubt this douchebag had a boss, but this was the one who was trying to put the hooks in me, the brain that would be trying to angle my next twist. The rest of these guys—while no doubt viscous deviants—were just soldiers. By the looks of things, my adversary didn't seem to have a second in command.

After a few moments inside, he stomped back outside holding the colorful shirt I'd worn the night before, the one from under the SUV's back seat. He had it to his nose, smelling me. I'd never seen somebody do that—it was a little freaky.

He took the shirt from his nose, cocked his head, and turned his dark eyes in my direction. Even from there I could see the eyes were black and flat like a shark's. It was like he knew I was there watching, like he could smell me on the breeze. I slunk back away from the edge of the embankment. He was no dummy; my adversary knew I might be watching, and where else but from the top of the ravine? If he took the bait that Trudy was alive, he might have even imagined that both of us had narrowly escaped somehow when we caught a glimpse of his goons' approach.

I knew not to push my luck and take another look. *This creep was smelling my shirt.*

I jogged south along the twisty roads dotted with bungalows tucked in the forest. At the river's edge there was a path, and I took it south, the saddle bag of sparks bouncing on my shoulder. The path brought me to a concrete wall that was the edge of a raised parking lot for an apartment complex. I climbed the rope I'd left there, unhooked it from the parapet, and rolled over the parapet into the parking lot. There was a pattern of decorative holes in the wall, and I watched for a few minutes to see if I was followed. Why? To see if they followed me, tracked me, known that I was watching them, that I was alone, and not with Trudy. It's important to know what your enemy knows, and more importantly only let him know what you want him to know. I wanted the Kurac to continue believing I was trying to keep her alive and running for my life. I wanted them to think I was weak.

They didn't show.

I trotted over to the Nighthawk, fired her up, and curved out of the parking lot. My path lay north, up River Road and past the street where the barn was.

I didn't dare turn my head that direction as I passed. What if that shitbag was standing there smelling my shirt, waiting for me?

Stomach in knots, I throttled the bike across the George Washington Bridge, the sky laced with steel cables and the huge span stabbing over the river at the heart of Washington Heights in Upper Manhattan. The sun was high and bright over the glistening Hudson River, on which sailboats, tugs, and barges sliced the water.

I let myself wonder what I'd do if they caught up with me.

I had to plan for that, too.

THUS WE MAY KNOW THAT THERE ARE FIVE ESSENTIALS FOR VICTORY:

1. *HE WILL WIN WHO KNOWS WHEN TO FIGHT AND WHEN NOT TO FIGHT.*
2. *HE WILL WIN WHO KNOWS HOW TO MANIPULATE SUPERIOR AND INFERIOR FORCES.*
3. *HE WILL WIN WHOSE ARMY IS ANIMATED BY A COMMON PURPOSE.*
4. *HE WILL WIN WHO WAITS TO ENGAGE THE ENEMY UNPREPARED.*
5. *HE WILL WIN WHO HAS MILITARY CAPACITY.*

THUS THE SAYING: IF YOU KNOW YOUR ENEMY AND KNOW YOURSELF, THERE IS NO FEAR OF A HUNDRED BATTLES BETWEEN YOU. IF YOU KNOW YOURSELF BUT NOT THE ENEMY, FOR EVERY VICTORY, YOU SHALL SUFFER A LOSS. IF YOU KNOW NEITHER YOUR ENEMY NOR YOURSELF, YOU WILL LOSE ALL BATTLES.

—*Sun Tzu*, The Art of War

TEN

DCSNet 6000 Warrant Database
Transcript Cell Phone Track and Trace
Peerless IP Network / Redhook Translation
Target: Dragan Spikic
Date: Sunday, August 8, 2010
Time: 1101–1106 EDT

SPIKIC: TALK TO ME.

VUGOVIC: WE DID NOT GET HIM.

SPIKIC: GO BACK TO YOUR MOTHER'S CUNT, VUGO! HOW COULD YOU LET THIS HAPPEN?

VUGOVIC: EVERYTHING WENT AS PLANNED ON OUR END. WE TRACKED THE PHONE TO A BARN OFF THE MAIN ROAD. THE VET GOT THE CALL TO COME, EVEN AS MY MEN WERE MOVING IN ON THE BARN. IT SEEMS UNDERWOOD TOOK THE GIRL AND LEFT JUST BEFORE WE GOT THERE, SOMEHOW. I DON'T UNDERSTAND. AN SUV WAS THERE, BLOODY BANDAGES, HER CELL PHONE, THE CLOTHES HE WORE IN THE ROBBERY, EVERYTHING. JUST NOT THEM.

SPIKIC: YOU'VE BEEN UP YOUR ASS AND KNOW SHIT! YOU HAD BETTER 'UNDERSTAND' VERY QUICKLY, MY FRIEND.

VUGOVIC: WE ARE WORKING ON THE HOUSE AT THE BEACH, AND HIS APARTMENT CONTAINED SOME INTERESTING DETAILS. IT SEEMS HE WAS MILITARY. NAVY.

SPIKIC: SO WHAT DOES THAT TELL YOU? HE HAS A BOAT?

VUGOVIC: DISCHARGE PAPERS SAY HE WAS A LIEUTENANT. AND THERE WAS ACCOMMODATION FOR BEING WOUNDED. IT MAKES ME WONDER ABOUT UNDERWOOD. I FEEL OUR QUARRY MAY BE MORE FOX THAN DOVE.

SPIKIC: PARENTS, FIND HIS PARENTS OR FRIENDS AND TRUSS THEM UP LIKE GAME BIRDS. THAT WILL FLUSH HIM OUT OF HIS MOTHER'S ASS.

VUGOVIC: THERE WAS NO ADDRESS BOOK, NO LETTERS. THIS MAN HAD VERY LITTLE IN HIS PLACE OTHER THAN EXERCISE EQUIPMENT, A TV, CLOTHES—IT WAS LIKE A MOTEL ROOM, LIKE HE EXPECTED TO LEAVE ANY DAY. YET HIS LANDLADY TOLD US HE HAD BEEN THERE FOR FIVE YEARS.

SPIKIC: WHAT OF THE CUNT?

VUGOVIC: HER PLACE WAS THE SAME. AND SHE, TOO, WAS MILITARY, A NAVY DIVER.

SPIKIC: A DIVER? MAY GOD FUCK YOU IN THE EYES, VUGO, WHAT DOES THAT MEAN?

VUGOVIC: A NAVY DIVER IS SOMETHING LIKE SPECIAL FORCES. THEY BOTH WERE EX-MILITARY, SO TO MY THINKING THEY WERE USED TO LIVING THE MILITARY LIFESTYLE OF VERY FEW

POSSESSIONS, MOBILITY. THIS COULD BE MORE DIFFICULT THAN WE BARGAINED FOR. THESE ARE SOLDIERS.

SPIKIC: THEY ARE NAVY AND THEIR CUNTS CAN'T HOLD WATER! IF YOU CAN'T FUCK THEIR MOTHERS ON THEIR FATHERS' GRAVE YOU ARE NO BETTER, AND GOD WILL FUCK YOU AND MAKE YOU HIS SPITTOON! FIND THEM! YOU WERE A SOLDIER, AND YOU ARE A SOLDIER! WOLVES EAT WOLVES! FIND THEM!

END

ELEVEN

It was two that afternoon by the time I wedged my bike into a legal space on Main Street in Flushing. It was my third stop, at East Trading Jewelers in Flushing, Queens. On a Sunday afternoon, the Chinatown thoroughfare was jostling with Asians of every stripe on errands. Trudy and I used to have some incredible meals here after seeing Doc Huang. I could never remember what it was called—Spicy and Tasty? Tasty and Spicy? The place had the most incredible string beans with minced pork. Never much of a string bean fan, either of us, and this was our favorite dish, along with the sesame dan-dan noodles. Both of which were good dishes for Trudy to learn how to use chopsticks. I'd never have a chance to eat there again.

Yet my plans had to include making sure I kept my energy up. At a food cart I grabbed a twenty-ounce cola.

Sipping sugar and caffeine, I pushed into East Trading Jewelers, the display cases glowing with gold, the walls festooned with pictures of wedding rings and moist brides.

"I help you today?" A plump Chinese girl with too much eye shadow was behind the counter. She was squeezed into one of those silk sheath dresses.

"Doc Huang is expecting me."

"Yes, please, this way."

I followed her wiggle through some back curtains past a small lunch room and bathroom to an office door with a Chinese good-luck emblem tacked on it. She rapped a knuckle on the door.

"Come!"

She closed the door behind me as I stepped into Doc Huang's lair, the walls lined with locking cabinets above low tables fitted with lamps and magnifiers. Fluorescents under the cabinets ringed the room with light. In the middle of the room was yet another table with a lamp and a magnifier and a plump Chinese woman in a pink pantsuit: Doc. She had taken off her magnifying goggles and held them with one hand. In the other she held a wedding ring with a modest brilliant-cut stone that flickered under her lamp.

She tilted her big head at the ring. "This stone is crap. My cousin wants a thousand for it, and my family will be pissed if I don't give him the thousand. What would you do?"

"I wouldn't give him the thousand. I'd tell him all the reasons why: the muddy color, the uneven faceting. I'd tell him I was doing him a favor by giving him five hundred and that if he accepted the money, it was on condition he told the family he got the thousand. If I'm going to take grief from the family, I might as well take it for giving him nothing at all."

Doc laughed softly, her chest heaving, and set the goggles and ring down. "Thanks, Gill, I like that answer—how are you?" She extended a hand, and I shook it.

"Fine."

"That's not what I hear from friends in Fort Lee."

There's a solid Asian contingent just across the GW Bridge. I had wondered if she'd call people there and check up on the latest news.

I tensed, my saddle bag feeling heavy on my shoulder. Teddy and Steve hadn't picked up the news. Then again, they were more or less straight businessmen. Doc was a little more connected.

She waved a hand at a rattan chair opposite her. "Don't worry, Gill, I haven't fingered you. The Kurac are no friends to the Asian community; they think we're all subhumans. I guess the Cubans haven't figured that they are subhumans, too, or maybe they wouldn't have flipped on you. I heard a Cuban squealed on you. Its people like the Kurac who make me question how there could possibly be a merciful God. Because I know your situation means I would be foolish to pay top dollar. For the Fifth Avenue sparks."

I eased into the chair, wanting very badly to light up a Winston.

She continued, gesturing to my saddle bag.

"I understand you have some very special sparks in there. The Britany-Swindol sparks."

"Not on me."

"Hm." Doc leaned back in her chair, away from the light, just a silhouette with sparkling eyes. "What say we forget about the Fifth Avenue junk? You might as well take that wherever you're going. You can sell that as easily here as in Sweden. Did you have plans for the big stones?"

"Not yet. I've had a lot on my mind. That's too tricky for me even to think about."

"You may not have been thinking about it, but I have."

I guzzled some of my cola and then skipped ahead a few questions. "How would you unload them? Israel?"

She shook her head. "China, dummy. The conversion rate is quite favorable for them at this time."

"I'm a reasonable person, Doc, you know that. But I'm not going to be a pushover. There's going to have to be serious money." I stood. "This has got to be my ticket out. I'll stash it for a rainy day if I have to."

"Relax. Sit."

"I can't relax, Doc, you know that, there is no relaxing for me. For all I know those bastards are right outside. My brain is moving in eight directions at once trying to stay ahead of them, trying to keep them from putting my hands in meat grinders."

"It's not your hands you should be worried about." She sighed. "Why would I even be discussing this opportunity if I had the Kurac in the wings? C'mon, Gill. I can help you. And Trudy. How is she?"

"Not great."

Doc bowed her head. "She seen a cat doctor?"

"I tried, but it was a setup."

"Damn those Cubans. Look, I can give you the name of a Chinese herbalist. He's right around the corner. I can call and ask him to fix you up with something. That stuff they do really does work."

"What makes you think I can trust him?"

"I'll dial, you listen until the herbalist answers, okay? That way you'll know it isn't the Kurac."

I thought about it a moment.

"What's this going to cost me?"

Doc leaned into the light, her eyes in deep shadows from the lamp, her smile slight.

"I want you to trust me. Let me broker the Britany-Swindol sparks to Hong Kong."

"Since you know my situation, you can use that to squeeze me."

"I could. But you know what?"

I raised an eyebrow, waiting.

"Gill, I despise those fuckers with every fiber of my being. I want you to get away with this. Yes, I want to make money."

"What happens when the Kurac find out you had a hand in taking their gems? They will."

Doc cocked her head. "The Corporation may fear the Kurac, and the Russians may be their friends. My friends from Hong Kong neither fear nor befriend these bastards. In fact, some of them would welcome the opportunity to confront them. Gill, I'm giving you and Trudy a path out. You let me broker the Britany-Swindol take to Hong Kong, and we'll take care of these Kurac for you, too."

"Sounds like your people want this as much to entrap the Serbs as anything else. I know the Hong Kong friends are probably still pissed about the smash-and-grab operation the Kurac pulled in Macau."

"Yes, that was my friends' store, the one they used to move *their* merchandise. You see? You have done to the Kurac what the Kurac did to my friends in Hong Kong, and so they want to complete that payback by taking possessions of the sparks. They will get you and Trudy out of the country, complete with paper. And pay you for the gems, less my fee, of course. Gill, look at me, what more could you ask for?"

I kept my eyes on the far wall, and finished my soda. "I won't feel comfortable unless we do this in stages, Doc. I know you may mean well, but I don't know your friends. Nobody in the business can really vouch for people like that. They're takers, not givers. I'll first need the paper, as a gesture that they mean what they say. With plane tickets to Iceland for tomorrow night in the names on the paper. And I'll need that tonight."

"Passports by tonight?" Doc leaned back again with a groan. "Iceland?"

"Well, Doc, just how long am I supposed to dance before I get tripped up? I have to sleep eventually, but with these Serbian dirtbags on my case I don't see that happening. I don't see me staying in one place more than an hour. Yes, I need to see those tonight, and we'll do the exchange tomorrow afternoon."

"What about photos?"

"There's a passport-photo guy down the street—I'll drop over and be right back." I slid my saddle bag off my shoulder, and fished around inside. "Here's Trudy's passport photo." I handed it over as Doc picked up the phone and dialed. "Make our names Mike and Marcia Thomas."

"I will still have to check with Hong Kong."

I pulled a wad of tissue from the knapsack and laid it on the desk in front of her.

"They're going to make a good faith gesture, now I'm making a good faith gesture."

Doc spoke rapidly into the phone and hung up. Leaning over the paper, she unfolded it with one hand while lowering the magnifying lamp with the other. Diamonds flashed as she flattened the paper—it was a pair of Britany-Swindol crossover drop pendants, fully encrusted in sparks. Retail? Probably mid-twenties.

"Doc, you check that against the hot sheets, you'll see it was from the Macau operation pulled by the Kurac. This way your friends in Hong Kong will know I've got the assets, safe and sound. I'll need the Mike and Marcia paper and Iceland tickets delivered. Call the number I called you from and leave a message when they're ready. I'll call back with the drop-off instructions."

Doc finally lifted her eyes from the earrings to me, and smirked. "You know, Gill, I hope you pull this off, I really do. Have you ever heard of *yuanfen*?"

I shook my head.

"*Yuanfen* is the ancient Chinese idea that two people are destined to meet."

"Like lovers?"

Doc pursed her lips. "Sort of. It includes repeated chance meetings of strangers and any big, life-altering joining of two people. I think you and I have *yuanfen*. This deal is huge, and because we met and are friends, you and Trudy will get safely out of the country and out of the business. This is no life for people in love."

"So this mess is all the work of fate? I wish it were that easy, that there aren't responsible parties. It would make it easier. So where's this herbalist?"

"The herbalist is on Union Street, around the corner. Mr. Zim. Make Trudy well. We'll make this work with the Hong Kong people, one way or the other."

I attempted a smile.

"Odds are on *the other*."

TWELVE

DCSNet 6000 Warrant Database
Transcript Cell Phone Track and Trace
Peerless IP Network / Redhook Translation
Target: Tito Raykovic
Date: Sunday, August 8, 2010
Time: 1405–1408 EDT

TITO: IDI?

IDI: YES, HOW ARE YOU, DEAR?

TITO: WHERE HAVE YOU BEEN? MY GOD, I WAS WORRIED.

IDI: SPIKIC WANTED TO SEE ME.

TITO: [UNINTELLIGIBLE]

IDI: OF COURSE, ABOUT THE ROBBERY.

TITO: FUCK A RODENT! WHAT DID YOU TELL HIM? WHY DID HE NOT ASK ME?

IDI: YOU HAVE PANTS FULL OF CRAP, TITO, YOUR COCK FOLDED IN TWO. IMAGINE IF YOU HAD SPOKEN WITH HIM? HE WOULD SEE YOUR PANIC AND ASSUME YOU ARE GUILTY.

TITO: IS IT WRONG TO WORRY? NO, IT IS RIGHT THAT I WORRY. GRAVEDIGGERS LICK SPIKIC'S TESTICLES. IF HE BLAMES US, HE WILL KILL US.

IDI: THANKS TO ME HE DOES NOT BLAME US.

TITO: HE DIDN'T TOUCH YOU, DID HE?

IDI: AND WHAT IF HE DID? WHAT WOULD YOU DO ABOUT IT?

TITO: TELL ME!

IDI: WHY SHOULD I TELL YOU ANYTHING, YOU FAT LITTLE LIZ-ARD? WHERE HAVE YOU BEEN WHILE I WAS PUTTING THINGS RIGHT WITH SPIKIC? CURLED UP IN A BOTTLE, I HAVE LITTLE DOUBT. YOU WERE THE ONE WHO HELD THEIR COCKS. YOU NEVER SHOULD HAVE GOTTEN IN BUSINESS WITH THESE CRIMINALS TO BEGIN WITH.

TITO: THAT CUNT DOESN'T HOLD WATER, YOU WANTON FE-MALE DOG! WERE IT NOT FOR YOU AND YOUR FURS AND DIAMONDS, I WOULD NOT HAVE NEEDED THE MONEY THEY PAY. I AM A WEALTHY MAN WITH LARGE DEVELOPMENT DEALS, BUT YOU—A FARMER'S DAUGHTER—MAKE ME POOR WITH YOUR FANCY WAYS AND OPERATIONS TO MAKE YOUR-SELF A GODDESS. AND BY MY MOTHER'S CUNT THAT DOG LIVES BETTER THAN A SULTAN!

IDI: DO YOU NOT DROOL OVER MY BREASTS AND TAKE MY LIP ON THAT BUG'S COCK OF YOURS? I BEND OVER PLENTY FOR YOU.

TITO: WHAT I DID WAS A FAVOR FOR THEM AND FOR YOU AND FOR US. DON'T PUSH ME, IDI! EVEN I HAVE LIMITS.

IDI: YOU STILL HAVE NOT ANSWERED THE QUESTION. WHAT WOULD YOU DO?

TITO: DID YOU LET HIM FUCK YOU?

IDI: ANSWER THE QUESTION, BUG COCK!

TITO: I WOULD KILL YOU AND HIM!

IDI: [LAUGHTER]

TITO: HELLO? HELLO? WANTON FEMALE DOG!

END

THIRTEEN

DOWN THE BLOCK WAS a stationer that did passport photos. I did my best to slick my hair all the way back, got the photo, and dropped it back at Doc's with the plump counter girl.

I made my way to Union Street and the door to Mr. Zim. There was a neon sign in the window: ACUPUNCTURE—CUPPING—HEALING. These Chinatown herbalists do their magic in normal retail shop space, and this one could easily have been a beauty shop or travel agency. Except there were acupuncture charts on the walls and dark shelves lined with jars full of dried roots, berries, twigs, and who knew what. In front was a counter stacked with bright Chinese boxes of elixirs and a mortar and pestle; in back was an examination table, a Chinese screen, and a rollaway instrument cart loaded with acupuncture needles, cups, and incense. The place smelled like tea and licorice.

Behind the counter was a chipper man with a wrinkled head, the kind that looked like a dried apple on a stick. Except it had black hair with white roots and matching wispy beard. Bad dye job. Vanity is boundless.

Mr. Zim removed his specs: "Huang called." And then he peered over my shoulder at the shop window to make sure nobody had followed me. "For this service I charge a thousand."

"A thousand?"

"What would cat doctor ask?" He wagged a finger at me. "Much more."

"Can you help?"

"Depends."

"On?"

"If she not dead."

"Bullet went through right here, came out the other side." I pointed to my side. "Now it's all blown up and yellow. She has a fever."

"Not good." He shook his head, and wagged his finger again. "Wait. Few minutes."

He went past the examination table and around the corner, out of sight.

I stepped out front, burned a Winston, and fished around my pockets for ten hundreds. When I was done Zim was at the counter with a box of slim glass vials, a jar of something slimy, and a bag of something crispy. His instructions were elaborate. The basics were to administer one vial an hour orally, put the slimy stuff on Trudy's wound with a hot compress every two hours, and dampen and smolder the crunchy stuff and fan it over her frequently. I loaded it all into my saddle bag.

"And if she doesn't improve?"

"Better get to hospital. Or cemetery."

I tugged on my lower lip a moment. "Zim? If this doesn't go well, it will have to be the cemetery. You have anything that could make it easier?"

He took off his specs again, and looked out the front windows. "Of course."

"Quick and painless. And small."

He eyed me very carefully. "This for her? Or you?"

I gulped, my eyes moist. "Does it matter?"

"Only to you." He reached for a jar on a lower shelf, and from inside pulled two regulation-sized sticks of gum wrapped in yellow paper with red Chinese characters. "Chew, and go in peace. Forever."

I dropped the thousand dollars on the counter and left.

Around the corner I dropped the crap Mr. Zim gave me in a dumpster.

Except the gum.

FOURTEEN

I HAD NO INTENTION of going to Iceland, but it didn't hurt to let Doc's Hong Kong friends think I was. Yet why not Iceland? It wasn't like Antwerp or London or Tokyo, where they would expect there to be a lot of connected goons, and it was the sort of place that would make a good jumping-off place to Europe and beyond. No doubt they would be flying people there to sandbag me when I came out of the airport. Just a few less to try to sandbag me in New York. Of course, as the mission proceeded, I would have to weigh my options and consider alternatives, but getting out of town for a while was a given. Australia might be far enough. I looked forward to drinking and sleeping on a long flight to the ends of the earth, a place where I could stand at the planet's edge and stare into oblivion for a while catching fading glimpses of Trudy.

Bric-a-brac stores in Flushing have almost every known product to mankind, and much of it spills out the front onto sidewalk bins and hangs from the awnings. I ducked into one of these places and picked up an oversized belly bag, the kind tourists strap around their midsection. Another purchase was a bill pen, the kind you mark bills with to see if they're real, and a large pack of Wrigley's. I put the gum and pen into the belly bag and strapped it on. The saddle bag I strapped back onto the Nighthawk.

Tito's watch said three thirty.

I fired up the bike and hit a gas station on College Point Boulevard before jumping on the Whitestone Expressway to the Van Wyck Expressway south. I snaked my way past Flushing Meadows Park in heavy traffic through the Grand Central Parkway interchange aimed at JFK, New York's international airport. Sunday afternoon traffic was heavy with beachgoers, picnickers, weekenders headed home from the last of their weekend fun.

At a short-term parking garage, I motored to the corner highest and farthest from the entrance to the terminal, where there were a lot of tired people coming off their Sunday afternoon flights from summer vacations.

I parked the bike and grabbed the plastic socket wrench box with the Britany-Swindol assets. In the back stairwell I found a fire hose cubby built into the cinder brick wall. I opened the access door. There was an almost empty pint of vodka and some other litter that I cleared out so I could inspect the tag on the hose. The fire-deterrent system had been tested every six months for the last few years, and the most recent date was the end of June. The next inspection was four months off. The flat hose was folded accordion-style on an armature that swung out so that a fireman could easily unfurl the hose out of the cubby. I tucked the socket wrench box into the back of the cubby and swung the hose back into place, closing the door. The socket wrench box was blocked from view by the hose and couldn't be seen through the cubby door's glass. Unless some moron happened to mess with this fire hose box in the next twenty-eight hours, the Britany-Swindol sparks were safely stored at my escape point. Monday would bring mostly business travelers, and they hardly had time to explore the garage stairwells, especially the ones farthest from the terminal.

Back at the Nighthawk, I slid Mr. Zim's fatal sticks of gum into the normal gum wrappers and then into the end of the Wrigley's pack, marking their ends with my thumbnail. The two sticks of gum they replaced I put in my mouth and matched a Winston.

I checked Tito's Patek Philippe. Four thirty. With any luck, the Serbs would be combing Long Beach Island looking for the beach house where they imagined me nursing Trudy. That would make New York and the Gold Coast safer for me. How long would they stay focused on that diversion before they turned elsewhere? Especially if Teddy, Steve, or Doc ratted me out? Doc was the loose cannon. What was to keep her from setting up the exchange with her Hong Kong friends and then handing me over to the Serbs? For all I knew, the Macau heist was sanctioned by the Hong Kong friends, an insurance rip-off. In a few hours I'd carefully take delivery of the paper and tickets, which, if a double cross didn't come down then, would at least let Hong Kong think I was a hundred percent on board with their schemes.

Heading back north I exited the Van Wyck onto a business strip in a residential area where I thought I remembered a diner next door to a motel. I'd stayed at the motel once after an operation where I made the tactical error of letting an elevator camera take a picture of me. Part of why I don't like leaving an operation by elevator. It wasn't a very good picture, but to be safe I had to stay out of New Jersey for a week until they stopped running my picture on Channel 12.

My memory didn't fail me. I parked at the diner and turned on Phone #2, which I'd used to call Teddy, Steve, and Doc. I walked across the street and dropped the phone into a trash can in front of the motel. Back in front of the diner I bought a newspaper from a metal box. Inside the diner I got myself a booth at the tinted window where I could keep an eye on the trash can over the top of my paper.

Coffee tasted like mud, and it was all I could do to swallow a burger deluxe worth of carbs and greasy protein. I didn't care if I ever ate again, yet I needed the energy and I needed to stay awake. Other than a cola, cigarettes, and Wrigley's, dinner was the first meal of the day.

The waitress had served me about a gallon of coffee over an hour and a half before a Chinese kid in a leather vest appeared in front of the motel smoking a cigarette. He stole long looks at the front of the motel while alternately checking his watch, and finally decided to go into the motel office. He came back out and went through the parking lot looking at license plates. The desk clerk had been no help in telling the kid which room I was in.

I went to the bathroom to get rid of some coffee. When I got back to my booth the kid had returned to the front of the motel and was standing next to the trash can, his cell phone to his ear. Phone tucked back into his shirt pocket, he faced the motel and waited.

His head snapped toward the trash can. They had called Phone #2 to see if I would pick up, to see if they could get an idea what room I was in, maybe to make me come out of my room, I had no idea. The kid soon had my phone in one hand and his in the other.

My waitress was relieved that I finally paid my check and that I actually tipped her well. I exited to the parking lot through a side entrance away from the motel.

Helmet under my arm, I turned the corner of the diner. The kid was ten feet ahead, walking around the diner, looking at the cars. And then he looked at me.

He tried ducking his head, reaching for his cell phone, pretending he hadn't recognized me.

I called out to him. "Excuse me, pal, can you tell me how to get to the Whitestone Expressway?"

Indecision on the kid's part caused him to hesitate, and that put me close to where he was standing. Close enough.

I pointed behind him. "Maybe your friend knows."

He was just a kid after all.

My helmet caught him in the back of the head when I swung it, and his phone clattered across the macadam as he fell. I jogged over and plucked the phone from the ground, just as he was trying to stand. The second blow was to the side of his head. I threw his phone over a fence into a yard.

"Hey!" Two white older men with bellies and sport shirts approached. "What goes on?"

"Fucket." I pointed at the ground where the kid lay squirming. "Kid tried to rip me off. Tried to hold me up."

One said, "No shit?"

The other said, "It's a Chink! I didn't think they did that."

"Can you guys watch him while I get a cop?"

They puffed their chests. Almost in unison they said, "We're vets!"

"I'll be right back."

As the two duffers stood over the kid, I wheeled my bike out around the corner to the boulevard, fired her up, and found the Whitestone without any directions. I felt sorry for the kid. But he would have learned his lesson one way or the other, if not me, someone else, and it may have cost him his life instead of a swollen head and a reprimand.

Tito's watch: six twenty.

The Whitestone Bridge's span arced out before me, sun low on the left making long shadows of the cables. To my right and a mile away the Throgs Neck Bridge glistened with traffic, its span straddling the East River as it opened up into Long Island Sound and a clutter of sailboats.

Doc's Hong Kong friends clearly had the ability to track my phone, just like the Kurac, and comparably devious. At least they were all about their own interests, and countered the Kurac interests. By sucker-punching their kid at the diner I'd just let Doc's friends know that I was no dummy, so maybe later when I got the paper and the tickets they would play straight. That was a big maybe.

The Kurac would soon realize the beach house was a ruse and be back in play, and I'd have to do some fancy dancing to stay clear of them long enough to make the exchange with the Chinese at JFK the following night. Yet two adversaries with disparate interests could be useful.

With both off-balance, it was important to seek out weak spots and gain human intelligence if possible.

FIFTEEN

INVESTIGATIVE DATA WAREHOUSE
SPT SUBSYSTEM
DATE: SUNDAY AUGUST 8, 2010
TIME: 1830 EDT

NCES / DOE EDUCATION BIO: UNDERWOOD, GILL
DOB AUGUST 23, 1971, BETHESDA, MD
CLIFTON ELEMENTARY, CLIFTON, NJ (NIA) 1977–1983
CLIFTON JR. HIGH, CLIFTON, NJ (NIA) 1983–1984
CLIFTON HIGH, CLIFTON, NJ (GPA 1.5) 1985
VALLEY FORGE MILITARY ACADEMY, WAYNE, PA GPA 3.9
   1986–1989

SAT: 690/720

FAIRLEIGH DICKINSON UNIVERSITY, MADISON, NJ 1989–1993

HISTORY GPA 4.0

ARREST RECORD: JUVENILE (SEALED)

SIRPNet BIO: UNDERWOOD, GILL

US NAVY: ENLIST, NY, NY JULY 1993

ASVAB SCORE: AFQT 95%

PHYSICAL: PASS

CAREER CLASSIFICATION: INTELLIGENCE

PRE-ENLIST INTERVIEW: ADDT'L TESTING—IQ 135

GREAT LAKES NAVAL TRAINING CENTER: REPORT SEPTEMBER 1993

A-SCHOOL: OFFICER'S CANDIDATE SCHOOL (OSC) NEWPORT, RI JANUARY 1994

COMMISSION: ENSIGN, JUNE 1994

ASSIGNED: BAHRAIN, OFFICE OF NAVAL INTELLIGENCE, AUGUST 1994

REASSIGNED: NAPLES, ITALY, OFFICE OF NAVAL INTELLIGENCE, COUNTERINTELLIGENCE UNIT, AUGUST 1996

PROMOTION: LIEUTENANT (GRADE) AUGUST 1996

REASSIGNED: PEARL HARBOR, HI, OFFICE OF NAVAL INTELLI-GENCE, CONTINGENCY OPERATIONS UNIT, MAY 1997

LIAISON: CENTER FOR NAVAL INTELLIGENCE, ALEXANDRIA, VA 1998

REASSIGNED: JOINT INTELLIGENCE CENTER, BAHRAIN, DECEM-BER 2001

REASSIGNED: NAVY SEALS, TACTICAL LIAISON, MARCH 2002

WOUNDED: IN ACTION, CITATION, MAY 2002

HOSPITALIZED: PORTSMOUTH NAVAL MEDICAL CENTER, PSY-
CHIATRIC CENTER, JUNE 2002
PROMOTION: LIEUTENANT (FULL) JUNE 2002
REASSIGNED: CENTER FOR NAVAL INTELLIGENCE, COUNTER
INTELLIGENCE INSTRUCTOR, NORFOLK, VA JANUARY 2003
DISCHARGE: HONORABLE, JANUARY 2004

NCES / DOE EDUCATION BIO: ELWELL, TRUDY
DOB MARCH 17, 1974, SCARSDALE, NY
SCARSDALE ELEMENTARY, SCARSDALE, NY (NIA) 1980–1986
WESTCHESTER JR. HIGH, SCARSDALE, NY (NIA) 1986–1987
WHITE PLAINS HIGH, WHITE PLAINS, NY (GPA 3.5) 1987–1991
SAT: 650/710
PRINCETON UNIVERSITY, PRINCETON, NJ 1991–1995 BFA GPA 4.0

ARREST RECORD: JUVENILE (SEALED); DRUNK AND DISORDERLY,
HONOLULU, HI AUGUST 1997; TRESPASSING, DRUNK AND
DISORDERLY, RESISTING ARREST, PANAMA CITY, FL, APRIL
2000.

SIRPNet BIO: ELWELL, TRUDY
US NAVY: ENLIST, WHITE PLAINS, NY JUNE 1995
ASVAB SCORE: AFQT 97%
PHYSICAL: PASS
CAREER CLASSIFICATION: ANALYST
PRE-ENLIST INTERVIEW: ADDT'L TESTING—IQ 110
GREAT LAKES NAVAL TRAINING CENTER: REPORT SEPTEMBER
1995
A-SCHOOL: OFFICER'S CANDIDATE SCHOOL (OSC) NEWPORT, RI
JANUARY 1996

COMMISSION: ENSIGN, JUNE 1996

ASSIGNED: NAVAL DIVING AND SALVAGE TRAINING CENTER (NDSTC) PANAMA CITY, FL JULY 1996

FLEET TRAINING: PEARL HARBOR, HI, OFFICE OF NAVAL INTELLI-GENCE, CONTINGENCY OPERATIONS UNIT, APRIL 1997

PROMOTION: LIEUTENANT (GRADE) AUGUST 1999

ADVANCED TRAINING: NAVAL DIVING AND SALVAGE TRAINING CENTER (NDSTC) PANAMA CITY, FL APRIL 2000

SPECIALIZED TRAINING: JOINT INTELLIGENCE CENTER, BAHRAIN DECEMBER 2001

WOUNDED: IN ACTION, CITATION, MAY 2002

HOSPITALIZED: PORTSMOUTH NAVAL MEDICAL CENTER, PSYCHIATRIC CENTER, AUGUST 2002

DISCHARGE: HONORABLE, OCTOBER 2002

SIXTEEN

I WENT TO THE Grand Excelsior and asked the desk to ring Tito's apartment.

There was no answer.

"Any idea where I might find him?"

The droopy clerk knit his brow. "Tonight?"

"Yes."

"Most nights you can find him at Benito's."

"Have you seen his wife today?"

"Who are you?"

"A friend." I turned toward the doors. "Thanks."

Benito's was one of the few decent Italian restaurants on the Gold Coast. It was on the first floor of a high-rise called the Galaxy, which was an early real estate anchor atop the Palisades that came complete with its own retail plaza, pharmacy, liquor store, restaurants, and movie theater. It was built when there was nowhere else to shop or eat close by. While it once had pretensions of glitz, the Galaxy—having been there since the beginning of time—had a mostly elderly population. An assisted-living facility had moved in across the street for easy transition. Almost everybody there seemed to own a dog, and while there were scooper laws in effect, the sidewalks and parapet around there stank of animal piss.

I'd never lifted any sparks at the Galaxy. Twenty years ago, had I been in the business, I might have. Stealing from old ladies and frail men was something I didn't do. There were plenty of younger morons with piles of sparks splayed on the dresser.

Benito's was tucked into the lower-right façade, paneled in wood and comfy with squeaky, red-vinyl banquets. A dark wooden bar was in back, where Tito—in a rumpled suit—sat on a stool. In front of him was a scotch and his cell phone. Around him the restaurant was busy enough for a Sunday evening, but most of the elderly crowd had eaten at five and were already upstairs soaking their dentures.

Tito's face was flush from the bender he was on. The Hispanic bartender with the giant mustache seemed a little on edge, probably about whether his customer should continue to be served, and he eyed me nervously as I sat next to Tito.

A napkin was placed on the bar in front of me. I could have used a bourbon. A big one. That couldn't happen until I was on my way to the edge of the earth.

"I'm on the wagon tonight—seltzer and lime, please." The bartender's mustache twitched, and he looked briefly relieved.

I held my wrist in front of Tito. "This your watch?"

Tito blinked hard. "No, I don't know what time it is."

"No, what I meant was, is this your watch, the one on my wrist?"

Tito focused on my wrist and then almost tipped backward off his stool. I grabbed him by the lapel to keep that from happening. "Steady!"

He blubbered, "Is that my watch?"

"Sure looks like it, doesn't it. I found it on your dresser. Patek Philippe. Nice. Here." I took it off and handed it to him.

Tito took the watch, squinted blearily at it, then turned his eyes to me. "Who are you?"

"Come on, Tito, who else would have your watch but a thief?"

His eyes widened and they began to search the room, perhaps for the police or the Kurac. He didn't seem to know what to do, but knew that he should take action.

"Steady, my friend, steady. You're not calling the police, or the Kurac."

The bartender set my seltzer in front of me. I said to him, "See, I found Tito's watch!" The bartender smiled politely and drifted to the far end of the bar. Tito was my problem now.

"You are very stupid coming here with my watch!"

"Didn't you want your watch back?"

He clenched his jaw and hissed. "I want it all back!"

I laughed. "Oh no you don't. Imagine what the Kurac would say when you handed them back their gems? Oh, they'd take them, and then they'd take you to a basement room and go to work on you with bolt cutters and a curling iron."

Tito shuttered so violently that half his drink sprinkled onto the bar. "What?"

"They'd think you took them and got scared and tried to give them back." I put a hand on his shoulder. "Tito, look, I can't give

82

them back any more than you can. They already suspect you, right?"

"No! My wife, she told them ..."

"Your wife?"

"Yes, Idi." His eyes went icy. "She told them I was not involved."

"Really. Are you sure?"

"Sure of what?"

"That your wife told you the truth?"

He took a deep breath and reset his jaw. "Why have you come here?"

"Because you and I are riding the same bus."

"How? You stole from me and you stole from them! I did nothing. I am a victim!"

"Shhh, no need to shout. Okay, so if you're a victim, whose victim are you? Mine?"

"Yes!"

"Let me ask you, Tito, why were the Kurac sparks in your safe?"

"I was doing a favor."

"Favors are free, my friend. No, you were getting paid. And you needed the money, right? Let me take a guess. Was the money to cover real estate losses? For new investment property? Or maybe to cover Idi's expensive lifestyle? All that Cartier jewelry doesn't come cheap. And I'm sure her breasts cost a bundle."

I could hear his teeth grind. "So you have come to torment me, is that your purpose?"

"Nope. I just thought we might be able to help each other."

"If you want to help, give back what you stole, thief!"

"I think I did you a favor last night."

"A favor!" He wiggled his empty glass at the bartender, who came reluctantly back toward us. I gave the mustache a nod that it was okay, suggesting I'd take responsibility for Tito. More scotch was poured, and I shoved a twenty across to pay for it.

"The Cartier stuff was insured, am I right? So what will you lose? Well, maybe you'll lose Idi, but that was inevitable. You really couldn't afford her anyway, am I right? Very few men could or even should. And let's be honest: she's not the kind of person a man wants as his wife. I mean, aside from her obvious charms. When has she ever cooked you a meal? And do you trust her? Really trust her? Why was it her who explained things to the Kurac? Maybe she actually works for them."

"She has gone to the Kurac boss and not returned." Tito slumped. "Now why is it you torment me, too?"

"I'm here to help, and I already have, you just don't know it yet."

"Go away. I don't want to talk to you."

"It's too late for that. You have to talk to me now. Imagine if the Kurac found out we were here drinking together? Smile." I held Phone #2 at arm's length and took our picture.

He had another violent shudder, his eyes wide with horror.

"I see you're beginning to understand now, Tito, and that's good. Look, they're chasing me, not you, and there's no connection between us other than this little visit and that watch. Too late, the bartender saw me give it to you. And I have the picture. I need you to help keep the Kurac chasing me."

Tito looked thunderstruck. "Why?"

"What do you care as long as they're not looking your way? Can you tell me some of their names? Who runs the show?"

"You are insane!"

"Am I? Well, maybe. At this point it can only help you to tell me. No skin off my nose if they get that picture, come and talk to the bartender. In fact, that would shift their attention to you away from me."

He seethed: "I should kill you right here." In his hand was a small automatic, a fancy thing with a white handle.

"Put that away before someone sees it. If you kill me, then what?"

"I say to the Kurac that I caught you! I deliver you to them!"

"That wouldn't look good at all. Not to the Kurac, who would see it as a falling out among thieves. I don't have the gems on me so they would still be missing. And police might take exception to you killing me. Remember them? Those are the ones who would put you away for life for murder."

Tito's impotence was reaching the boiling point, and for a second there I thought he was going to shoot me—I was pushing him too hard, he was at the brink of not caring what happened, of only caring about taking decisive action.

I said, "Look, Tito, don't do this, prison will only make your life worse than it is now. I'm not the problem. Idi is your problem. The Kurac is your problem. Let's take care of the real problems and make your life better. Tell me their names and something about them."

The gun went back into his jacket, tears rolling down the poor slob's cheeks.

"Was it wrong to want a beautiful woman?"

"No man in his right mind would walk away from a woman like Idi, Tito. You can't blame yourself for that. Any man would do the same. Only once you realize that she doesn't make you happy, that she really only makes you miserable, you have to move on and find someone else. You have to take action, not with a gun, but with a lawyer. Tell me about the Kurac."

"The top man is Dragan Spikic. He runs the show from the shadows, arranges to sell the gems." His voice was low, flat, and defeated.

That name sounded vaguely familiar. "Sell to the Israelis?"

"Of course."

"Was the deal supposed to go down soon?"

"All I know is they were coming to pick up the gems today. How did you know?"

"Know what?"

"To steal them last night? I must know: are you with Idi?"

I put a hand on his shoulder. "I am not with Idi. All I knew was that Idi wore a lot of expensive jewelry and that I wanted to take it."

"Why?"

"Why what?"

He sniffled. "Why do you take things like that?"

I had to think a few seconds about that.

"Is it for the money?"

Finally, I said: "I take it because I can."

"Do you not realize that stealing in this way hurts people?"

"People hurt themselves by being careless, by not realizing what's important."

He squinted. "And what is important?"

"People seem to think jewelry, money, flashy cars, and expensive suits are important. Or that their jobs or missions are important. But there's only one important thing in this life."

"You mean sex?"

"Love, Tito. It is more valuable and harder to attain and hold onto than any gems. Find it. Keep it locked in your heart where no thief can take it away. Who is the one in the ponytail?"

"Vugovic."

"He answers directly to Spikic?"

"Yes."

"When did these guys get in town?"

"Last week, from Rome. The gems needed only be in my apartment a short time while they met with the Jews to cut a deal."

Obviously Roberto was dialed in and knew these honchos were coming long before they got to New York. No doubt through the Corporation's connections, possibly with the Israelis.

"How tight are they with the Russians?"

"I don't know those things. They are not friendly with the Corporation. I overheard one of them saying that they kidnapped one of their men to find out more about you."

"Ramón?"

"I think so."

Roberto would have fits over this. Unless of course he knew Ramón was a leak in his organization. Roberto was a wise man. If I had to guess he'd see poetic justice in Ramón's fate. The Kurac promised Ramón money to tell what he knew, and when he had nothing else to tell them, they grabbed him and squeezed him some more, because people always tell more when faced with torture. That's how the Kurac think. Always with the torture.

"Where do the Kurac stay?"

He hesitated. "I will not say. If you visit them as you did me, then what? They will know I talked to you, they will…"

I put a hand on his shoulder. "I'm not going to confront them. Tito, the more they focus on me, the less they will even think about you."

Tito groaned. "What does anything matter now?" His hand stroked the automatic in his jacket pocket. "They have rented a penthouse apartment at the Grand Excelsior, upstairs from me. They were staying near their treasure."

Which was how they could show up so soon when the alarm went off.

"Spikic: he stay there too?"

"No. I do not know where he is. But if I had to guess I would say he is in Manhattan. He is careful not to stay close to the gems, and likes to live well, better than those who work for him. But I do not think he even lets his men know exactly where he is. It is possible…"

"Possible?"

"Spikic may be a conflict commander. In hiding. This is what I have heard."

"One indicted by The Hague?"

Tito shrugged. "Many have been."

"You ever talk with Spikic? On the phone?"

"No, just Vugovic."

I stood, fishing out a tip from my change. "Good work, Tito, I'm proud of you. You overcame your anger with me and were smart enough to recognize what's in your best interest. But why should that be surprising? You're a successful and respected businessman around here. It's time you got your house in order and went back to respecting yourself. Now go home and get some sleep. I'll keep the Kurac off your back. Tomorrow is Monday.

Wake up to a new day, get yourself a lawyer to get Idi off your back. "

"Here. This is no good to me." Tito held out his watch sadly, and I took it. "It is on the list of items stolen. I cannot be seen with it."

"True." I nodded. "Buy yourself a *real* Patek Philippe with the insurance money. Just make sure the dealer is reputable, not like the last guy you bought this from."

"What are you saying?"

"The case is real, but it was salvaged. The insides are Timex or some crap. You can tell by the weight and the movement. No gems inside."

I left Tito at the bar with his mouth hanging open.

People get ripped off every day. They just don't know it.

Down the block I stopped at a bench and opened Tito's phone. I'd lifted it off the bar. I copied some of his recently called numbers onto Phone #2, including one tagged as Idi's. One of them must be Vugovic's number.

Then I swung by the Excelsior and handed Tito's phone to the droopy doorman.

"Here, this belongs to Tito. He left it in my car. I was looking for him to give it back."

KNOWLEDGE OF THE ENEMY'S DISPOSITIONS CAN ONLY BE OB-TAINED FROM OTHER MEN. HENCE THE USE OF SPIES, OF WHOM THERE ARE FIVE CLASSES:

1. *LOCAL SPIES*
2. *INWARD SPIES*
3. *CONVERTED SPIES*
4. *DOOMED SPIES*
5. *SURVIVING SPIES.*

WHEN THESE FIVE KINDS OF SPY ARE ALL AT WORK, NONE CAN DIS-COVER THE SECRET SYSTEM. THIS IS CALLED "DIVINE MANIPULATION OF THE THREADS." IT IS THE SOVEREIGN'S MOST PRECIOUS FACULTY. LOCAL SPIES ARE THOSE WE EMPLOY FROM THE INHABITANTS OF A DISTRICT. INWARD SPIES ARE OFFICIALS OF THE ENEMY. CONVERTED SPIES ARE THOSE ENEMY'S SPIES WE USE FOR OUR OWN PURPOSES. DOOMED SPIES THAT DO CERTAIN THINGS OPENLY FOR PURPOSES OF DECEPTION, AND ALLOW OUR SPIES TO KNOW OF THEM AND REPORT THEM TO THE ENEMY. SURVIVING SPIES, FINALLY, ARE THOSE WHO BRING BACK NEWS FROM THE ENEMY'S CAMP. NONE IN THE WHOLE ARMY IS IT MORE IMPORTANT TO MAINTAIN INTIMATE RELATIONS WITH THAN SPIES. NONE SHOULD BE MORE GRACIOUSLY REWARDED. IN NO OTHER ENDEAVOR SHOULD GREATER SECRECY BE PRESERVED. SPIES CANNOT BE USEFULLY EMPLOYED WITHOUT A CERTAIN INTU-ITION AND SAGACITY. THEY CANNOT BE MANAGED WITHOUT KIND-NESS AND STRAIGHTFORWARDNESS. WITHOUT SUBTLE INGENUITY OF MIND, ONE CANNOT MAKE CERTAIN OF THE TRUTH OF THEIR REPORTS.

—*Sun Tzu*, The Art of War

SEVENTEEN

EUROPEAN ORGANIZED CRIME TASK FORCE
MEETING MINUTES
1800 EDT SUNDAY AUGUST 8, 2010

ATTENDANCE: LOG ATTACHED

Re: Kurac gem theft conspiracy—recent developments re: G. Underwood

EOCTF Agents Brown and Acosta apprised superiors on interceding on Kurac kidnapping and torture of "Corporation" soldier Ramón Vasquez at approximately 1300 EDT @ the Lincoln Motor Lodge, Tonnelle Avenue, North Bergen, New Jersey. Paramedics called to aid R. Vasquez redirect to hospital, protective services alert to process medical secure. Apprehended: Dusko Ilimic, Serbian national. Passport/visa: business. Evidence team and security arrived to process crime scene, to include 9mm automatic handgun, pruning shears, 12v car battery, jumper cables. Appears abductee was "chimped" [fingers and toes removed with shears] to extract information on G. Underwood whereabouts. Interrogation of D. Ilimic as yet unproductive. Interpol ID of D. Ilimic: Tupo Muvolivic, convicted of gem theft in Frankfurt, prison escapee, served two years, outstanding warrant. Tattoos match description. Filed with ICE to commence extradition to Germany. Interrogation to recommence.

1. Agents Kim and Bola of Intel Surveillance section report tactical database ref data re: Asian OCF—Nee Fat Tong, Hong Kong to intercept G. Underwood for Kurac gems. Details as yet unavailable, surveillance subsystems targeting. Data also indicates "Corporation" knew Ramón was leak and promoted his abduction by leaking that Ramón was not in full disclosure to the Kurac re: G. Underwood.

2. EOCTF Supervisor Palmer initiates discussion of G. Underwood location. Finding Underwood key to putting Kurac and gems in same place for prosecution. G. Underwood burglary resulted in lost opportunity to make arrests of Kurac upon exchange of Britany-Swindol gems to Israelis.

3. Agents Kim and Bola of Intel Surveillance section report G. Underwood and Trudy Elwell registered cell phones not in use. Calls from G. Underwood to veterinarian via prepaid phone, surveillance and ping not yet successful on G. Underwood prepaid phone; consensus is that G. Underwood likely changing prepaid phones and turning them off/removing

batteries between use. Agents were dispatched to respective apartments of G. Underwood and T. Elwell, which Kurac had already searched for data. No computers or personal effects of any use. Navy commendations on wall, see attached for complete inventory. Intercepts indicate Kurac found no computers or useful personal effects. DNA samples obtained from hairbrushes, forwarded to Baltimore labs for analysis.

4. EOCTF Supervisor Palmer initiates discussion of injured T. Elwell condition, possible to locate through medical community.

5. EOCTF Agents Brown and Acosta apprised superiors possibility T. Elwell may already be dead even though Kurac intercepts indicate they believe she is alive.

6. Intel Profiler Agent Laurenta provided input on G. Underwood M.O. A quick study of his Navy file suggests G. Underwood will employ highly evasive tactics to include multiple layers of subterfuge. As Navy intel officer, the record indicates that G. Underwood was a fundamentalist military tactician and adherent of the ancient Sun Tzu text "Art of War." Navy ops employed revised tactics in raid with G. Underwood supervision, multiple casualties, G. Underwood severely injured, tactical operation and G. Underwood's program deemed failure. G. Underwood spent time in psychiatric hospital for PTSD and depression. Unclear how he transitioned to crime, how he met T. Elwell, possibly in hospital as they were admitted to Portsmouth Naval Medical Center approximately the same time in 2002. Profiler believes G. Underwood will follow his training and Sun Tzu text but to a fault. To "know enemy and self" 100% not possible, coinciding

errors in judgment likely as complexity of G. Underwood's deceit progresses. Agents to look for misstep that will signal progressive failures and apprehension by G. Underwood's pursuers.

7. EOCTF Supervisor Palmer: schedule reconvene @ 1300 EDT Monday, August 9.

*******************MEETING ADJOURNED******************

EIGHTEEN

It was twilight as I motored my bike to a Starbucks on River Road. With a large latte and a cookie in front of me, I lit up Phone #2 and called Doc. "Gill! I tried calling. You did not answer and there was no message machine."

I could have held her feet to the fire over the punk with the leather vest out in Queens, but what was the point?

"The paper and tickets: are they ready for delivery?"

"Yes. Where's the drop?"

"Boulevard East and 77th Street, North Bergen, east side of the street, under the street lamp. Put the money inside a volleyball so I'll know the courier, and I'll need the courier's phone number."

"I'm coming myself."

"Even better. But still put it in a volleyball."

"Where am I going to get a volleyball this time of night?"

"I'm sure that store on Main Street there in Flushing must have one."

"What if they don't? And how am I supposed to get the stuff inside a volleyball?"

"Swipe a volleyball from your kids if you have to. Just slice it and then put a piece of duct tape over the slice once you insert the passports and tickets."

"Is this really necessary?"

"That's the way it has to be. Can you be there in two hours?"

"I suppose so."

"Should I even ask you not to bring your friends from Hong Kong?"

"I'm on the up and up, Gill. You know me, I deal fair and square."

"Good to know. See you at eleven."

Phone #2 off and battery out. I gobbled down my cookie, and took the coffee with me. Sticking around to see if the Hong Kong friends were going to show up at the Starbucks didn't seem like a good idea. After the punk in the vest I had to assume they would ping my phone this time, too. If I hung around they'd be more careful in their approach and tighten their net more carefully as they moved in.

Time to purchase some camo. Not for hunting but for being hunted. I pulled into a CVS and waited half an hour before going in. That way I'd pretty much seen everybody who came out and went in other than the people who worked there. The Kurac wouldn't have any way of knowing I'd be there, but they were in the neighborhood, and I didn't want to risk any chance encounters with those snotbag goons.

Nice 'n Easy said on the box exactly what I wanted in a hair dye, and I bought something called Born Blonde Maxi. I wanted my hair to be almost white when I got done with it. Then I grabbed a Jets ball cap, a straw trilby from the seasonal section, and a pair of large sunglasses. They had shirts in back, crappy drab tropical ones on sale, so I tossed one in my basket.

It was getting late and I needed to get online and I needed a place to hide out overnight, possibly even sleep for an hour or two if I could manage it. If not maybe just rest, lie still for a couple hours, which is almost as good as sleep.

My laptop was hidden in my Screen Man truck in a commercial parking lot in back of a gas station on River Road, but I didn't dare go anywhere near it. Libraries were all closed.

I began to cruise the neighborhoods in Edgewater away from the river at the base of the cliff. I needed a dark house, one with those circulars and newspapers piled up on the front step. If they'd gone to the shore or the mountains for the weekend, they'd probably be home already, and it being August a lot of folks were on vacation for a week. Likely as not they would vacation Saturday to Saturday—that's how most vacation houses were rented.

A woman was on one porch picking up circulars, and I saw her move off toward a house two down.

I pulled over. The house she'd been at had a porch light on, and an upstairs light on behind the curtain, but all the other windows were dark. The only reason she would be over there lifting their circulars was if they were out of town and she was doing them a favor by not letting the circulars pile up, so it would look like they were home. If she was picking up circulars at that hour it probably meant they weren't coming home that night. The mailbox said: GARBER. There was an ACE SECURITY SYSTEMS sticker by the front door, but I recognized that as one of the many stickers on the market that are phony, for people who want to pretend they have an alarm system. A sign in the yard that had the name of a real security company would have had me move on.

I decided to play it safe.

I went to the door of the woman who was collecting circulars and rang the doorbell.

She cracked the door, the chain across the gap. She was older, with too much blond hair than she knew was good for her at that age. She wore a snuggie, and the TV flickered in the living room behind her.

"Hi, thought I'd stop by and let you know I'm staying at the Garbers' tonight."

"What?"

"I have the key."

"You do?"

"They told you, right? About Phil?"

"Phil?"

"That's me. Phil Greene." I pulled my wallet and showed her my Jersey license. "See? I live nearby, and my apartment building is being fumigated for bed bugs. They said I could drop in and stay the night."

"Fred didn't say anything about this to me."

"Well, how else would I know to come here unless Fred told me to?" I smiled. "I mean, sure, it could be I'm just driving around looking for a house to break into, and so decided to announce it to the neighbors and show them my driver's license. Right? You can call Fred if you want."

She relaxed a little, and I could see on her face that she didn't have a number to reach Fred.

"How long will you be there?"

"Just tonight."

"I'm not comfortable with this."

"I'm sorry Fred forgot to tell you I was coming. But he left me a key, so …"

"Phil Greene."

"I live just over in North Bergen. If anything goes missing or anything, tell the cops to arrest me."

She relaxed a little more, and almost smiled. "Leave the lights the way he has them."

I drifted back from her door. "I will. Good night." I saluted and went back to my bike for the saddle bag. Around back of the house I looked under the mat—no key. Not in a magnet box under the Weber grill, either. I turned over some stones in the garden until I found one that rattled. Fake rock with a key inside, which unlocked the back door. It amazes me that people think these gadgets fool burglars. Don't they think we go to Lowe's or get clever catalogs with these gadgets in them, knowing exactly what to look for? Don't they think we know the name of all the local security companies and know which stickers mean business?

The kitchen was late-model and smelled like dust and grease and needed the tops of the cabinets cleaned, probably a change of curtains. I opened the fridge with a dish towel. Just instinctive—I wasn't hungry, it's just what you do when you're about to make yourself comfortable in someone else's home: you want to see what's in the fridge. They had Oreos in there, and beer, and cold cuts, and some fruit that was past due. At least they'd gotten rid of the milk. I'd never seen anybody keep cookies in the fridge before. I took a sport drink and shut the door.

I didn't spend too much time on a tour of the Garber place. It was a split-level, three bedroom, one doubling as a den downstairs with a computer on the desk. The lights of the modem blinked next to it. With the desk lamp clicked on, I sat at the swivel chair, plugged in my secure flash drive, and fired up the CPU. Not the newest equipment, I only hoped it wouldn't be really slow. The Microsoft tune trumpeted from the speakers and I was in—no password protection. Not much of a surprise that people are even laxer with their computers than they are with their safes. I mean, who really expects someone to break into their home and use their computer?

The thermostat was turned pretty warm so I cranked up the AC. I was headed back to the den with the sport drink when the doorbell sounded. I looked through the peephole.

My stomach shriveled. Cops.

A very important part of being a successful thief is being able to talk your way out of situations with the cops rather than running from them. When you run, they catch you, and when they do, they are not gentle; you have given them an excuse to get physical. Also, by the very fact that you ran they know you are guilty.

Sport drink in my hand, I opened the door. "Hi."

One was a Hispanic female, the other a pimply white male, both young, thumbs in their belts next to their guns. The Hispanic said, "Can we see some identification?"

"Sure, it's in my wallet, so don't shoot or anything, okay? I guess Missus Whatshername thought I was a shady character." The cops didn't reply; they just flexed their jaw muscles. I handed them the wallet with my license.

"You know the Garbers?" She cocked an eye at me.

"Yup, they gave me the key." I held up the key. "And that's why I went over to the Whatshername house to tell her I was staying here tonight, because I didn't want to have to waste your time."

"You're not wasting our time," Pimples said. He didn't like me. She wasn't so sure.

"Look, officers, I've shown you my license, and that I live one town over, and you know I've done my best to make sure everybody knows I'm here on the up and up. You want to come in and look around?"

Pimples spoke before she had a chance. "If you don't mind."

I held the door open, and switched on a living room lamp.

"You always sit around in the dark?" she asked.

"I just got here. And I'm just staying downstairs in the den, no need to light the whole house up. I was just going to do a little work on the computer, have a snack, and turn in."

Pimples approached the step and looked down toward the den and glowing computer. I think if he'd had his way they'd search my belongings. The sparks, cash, and burglar tools would have been a deal breaker. But she turned toward the door.

"Just checking, Mr. Greene. Have a good night. Let's go, Andy."

They thumbed their belts all the way back to the squad car.

I indulged in a huge sigh. Then I took a long hot shower, remembering back when Phil Greene died. When I got out of the shower, the doorbell was ringing again. Still in my towel, I opened the door. It was the blond neighbor.

"I am so sorry, Mr. Greene, about calling the police. But I am responsible and I didn't feel right."

"That's fine, no worries."

"My name is Florence. My friends call me Florrie."

I smiled. "I'd shake your hand but then I'd drop my towel."

Florrie blushed, and laughed. "Oh, my, well…"

"But you did the right thing. If you don't feel right about something, call the cops. And I have nothing to hide. I could always go to a hotel, but Fred said…"

"Again, I'm so sorry, you seem like a nice person, but how am I supposed to know? It's always the nice ones."

"You're right, it is always the nice ones. Well, I…"

"You have enough to eat? I could fix you something."

"Thanks, Florrie, I'm just having a snack and turning in. Monday morning is just around the corner. Gotta get up early for work."

"Where do you work, Mr. Greene?"

"I'm the Screen Man. I repair screens, screen doors, install storm windows."

"Really? I've seen your van! You have a card? My screens are in terrible shape."

"I have them back at my apartment. Just look me up, and I'll come by and fix what needs fixing."

"Wonderful! Well, have a good night, Phil." She backed off the porch.

"Good night." I latched the door and threw on the useless chain, hoping that was the end of the visitors for the night.

Nice 'n Easy was as advertised, and I quickly had the goop combed into my hair waiting to work its magic. It said forty-five minutes was all it would take to make my hair snowy white.

I put on one of Fred's velour track suits—not a bad fit—and sat down at the computer. Typing in my password to the flash drive's encrypted browser, I accessed the private network tunnel and secure sessions service.

I typed into Google and went into my backup Gmail account, the one I only used at the library. I composed an email to tim@bernardscaybonefishlodge.com:

> Hi, Tim: I decided I might take you up on that fishing trip to your lodge. You must be shocked after all the times you invited me. Think you could teach me to bonefish? I'm between jobs with a severance package and am thinking about coming for a month to clear my head. Hope you can accommodate. Email ASAP as I am booking a flight for Nassau tonight. Looking forward to catching up with an old army buddy. Yours, Gill.

I wanted them to think Trudy was alive, that I was at the beach house, that I was dumb about phones, and that I was headed to Iceland. A misinformed adversary can be your best ally. The name on the passport was so generic that even if it fell into the wrong hands it would be of little use.

It seemed inevitable that when those Serb shitbags returned from their beach holiday they would get wind of what was going on and confront the Hong Kong friends. In fact, I hoped they would. Let them go after each other instead of me.

I went to the Bernard's Cay Bonefish Lodge website. It boasted that it catered to the hardcore fly-fishing angler as well as their "non-fishing spouse" who might like lounging by the pool, snorkeling, or combing the white sandy beaches. There were lots of grip-and-grin shots of people with silvery fish in the bright sun and blue waters, as well as happy couples hand in hand frolicking in the surf and sipping drinks by the sunset. That had been me, once, a jillion years ago, and never again. My only hope was that one day I might somehow think back on Trudy and be warmed by the memory instead of chilled. The regret was acid on my tongue, my mouth dry with fear of being alone.

The out islands of the Bahamas looked perfectly isolated, yet at the same time accessible by air and boat, and a guy with cash could keep moving. It looked like you could hit a new island every couple weeks for a year. I'd never really known what fly fishing was. I opened a new Explorer window to YouTube, where I found videos showing how it was done. Unlike the kind of fishing where the line is cast from the reel, fly fishing was all about using the plastic line to draw itself out by swinging it through the air. The casts looked freaky, like a slow whipping action. There were a lot of details to how it was done, and with what kind of equipment, but the exactness and complexity attracted me. It was tactical: the fish were adversaries to be outmaneuvered, and teamwork was often required. As a tactic for my situation, going to a remote location alone with a guide on a motorboat with lots of escape options was ideal. I'd fit right in.

It would help if I had the equipment when I went to complete my cover as a genuine traveling angler. I flipped out of YouTube and searched for a fly-fishing store in Manhattan. There was one in the Twenties on Fifth Avenue, and I jotted the address onto a gum wrapper. They booked trips to the Bahamas.

"BAHAMAS OFFSHORE BANK" also got me a lot of results. Apparently the banks in Nassau and Freeport aren't as shifty as those in Panama, but shifty enough. The home page of Warranty Trust Bank claimed to be "highly specialized," "respectable," and catered to "discriminating individuals." Anybody that feels the need to say they're respectable isn't. "Confidentiality is entirely protected by the Bahamas Banking Code." Translated, that means they can figure out a way to accept large sums of cash without setting off any alarms. That's what I wanted to hear. I didn't bother to write the address down on a gum wrapper.

I realized I was running late to meet Doc, so I plucked out the secure flash drive and turned off the CPU. Fred's tracksuit came off and I changed back into my canvas shirt and cargo pants—my new CVS shirt and trilby hat would be for Monday, once the Sunday duds were completely sweated out.

The Nice 'n Easy had to be rinsed from my hair, so I hosed off my head and toweled off. My wet hair was blond as straw, and I scrunched the Jets cap on top of it.

The rinse and gloss steps would have to wait until I returned. Saddle bag over my shoulder, I locked the Garbers' house and straddled my bike.

NINETEEN

DCSNet 6000 Warrant Database
Transcript Cell Phone Track and Trace
Peerless IP Network / Redhook Translation
Target: Dragan Spikic
Date: Sunday, August 8, 2010
Time: 2304–2308 EDT

SPIKIC: TALK TO ME.

VUGOVIC: THE INFORMATION FROM THE CUBANS WAS BAD. WE ARE COMING BACK TO THE CITY. UNDERWOOD NEVER CAME DOWN TO HIS HOUSE, AND IT CONTAINS NOTHING OF VALUE. I THINK UNDERWOOD USED THE CORPORATION TO FEED US MISINFORMATION, TO BUY TIME.

SPIKIC: SON OF A THOUSAND THREE-PUSSY WHORES! HE HAS PROBABLY ESCAPED, IDIOT!

VUGOVIC: THERE IS GOOD NEWS. THE RUSSIANS TELL US UNDERWOOD HAS ARRANGED TO SELL OUR GEMS TO THE HONG KONG PEOPLE.

SPIKIC: THIS IS GOOD NEWS? VUGO, MUST I COME OUT THERE MYSELF? YOU DISAPPOINT ME, HARD ROUND TURD.

VUGOVIC: [UNINTELLIGIBLE]

SPIKIC: WHAT WAS THAT?

VUGOVIC: SIR, THIS MEANS THAT UNDERWOOD WILL BE AT A CERTAIN PLACE AT A CERTAIN TIME TO HAND OVER THE GEMS. WE HAVE TO BE THERE TO INTERCEPT HIM.

SPIKIC: WHERE IS THE DROP?

VUGOVIC: WE DO NOT KNOW YET.

SPIKIC: FIND OUT.

VUGOVIC: WE WILL, AND THEN WE WILL BE THERE. BUT HE IS STILL IN THE CITY. HE GAVE THE CHINKS THE SLIP IN QUEENS.

SPIKIC: I SEE THE CHINESE CAN FIND HIM AND WE CANNOT. WHY IS THAT, VUGO?

VUGOVIC: IT HELPS THAT UNDERWOOD HAS GONE TO THE CHINESE TO SELL WHAT HE HAS STOLEN FROM US. IF HE CAME TO US I CAN ASSURE YOU WE WOULD NOT HAVE LET HIM SLIP AWAY, AND HE WOULD BE DINING ON HIS OWN TESTICLES AT THIS VERY MOMENT.

SPIKIC: I HOPE I DO NOT DETECT IN YOUR TONE THAT YOU TREAT ME AS YOU WOULD A GRANDMOTHER, OR YOU WILL FIND A MEAL OF YOUR OWN LOINS IN A POT OF ONIONS.

VUGOVIC: I HAVE NOTHING BUT RESPECT FOR YOU, SIR. I WAS JUST EXPLAINING.

SPIKIC: EXPLAIN ALL YOU WANT BUT FIND THOSE GEMS AND TEAR THE ENTRAILS FROM UNDERWOOD ACROSS THE ROAD. THE ISRAELIS ARE NERVOUS BECAUSE OF THE DELAY. THEY FEAR THE FBI IS LISTENING TO OUR EVERY WORD, THAT WE ARE SETTING THEM UP.

VUGOVIC: I DON'T THINK ANY OF US COULD HAVE ANTICI-PATED UNDERWOOD STUMBLING UPON THE GEMS AND TAK-ING THEM. IT WAS A CRAP IN THE PANTS, THAT'S ALL. NOW WE CHANGE PANTS.

SPIKIC: WHAT OF THE CUBAN WE GRABBED? HAS HE BEEN USEFUL?

VUGOVIC: THE COPS ARRESTED OUR INTERROGATOR AND TOOK THE CUBAN. BUT RAMÓN HAD NO BETTER INFORMA-TION EVEN WHEN CHIMPED. THE CUBANS WERE CONVINCED UNDERWOOD WENT TO THE BEACH.

SPIKIC: WHICH SOLDIER DID THE COPS GRAB?

VUGOVIC: THE STUPID ONE, DUSKO. HE DID NOT PROPERLY RE-STRAIN THE CUBAN'S SCREAMS AND SO GOT CAUGHT. LET HIM EAT HIS MOTHER'S PUSSY, THE HOMOSEXUAL BOSNIAK. HE KNOWS NOTHING THAT COULD HURT US, AND IS SOLID ENOUGH TO NEVER TALK ANYWAY.

SPIKIC: CUT HIM LOOSE. WHAT IS YOUR NEXT MOVE?

VUGOVIC: UNDERWOOD MUST STAY SOMEPLACE OVERNIGHT. A FRIEND, A MOTEL, SOMEPLACE. WE ARE WORKING THE HO-TELS. WE ARE ALSO TRYING TO FIND HOW HE MOVES ABOUT. TAXIS, BUSES PERHAPS. HE LEFT HIS VEHICLE. AND WE HAD SOMEONE WATCHING HIS VAN, THE ONE HE USES FOR BUSI-NESS, IN A PARKING LOT BEHIND A GAS STATION ON RIVER ROAD. HE HAS NOT GONE TO IT. WE DISABLED THE VEHICLE SO HE CANNOT USE IT, THOUGH I DON'T THINK HE HAS ANY INTENTION OF COMING ANYWHERE NEAR THE VAN SO WE HAVE STOPPED WATCHING IT. IN HIS GARAGE THERE WAS EVIDENCE OF A MOTORCYCLE. WE THINK HE MAY BE RIDING ONE, THOUGH NONE IS REGISTERED TO HIS NAME AND WE HAVE NO IDEA WHAT KIND YET. THE FRUIT ON THIS TREE IS STILL RIPE. WE WILL SHAKE IT DOWN, SIR, FEAR NOT.

SPIKIC: I ONLY FEAR FOR YOU, VUGO, IF WE DO NOT COLLECT THE HUNDRED AND FIFTY MILLION FOR THE GEMS.

VUGOVIC: THERE IS A POSSIBILITY THAT WE CAN TAKE FROM THE CHINKS WHAT THEY ARE GOING TO PAY UNDERWOOD.

ASSUMING THEY PLAN TO PAY HIM ANYTHING AND NOT JUST TAKE THE GEMS.

SPIKIC: I LIKE THE WAY YOU THINK. STAY ON IT. CALL ME IN THE MORNING WITH GOOD NEWS. I AM FUCKING TITO'S WIFE AGAIN NOW, SO DON'T BOTHER ME UNTIL THEN.

VUGOVIC: WE WILL BE VIGILANT.

END

TWENTY

SOUTH ON RIVER ROAD, I drove through the intersection of Bulls Ferry Road. Had I made a right there, up the steep and curvy road to the top and made a left, I would have arrived where Doc was waiting at 77th and Boulevard East.

Instead, I pulled over just south of Bulls Ferry Road next to a chainlink fence and gate. The bike's kickstand down, I dismounted and shouldered the saddle bag. The gate was loosely chained, so there was room enough to slip into the construction yard. Ahead in the dark before me loomed a large notch cut into the Palisades cliff. Developers like Tito were expanding the notch south so they could squeeze a mall right up against the cliff face, a sheer drop from Boulevard East. When I looked up in the dark I could see where Boulevard East bridged the top of the notch—at 77th Street. The streetlight there shimmered brightly.

I weaved between large CAT excavators lined up in the middle of the site and rang Doc.

"Where are you? I've been waiting, Gill. It's half past eleven."

"I was taking care of Trudy."

"How is she? Did the herbalist help?"

"He did. She's better, good enough to travel tomorrow."

"So where are you?"

"I'm here."

"I don't see you."

"Are you at the streetlight?"

"Yes."

"Is the stuff in a volleyball?"

"*Yes.*"

"Throw the ball over the fence."

"Over the fence? Down there?"

"Don't stall, Doc. Do it."

"Gill, stop playing games and let me hand you the stupid ball."

I stood at some brush at the base of the cliff. Looking up, I couldn't see Doc, but there was a chute in the cliff face leading down to me from about where she stood at the streetlight.

"Now who's playing games, Doc? Your Hong Kong friends are probably right there in the shadows waiting to sandbag me. Am I right? I better see that ball coming my way in five seconds. And don't even toss it if there's nothing inside. Because any monkey business and I'm walking. I'll take the sparks to the Italians, or the Corporation, any of a dozen others who …"

Above I saw the white sphere rise up over the fence and pass into the shadow of the cliff. At a ledge, it bounced out and away from the rock face, glanced off some bushes, and came to a rest about ten feet up the chute in some vines. It was good that I'd insisted on a volleyball—the white made it easy to see in the gloom.

I scrambled up the chute, knocked the volleyball down, and then stepped on it to burst the seal. Didn't seem to be booby trapped. So I shook out the contents: sure enough, they came up with the paper and the tickets.

"Got it, Doc."

"See? No double cross, Gill. This is on the up and up."

"We'll see about that. I'll call you tomorrow afternoon to arrange the exchange. My cut is ten million: two million in hundreds, the rest in Guatemalan bearer bonds."

Bearer bonds issued by U.S. banks became heavily scrutinized for obvious reasons, and no crooks use them anymore. Guatemala saw an opportunity and issued bearer bonds in denominations of two hundred thousand U.S. dollars. Guat bonds quickly became the tender of choice for cartels when they exchanged large sums.

"Guat bonds? By tomorrow?"

"That's a huge bargain, so don't dick me over, Doc."

"Gill…"

Phone #2: off, battery out. I tossed the flattened volleyball aside. Tucking the goodies in my belly bag, I jogged back to the Nighthawk. If I stayed there a second longer than I had to, likely as not the Hong Kong friends would be around my neck.

I slipped through the gate and hopped on my bike.

Behind me at Bulls Ferry Road I heard a roar. A black Hummer thundered down the steep road and exploded in sparks when it bottomed out at River Road. The Hummer restarted its engine, revving it.

I guessed the Hong Kong friends weren't going to let this go my way if they could help it.

I started the bike and kicked her into gear, racing south on River Road and away from my hideaway at Fred's. I put the spurs to the Nighthawk past the medical center on my left and the water treatment plant and car wash on my right. At the Bulls Ferry townhouses I made a left and slipped around the candy-striped arm barrier onto Lydia Drive.

I motored to the end of the lane and a T-intersection of sleepy townhouses nestled in the trees.

There was a screech behind me. The Hummer crashed right through the arm gate, headed my way.

Straight ahead was a path to the riverwalk, a ribbon of board-walk that hugged the river along the Gold Coast, a place for a peaceful stroll across from midtown Manhattan's glowing spectacle. My motorcycle fit easily down the path, and when I hit the riverwalk I made a right. If I'd gone left there would have been no place to go; the riverwalk was interrupted by the medical center and dead-ended. I hoped the Hummer didn't see where I went. Ahead the riverwalk went south about a mile and a half to the Port Imperial Ferry Terminal, and beyond. A man in a tracksuit smoking a cigar sat on a bench, a small dog at his feet.

"Hey, douchebag, you can't ride that here! This is the riverwalk. No motor vehicles. Can't you read signs?"

Behind me was the sound of a bulldozer coming through a thicket.

The Hummer burst through the path, shrubs and trash cans plowed out ahead of it.

The guy on the bench was on his feet, his cigar on the ground, dog hiding behind his legs.

I kicked the Nighthawk into gear and shot straight down the riverwalk, zipping by pleasant benches and period lampposts. About a third of a mile along, the brick pathway made a hard right turn, followed by a couple other ninety-degree turns and another straightaway about a quarter-mile long, until the next turns into the Port Imperial Ferry Terminal. Those turns would slow the Hummer down considerably. I hoped. The trick was to cover the third of a mile faster than the Hummer, or at least not get shot, as stupid as that would be for them to do. Bottoming out the Hummer was stupid, too.

I flew past other pedestrians taking the night air, lights coming on in some of the townhouses as they heard my Honda, the echo of the Hummer gaining. Fancy lampposts flicked by as I rumbled across two wood bridges, Manhattan a blur on my left beyond the bulkhead.

With the Hummer about three hundred feet back I made the first turn, my wheels chirping as the motorcycle fishtailed. A couple hundred feet along I made the next turn left along the walk and shot a glance back. The Hummer was still roaring along, gears howling as it rumbled around the turns.

I was pretty sure the riverwalk ended at Arthur's Landing and Pershing Road, which went back up the cliff to the top. There was some construction at Arthur's Landing, right at a restaurant of the same name that went bust. It was confusing how the barricades were set up there, and I hoped I could lose the Hummer permanently among the Jersey barriers. Even a Hummer can't barge through giant blocks of concrete.

The next switchback came at Riverwalk Place, where the brick walkway met a circular drive ringed with tall art deco monuments. I raced toward the circle, up a pedestrian ramp, and out the other side and back onto the riverwalk. I'd cut the corner. Right in front of a rent-a-cop car. I just saw the cop's eyes, wide and white, as I passed. I went right and then left again.

Behind me was a thump. I looked back. The little security car was sinking in the river, the Hummer regaining control after colliding with it. Bad luck for the security guy.

By the time I'd made the next turns, the ferry terminal was large before me, a giant curve of blue and luminous glass at the river's edge.

I changed my mind about Arthur's Landing when I heard a gunshot behind me. I'd rather not have done what I did next but there were few options. I squealed down the ferry parking lot drive to the traffic light at River Road. It was red, and there were cars passing in both directions.

Across the road was the light rail station, which serviced a two-car tram that connected Hoboken to the Port Imperial Ferry and destinations west. The system was only a couple years old.

The Hummer scuttered off the riverwalk and about eight hundred feet directly behind me. There were sirens in the distance.

I found my opening and shot across River Road's six lanes and onto the far brick sidewalk. I crossed through a small sculpture garden and a bus and taxi queue before I reached the pedestrian grade crossing to the train platform. This was the first set of tracks, the ones that headed west to the Tonnelle Avenue station deeper in New Jersey. The Port Imperial station was in front of me, new and slick-looking, all brickwork, with pitched-roof green canopies over the benches.

I looked at Tito's watch.

It was going on midnight.

The trains stopped running at midnight. At least I thought so.

To my left and south the tracks stayed hard to the side of River Road; to the right and north, the tracks turned west into a giant hole in the Palisades cliff face. The tunnel went for a mile or more through the Palisades and solid rock. Lights in the tunnel dotted the way into the distance until they seemed to come together. There was a set of tracks in each direction. What were the chances two trains would come, one in each direction, even if the trains were running?

I tried to picture the next stop heading west. It was the Bergenline Avenue station, which was completely underground and only accessible by elevator. If I tried to exit the tunnel there, how would I get my bike up onto the platform and into the elevators? I knew after that station and before Tonnelle station the tracks came out of the tunnel and were in an open cut. I thought maybe the Nighthawk might make it up those slopes. Either that or I would have to abandon the bike and climb over the fence.

Honking and squawking tires behind me meant the black Hummer was headed my way.

No trains in sight. I goosed the bike onto the tracks, heading for the tunnel.

I rumbled down the center of the tracks on the concrete ties until I could pop out to the side and ride on the gravel. The tunnel was well lit with orange overhead lamps. A warm, swampy breeze flowed through the tunnel from the meadowland marshes on the other side of the Palisades. Cameras at the entrance were trained on the tracks, along with a warning sign about the dangers of trespassing. I wondered if anybody was watching at that hour. I had to assume they were. There might be police waiting for me at the next station if I set off alarms. I paused. Was there another option? I suddenly didn't like this one, and looked back at the station.

That black Hummer was determined. It flattened a fence and rolled onto the tracks behind me.

I snaked the motorcycle around a fence and into the tunnel, next to the westbound tracks. The Hummer started after me. I roared down the tunnel, the Nighthawk's roar thundering off the walls and hammering my helmet.

A quarter-mile in, I slowed and looked back, the orange dots tracing back to the black tunnel entrance. The Hummer was hot on my tail.

That was the bad news.

The good news was that when I turned forward, a train was coming, going the other direction. I really wasn't sure the Hummer—wide as it was—could get past the tram. I could, of course, and raced past the tram, whose driver honked angrily at me until he saw the Hummer.

I heard the scream of the tram's brakes but didn't look back.

The Bergenline station was still new and slick-looking, with shiny tile and brushed aluminum. An angry black woman in a New Jersey Transit uniform was punching a fist at me as I passed, but I couldn't hear what she was barking. My ears were filled with the Nighthawk's reverb against the station walls. The bright lights of the station were behind me as I continued west into the orange glow of the tunnel. Ahead I could already see the night at the place where the tunnel exited the rock. I stole a look behind me. Nothing.

In the night air again, I found that there was a service road on the right side of the tracks, one made of fine gravel, so I hopped the bike onto it.

The slopes to either side of the tracks were thick with vines and brush. Even if I abandoned the bike, it would take me awhile to swim through all the vegetation, and I'd probably get terminal poison ivy.

In the distance I could see the Tonnelle Avenue station, and the flashing lights of cop cars.

Then some luck. The road I was on next to the tracks swung right and up the slope, though the brush, to the railway fence and a chainlink gate. Beyond the gate was a truck parking lot. The gate must have been a way for the railway to bring in maintenance vehicles.

My bolt cutters dropped the gate's lock. Engine off, I rolled my bike through the truck lot of the Peruvian food importer and to the road fronting the building. It was 51st Street. I looked both ways, figuring that any cop I ran into would be looking for a renegade troublemaker on a bike. I started her up, slowly made a right, and quickly found myself at the intersection of JFK Boulevard, made a left, then my first possible right, a left, a right: I was weaving my way quietly back north and east to Edgewater and Fred's place on small streets where I hoped to avoid cops.

I wondered if Fred had any Old Crow in his liquor cabinet. The night had almost done me in.

Stopping a block away from the Garber house, I shouldered my saddle bag and hiked uphill on the ribbon sidewalk past peaceful, slumbering homes. When I got to the intersection I looked carefully around the corner toward the Garber place.

All seemed quiet out front.

But at the next intersection down, I saw what looked like the nose of a patrol car, its reflectors shining in the yellow street light.

I circled around and walked up that block, past the little white houses. Ahead I could make out the stenciling on the back of the patrol car, EDGEWATER POLICE, and there were two cops sitting in it. Waiting. Watching Fred's.

I scratched my head. Were they watching it because of their earlier visit, just a hunch? Or was it because of my recent antics, someone marked down my plate, and even though it was long expired, maybe they had a record that the plates were never turned in, and the two cops who stopped by noticed a bike out front that was gone and so was I? Or were these cops on the payroll of the Corporation, or the Russians?

I sighed. Didn't really matter. I had to get out of Edgewater, and not on the bike; it was poison. Bad enough that every cop around was looking for it, but it had also been through a number of tollbooths and airport license-plate scanners. And who knew how many facial-recognition scanners had profiled me with the bike?

Going on one in the morning, it had been almost exactly twenty-four hours since I let Trudy slip into the grinders, and that thought made me even more exhausted as I trudged back down the hill toward River Road. I rigged up Phone #2 and called 411. I called a taxi and then unrigged the phone.

The walk to the Edgewater Ferry Terminal took only ten minutes, and a blue van with "GW Taxi" on the side was waiting for me.

The bald driver pointed at me through his open driver's window as I approached. "Manhattan, right?"

"Yup." I opened the back door, climbed in after my saddle bag, and slid the door closed. "Plaza Hotel."

The driver gave an approving nod. "Schmancy."

TWENTY-ONE

DCSNet 6000 Warrant Database
Transcript Landline Track and Trace
Havana Social Club Jukebox
Peerless IP Network / Redhook Translation
Target: Roberto Guarrez
Date: Monday, August 9, 2010
Time: 112–122 EDT

ROBERTO: MIGUEL, CLOSE THE DOOR. SO, MR. VUGOVIC, I HOPE
YOU AMUSED YOURSELVES WITH OUR RAT, RAMÓN. PLEASE
SIT. CAN WE GET YOU SOMETHING TO DRINK?

VUGOVIC: I DON'T DRINK.

ROBERTO: NOT EVEN WATER? AH, YES, KURAC. BARELY HUMAN.

VUGOVIC: WHAT CAN YOU TELL ME ABOUT UNDERWOOD?

ROBERTO: [LAUGHTER] AND WHY IN THE NAME OF MOTHER MARY SHOULD I HELP THE KURAC? YOU WAKE ME IN THE MORNING AND KEEP ME UP AT NIGHT. YOU COME TO MY TOWN AND CREATE TROUBLE. YOU SNATCH ONE OF MY MEN—GRANTED, A PIGEON I NEEDED CULLED FROM THE FLOCK—AND CHIMP HIM. IMAGINE IF I CAME TO YOUR TOWN AND DID THE SAME? WERE IT NOT FOR OUR GOOD RELATIONS WITH THE RUSSIANS, YOU AND YOUR CREW WOULD ALL BE EATING PHONE BOOKS IN THE LANDFILL.

VUGOVIC: WHAT CAN YOU TELL ME ABOUT UNDERWOOD?

ROBERTO: THE WAY THE CORPORATION OPERATES HERE ON THE GOLD COAST, OR AT THE AIRPORTS, IS THAT SOMEONE WHO WANTS A FAVOR NEGOTIATES WITH US. THERE IS GIVE AND TAKE. BUT IN THE END THE TERMS ARE THE CORPORATION'S. NOBODY DEMANDS ANYTHING FROM US. I WOULD HOPE YOUR BOSSES HAVE BETTER MANNERS. EVEN THE RUSSIANS CAN MANAGE THAT. I WILL ASK AGAIN, AND IF YOU STILL HAVE NO MANNERS THEN WE ARE FINISHED HERE. GIVE ME A REASON TO HELP YOU FIND UNDERWOOD.

VUGOVIC: YOU WANT SOME SORT OF PERCENTAGE?

ROBERTO: [CLAPPING] VERY GOOD, MR. VUGOVIC! YOU SEE, WAS IT THAT HARD TO BE CIVIL? MY UNDERSTANDING IS THAT THESE GEMS ARE WORTH ABOUT ONE HUNDRED AND FIFTY MILLION TO THE ISRAELIS. YES?

VUGOVIC: [UNINTELLIGIBLE]

ROBERTO: [LAUGHTER] YOU THINK YOU ARE THE ONLY ONES WITH SPIES? THE ONLY ONE WHO KNOWS THINGS? THE CHINESE ARE WAY AHEAD OF YOU. CIGAR?

VUGOVIC: I DON'T SMOKE. THE CHINESE? WHAT CHINESE?

ROBERTO: WHAT IS THE CORPORATION'S CUT?

VUGOVIC: FIVE PERCENT OF WHATEVER DEAL WE STRIKE WITH THE ISRAELIS. BUT ONLY IF WE CATCH UNDERWOOD BY

NOON TOMORROW. OTHERWISE THE DEAL IS OFF. WE NEED TO GET UNDERWOOD IMMEDIATELY.

ROBERTO: HE WASN'T AT HIS BEACH HOUSE?

VUGOVIC: DO WE HAVE A BARGAIN?

ROBERTO: TEN PERCENT. THAT IS A STANDARD FINDER'S FEE.

VUGOVIC: SEVEN AND WE HAVE A DEAL. OTHERWISE I WALK.

ROBERTO: I AM EXTENDING MY HAND—YOU WON'T SHAKE IT?

VUGOVIC: I DON'T SHAKE HANDS.

ROBERTO: [LAUGHTER] REALLY, YOU KURAC HAVE COMPLETELY LOST YOUR SOULS, HAVEN'T YOU? IT IS A BARGAIN THEN. WHAT DO YOU WANT TO KNOW?

VUGOVIC: ABOUT THE CHINESE.

ROBERTO: THEY ALMOST GRABBED UNDERWOOD ABOUT AN HOUR AGO, ABOUT TEN BLOCKS FROM THIS SPOT.

VUGOVIC: EXPLAIN.

ROBERTO: THEY HAVE A DEAL WITH UNDERWOOD TO TAKE THE GEMS FROM HIM. THEY DELIVERED TRAVEL DOCUMENTS AND AIRLINE TICKETS TO HIM, BUT ATTEMPTED TO SEE IF THEY COULD TAKE A SHORT CUT TO THE GEMS AND SAND-BAG GILL. HE WAS ON A MOTORCYCLE, AND A CHASE BEGAN. A CHINK WHO TRIED TO FOLLOW GILL IN QUEENS GOT A BEATING FOR HIS TROUBLE EARLIER IN THE DAY, AND THIS SAME CHINK WAS STILL ANGRY WHEN HE WENT COWBOY AND LET THE PURSUIT GET OUT OF HAND. THEY ACTUALLY TRIED TO SHOOT GILL. THE TONG HAS LET THE COWBOY SIT IN JAIL TO MAKE SURE HE IS OUT OF THE WAY UNTIL THEY CLEAR UP THINGS WITH UNDERWOOD. THEY DON'T WANT HOTSHOTS RISKING THE LOSS OF A HUNDRED AND FIFTY MILLION.

VUGOVIC: THIS ALL HAPPENED TONIGHT? HERE?

ROBERTO: GILL LED THE CHASE ALONG THE RIVERWALK, AND THEN DROVE INTO THE WEEHAWKEN TRAIN TUNNEL, AND THE CHINESE FOLLOWED HIM THERE, TOO, BUT A TRAIN CAME THE OTHER WAY AND THERE WAS ALMOST A VERY BAD

COLLISION. THE POLICE WERE EVERYWHERE AND I WAS GETTING CALLS ALL EVENING ABOUT IT. THAT IS THE ONLY REASON I AM STILL AWAKE AT THIS HOUR. QUITE AMUSING IN A WAY. MOSTLY BECAUSE THIS WAS ALL HAPPENING WHILE YOU WERE DRIVING BACK FROM A FRUITLESS SEARCH AT THE BEACH. MEANWHILE, THE CHINESE ALMOST HAD HIM. I CAN SEE YOU DON'T FIND ANY OF THIS AMUSING OR IRONIC.

VUGOVIC: I DON'T LAUGH.

ROBERTO: ONLY WHEN YOU BEAT PROSTITUTES DO THE KURAC LAUGH AND SING. I HEARD WHAT YOUR MEN DID IN NEWARK. THE ITALIANS AREN'T HAPPY.

VUGOVIC: WHAT WAS THE NAME OF THAT CHINESE, THE ONE WHO CHASED GILL?

ROBERTO: I DON'T KNOW. HE IS BEING HELD AT THE WEEHAWKEN POLICE STATION, WILL PROBABLY BE ARRAIGNED BY HUDSON COUNTY TOMORROW MORNING.

VUGOVIC: CAN YOU TELL ME HOW WE MIGHT FIND UNDERWOOD AND IN TURN YOU MIGHT EARN YOUR SEVEN PERCENT, CUBAN?

ROBERTO: YOU HAVE BEEN TO HIS AND TRUDY'S HOMES AND FOUND NOTHING. NOT SURPRISING, THEY WERE PROFESSIONALS. YOU MIGHT TRY HIS VAN, THE ONE HE USES FOR WORK. IT IS PARKED IN A LOT ON RIVER ROAD BEHIND A GAS STATION AND REPAIR SHOP. IT IS WHITE AND SAYS "THE SCREEN MAN" ON THE SIDE.

VUGOVIC: WE KNOW ABOUT THE VAN. TELL ME MORE ABOUT THIS WOMAN, TRUDY.

ROBERTO: MILITARY, LIKE GILL.

VUGOVIC: WHERE DID THEY MEET?

ROBERTO: SHE WAS A REAL ESTATE AGENT. HE USED HER TO ACCESS APARTMENTS HE TARGETED AS A PROSPECTIVE SOURCE FOR SPARKS. ONLY SHE DIDN'T KNOW AT THE TIME THAT'S WHAT HE WAS DOING.

VUGOVIC: SPARKS?

ROBERTO: JEWELRY. IT IS A LOCAL TERM. THEY SPARKLE, AND BE-CAUSE THEY ARE STOLEN, THEY ARE ALSO HOT. LIKE A SPARK. TRUDY BECAME SUSPICIOUS OF GILL AND CAUGHT HIM. RO-MANCE STEPPED IN.

VUGOVIC: HE FUCKED HER.

ROBERTO: [SIGH] DO YOU UNDERSTAND NOTHING? SHE WAS IN THE NAVY, A DIVER. SHE LIKED DANGER, AND SO SHE LIKED A DANGEROUS MAN. HE LIKED A DANGEROUS WOMAN. THERE WAS SOME BACK AND FORTH, BUT SHE WANTED IN ON HIS BUSINESS. REALLY QUITE EXTRAORDINARY TO HAVE A ROMANCE THAT WAS FOUNDED ON BURGLARY, ON SLID-ING DOWN ROPES AT NIGHT FROM TALL BUILDINGS. THEY WORKED PERFECTLY TOGETHER, AND SEEM VERY MUCH IN LOVE.

VUGOVIC: SO UNDERWOOD WILL DO ANYTHING TO KEEP HER ALIVE?

ROBERTO: THAT WOULD GO AGAINST THE CLAUSE.

VUGOVIC: THE CLAUSE? EXPLAIN.

ROBERTO: THE CLAUSE IS PART OF THE CONTRACT ONE SIGNS WHEN ONE FALLS UNDER THE INFLUENCE OF OUR ENTER-PRISE. IT IS ONLY FIGURATIVE. THERE IS NO PAPER TO SIGN, BUT IT IS JUST AS BINDING. IT HAS BEEN A PART OF THE COR-PORATION SINCE THE BEGINNING, AND HAS BEEN ADOPTED WIDELY AMONG ALL PROFESSIONALS OPERATING AROUND HERE. THE CLAUSE RECOGNIZES THE FUTILITY OF LETTING ANY MEMBER OF A PROJECT BE GRABBED BY THE POLICE IF AVOIDABLE, TO INCLUDE AVOIDING HOSPITALS.

VUGOVIC: DID GILL FIND ANOTHER CAT DOCTOR?

ROBERTO: PERHAPS THE CHINESE FOUND HIM ONE, I DON'T KNOW. BUT HE WILL NOT TAKE HER TO A HOSPITAL, AND AT A CERTAIN POINT HE WOULD LET HER DIE.

VUGOVIC: I THOUGHT HE LOVED HER?

ROBERTO: SEE? YOU DO LAUGH, IF ONLY A LITTLE. GILL LOVED HER ENOUGH THAT HE WOULD NOT DISHONOR HER BY VIOLATING THE CLAUSE. HE IS SMART ENOUGH TO KNOW

THAT POSSIBLY SAVING HER ONLY TO PUT THEM BOTH IN PRISON IS A POOR OPTION.

VUGOVIC: DID THEY HAVE ANY FRIENDS? WAS THERE ANY PLACE THEY WENT TO EAT AND DRINK?

ROBERTO: LIKE MANY FRIENDS OF THE CORPORATION, THEY COULD OFTEN BE FOUND TOGETHER AT NAPOLI ON MAIN STREET IN FORT LEE. IT IS A RESTAURANT, AND THERE IS A BAR. I DOUBT GILL WOULD GO THERE NOW. HE WILL NOT WANT TO BE SEEN.

VUGOVIC: HE MUST BE TIRED AFTER HIS CHASE THROUGH THE TRAIN TUNNEL AND NEED REST. IF HE GOES TO A HOTEL HERE WE WILL HEAR ABOUT IT. THIS WOMAN TRUDY MUST BE WITH A FRIEND, SOMEONE WHO IS TAKING CARE OF HER. THIS IS WHERE HE WILL GO.

ROBERTO: INTERESTING THEORY, BUT I THINK HE WILL KNOW BETTER THAN TO MAKE A MOVE SUCH AS THAT. HE WILL NO LONGER BE RIDING THAT MOTORCYCLE. THE POLICE HAVE THE PLATE, AND AFTER THAT CHASE ARE STOPPING EVERY MOTORCYCLE THEY SEE.

VUGOVIC: THAT MUST MEAN HE WILL TAKE A CAB.

ROBERTO: [CLAPPING] BRAVO, MR. VUGOVIC. I WOULD GUESS HE WILL LEAVE NEW JERSEY AT THIS POINT, THINGS ARE TOO HOT HERE FOR HIM NOW WITH THE POLICE LOOKING FOR HIM AS WELL AS THE KURAC AND THE CHINESE. CATS SEEK A JUNGLE TO ELUDE THE HUNTER.

VUGOVIC: HOW DO I FIND THESE CHINESE, THE ONES WHO ARE PURSUING UNDERWOOD?

ROBERTO: IF I HAD TO GUESS, I WOULD SAY UNDERWOOD MADE CONTACT THROUGH EAST TRADING JEWELERS. DOC HUANG.

VUGOVIC: I MAY NEED YOU AGAIN.

ROBERTO: NOT UNTIL MORNING. I AM AN OLD MAN, I LIKE SLEEP VERY MUCH.

VUGOVIC: OLD ENOUGH THAT YOU STILL DEAL WITH THE CIA? THEY MIGHT KNOW WHERE GILL IS.

ROBERTO: THE BAY OF PIGS WAS A LONG TIME AGO. I WAS ONLY TWENTY-THREE WHEN I LEFT HAVANA WITH MY FAMILY. EVEN IF THAT WERE SO, I DOUBT SPIKIC WOULD WANT THE CIA INVOLVED.

VUGOVIC: WHY DO YOU SAY THAT?

ROBERTO: I'M JUST GUESSING THAT SPIKIC MAY BE A WANTED MAN IN SOME SECTORS.

VUGOVIC: WHO TOLD YOU THAT?

ROBERTO: AS I SAID, JUST A GUESS. AND NOW, IF YOU DON'T MIND, I'D LIKE TO GET SOME SLEEP.

VUGOVIC: WE HAVE AN OLD SAYING: SLEEP IS FOR THE DEAD.

ROBERTO: HOW CHARMING. WE HAVE A SAYING AS WELL: A MAN WHO SLEEPS WELL LIVES WELL. GOOD EVENING.

[PAUSE—BACKGROUND SOUNDS UNKNOWN]

ROBERTO: MIGUEL? DO YOU THINK THE JUKEBOX IS ON?

MIGUEL: YES. WHETHER THEY WILL HEAR WHAT WE HAVE SAID IS UNKNOWN.

ROBERTO: WHERE IS THE MICROPHONE?

MIGUEL: IT DOES NOT MATTER. SPEAK ANYWHERE IN THE ROOM AND THE JUKEBOX WILL HEAR YOU. THE BUG IS VOICE ACTI-VATED, AND IT SENDS THE SIGNAL ON THE SAME PHONE LINE THAT THE JUKEBOX USES TO PLAY MUSIC.

ROBERTO: TRULY AMAZING. REMEMBER WHEN THEY USED TO HAVE RECORDS IN THEM THAT DROPPED INTO PLACE AND THE NEEDLE SWUNG INTO PLACE?

MIGUEL: I AM SORRY. I DO NOT.

ROBERTO: THEY STILL HAVE THEM IN HAVANA. I FEEL IDIOTIC TALKING TO A JUKEBOX.

MIGUEL: THEN TALK TO ME.

ROBERTO: WHO DO YOU THINK LISTENS TO THIS DEVICE?

MIGUEL: I DO NOT KNOW.

ROBERTO: THE FBI?

MIGUEL: PERHAPS.

ROBERTO: HELLO, FBI. I HOPE YOU ARE LISTENING AND THAT YOU WILL FOLLOW THE KURAC. I AM DOING YOU A FAVOR, PLEASE REMEMBER THAT. WE LOOK FORWARD TO YOU RIDDING US OF THE KURAC, THE SOONER THE BETTER. AND BECAUSE I KNOW I WAS BEING RECORDED, NOTHING I SAID TO SUGGEST THAT I WAS IN ANY WAY INVOLVED WITH A CRIME SYNDICATE IS TRUE. I MADE IT ALL UP TO KEEP HIM TALKING SO YOU CAN LISTEN, AND ANY STOLEN MONEY THAT VUGOVIC WOULD GIVE ME I WOULD REPORT DIRECTLY TO THE POLICE. NOT THAT THEY HAVE ANY INTENTION OF HONORING ANY KIND OF DEAL WITH ANYONE. I AM A COMMUNITY LEADER AND BUSINESSMAN, AND AS FAR AS I KNOW THE CORPORATION IS A MYTH.

MIGUEL: WHAT ABOUT UNDERWOOD?

ROBERTO: IF HE ALLOWS HIMSELF TO BE CAUGHT, THAT IS HIS FAULT. SOMETHING TELLS ME THE CAT WILL FIND A WAY TO SLIP BACK INTO THE JUNGLE. LET'S GO. MY PILLOW CALLS ME.

END

127

TWENTY-TWO

WHY STAY AT ONE of the most expensive hotels in town? Because they have the best security, though I didn't kid myself that they could actually stop any of my pursuers. I asked for a room on the thirteenth floor, the one with the ledge. It needed to be between two empty rooms, which I told the desk clerk was because I was a light sleeper. Price: twelve hundred and change a night. I paid with a credit card to make sure my pursuers could find me before too long, even if the hotel security did slow them down.

The lobby is like pictures you see of palaces in Europe, with a white vaulted ceiling and chandeliers, everything trimmed in gold, the furniture plush, all the staff in spiffy uniforms and alert. Fucket, they sure as hell better be like that at twelve hundred a night.

I walked to the ornate elevators, which looked like they should be in a museum.

There wasn't much traffic in the lobby at two thirty in the morning on a Monday: mostly hotel staff, and they tried their best not to look at me like I had two heads. In my canvas shirt, cargo pants, white hair, and carrying a saddle bag, I didn't exactly look the type to stay at the Plaza. That was good. The bellhops and staffers would remember the shabby man with the messy white hair and Jets cap when the Kurac arrived and started asking questions. Maybe the staff guessed I was an aging rock star.

For twelve hundred dollars I imagined the presidential suite. More like the governor's suite. Governor of Rhode Island. It was just a hotel room with a small sitting area, a "butler's pantry" (kitchenette), fancy tile bathroom, better linen, and a window. I put a Do Not Disturb tag on the door handle and looked out the window. There was a healthy ledge at that floor. I took a quick shower. Shampoo helped remove the weird acid smell the Nice 'n Easy left in my hair. Drying off, I looked at myself in the mirror, at the blond dude with the angry old scar across his belly and blood-shot eyes. Damn, it had been a long road. And the road seemed to stretch out far into the distance, like across a high desert, and I had to walk it by myself. My jaw muscles tightened as I thought about Trudy. To see her just one more time, to have her curl up next to me and smell her, and to sleep ...

My breath came short. My vision swam. A panic attack was creeping up on me, so I slapped myself, hard, and turned away from the mirror. That helped, so I got busy, which helped some more.

The Jets cap and canvas shirt went into the trash can along with the saddle bag littered with gum wrappers, rope, and bolt cut-ters. I stuffed a handful of unsold sparks and cash into my belly bag next to the three passports (Michael Thomas, Marcia Thomas, and Phil Greene) and ticket to Iceland. The crumpled straw trilby was my new hat, and I slipped on the drab tropical CVS shirt. But the cargo pants were all I had, and some of the pockets were stiff with wads of cash. My spring steel kit in my teeth, I examined the window lock, then opened the window and crawled outside. There was practically no breeze, even thirteen stories up. I turned south on the ledge. Below me to the left was Grand Army Plaza, complete with fountain and Fifth Avenue on the other side. It was a short distance to the next window, and I cupped my hands over the glass. The bed wasn't made. That meant the maid might come in at any time to remake it.

So I crawled slowly backward to my room's open window and back inside before crawling out the opposite direction, toward 59th Street and Central Park. The park's dark trees were dotted with streetlights that stretched north into the distance like a black starry night rolled out onto the earth's surface. Like a giant hole of outer space that I might have been able to leap into and fall through the vast nothing surrounded by the solar system, the galaxy, the universe, to drift in the void with Trudy.

At the next window I could see the bed was neatly made. Unless there were any other characters slinking around at two thirty in the morning looking for a room at the Plaza—which seemed unlikely—nobody else would check into that room until the next day's check-in time, which was three in the afternoon. I would be long gone by then.

For most people, crawling back and forth along a high ledge would freak them out. Keeping your cool is all a matter of maintaining perspective, of concentrating on the ledge and not what is below it. If I actually looked down and thought about falling, I think I would have. You train yourself not to think about that possibility any more than you would about your morning coffee being poisoned. There's sort of a zone you put yourself into, almost like a meditative state, and it's all about what is close to you, not far away. Part of maintaining your perspective while crawling on ledges is to avoid backing up if you can avoid it. I'm not sure why, but backing up seems to invite vertigo. So it is always best to find a place to turn around even if it means extra work. In this case I didn't have that luxury, so I backed up slowly.

From my kit I pulled a dowel and tried to simply lift the window. It was locked. A moment later it wasn't—I had slipped in a hooked piece of spring steel, worked it under the latch, and pushed. I climbed over the sill into the room, turned around, and crawled back to my first room one last time to re-latch it with the spring steel, locked from the inside.

Did I worry that anybody had seen me crawling around out there? No. One thing you learn doing high-wire work is that nobody at ground level spends any serious amount of time looking up. Even during the day. And people in other buildings don't spend a lot of time adjusting their focus beyond what's in their apartment. Especially at that hour. The windows across the way were dark.

In my new room I turned on the television, sound off, to light the room. This compact suite was near the corner of the building and so was in an "L" shape. I went to the front door's peephole and had a clear view toward the door to my first room. Keeping my eye at the peephole for hours didn't sound like much fun, and the bed beckoned. If I could get sleep, I knew I should. At the same time it would be instructive to see who showed up at that door across the way, and how soon. Timing from then until I made my escape might be critical. I needed to know how tight the tolerances were.

With the safety hasp secure on the door, I stretched out on the bed and immediately felt my muscles begin to melt. Aside from all the moving around, I had been wound up emotionally. My mind raced with all that had happened, so I tried to concentrate on something from before all the craziness, before Trudy, back to my childhood, to something fun and simple. I tried to remember the taste of salt water taffy, of the interior smell of my Dad's old Renault, to the sounds of my father playing the piano at night and singing along like he was a band leader at some fancy hotel in Milwaukee where he grew up. Sometimes my folks would have friends over after I turned in. I lay snug in bed listening to their gentle laughter and the ice cubes tinkling in their highball glasses as I fell asleep.

The wall behind me jolted me from near-sleep.

I was at the peephole a moment later.

The door to the first room was open, shadows of people moving around inside, but no voices.

A black woman and a Hispanic man soon came out and carefully closed the door behind them. They were both in FBI windbreakers that they were in a hurry to remove and push into shoulder bags before moving past my peephole and out of sight.

I got a good look at them. She had angular features, swept-back hair, and a crooked mouth. He had a heavy brow and frame, low hairline, not particularly tall.

I rubbed my jaw, trying to iron out this wrinkle. The Bureau hadn't showed up to the party over Tito's missing Cartier sparks. If the FBI were on to me, they had to be after the Britany-Swindol sparks, and the only way they would know I had them was if they first knew the Kurac had them. And if they knew the Serbs had them in New York, it most likely meant that they weren't just spectators. They intended to intercept them and bust the Kurac. Probably at the point of sale to catch them red-handed. And then I came along and screwed up everybody's plans. I wondered if Roberto knew about this, too, and decided to keep it to himself.

My brain did a flip, thinking about how much more complicated this made the mission. It was one thing to play cat and mouse with goons, and another with the Bureau. The FBI could stop an airplane on the runway, stop it from taking off, stop me from getting away. I had little doubt they had been listening in on everything the Kurac had said on their phones, maybe the Hong Kong friends too, and had a complete bio on Gill Underwood. They found my room because they had a tag on my credit card so that as soon as it was used they got an alert. The Kurac would be a step behind because they had to go through the Russians.

You might have thought that these syndicates would be as savvy as me about the phones, about not using them so freely. But they generally weren't, at least not at that point; it wasn't widely enough understood how sophisticated surveillance had become. Yet I'd had firsthand experience with the information that government data mining and SIGINT could provide. Believe it or not, and counter to their mandate and Title 50 of the United States Code that restricts spying on ordinary citizenry, the FBI, the CIA, and the NSA—between them—literally record everything that is said. Both over the phone and in many cases out in the open, by satellite. Everything texted or emailed is of course also stored and studied by software. This surveillance is of all U.S. citizens, and of course many, many people overseas, though I'm sure if you live in a yurt tending yaks or in a thatched hut collecting açai you may not be targeted. Whether an actual person actually listens, analyzes, and acts on what it recorded and the software flags is another matter. I don't think they or the software care if you are cheating on your spouse or conducting shady business practices. Not yet, anyway.

Three adversaries might not seem that much worse than two, but mathematically it actually complicates the combinations of things to go wrong from four to nine permutations.

I sank down in front of the TV. On the screen was a telemarketer trying to sell a miracle rag.

Another movie flashed through my mind, another I didn't know the name of. I saw a lot of them when I was at Portsmouth Medical cooling my heels. A gunslinger comes to a town split down the middle by two competing gangs, and this part I remember: the Rojos and the Baxters. The Rojos ambush a Mexican army payroll convoy and try to make it look like the Baxters did it. Meanwhile, our gunslinger joins both gangs without the other knowing; his loyalties are only his own. He plays one against the other so that the Baxters are destroyed. To make the Rojos show their hand, the gunslinger unearths a dead Mexican soldier who he positions outside of town as a survivor of the payroll heist and potential witness. While the Rojos ride out of town to dispatch this supposed witness, our gunslinger searches for and finds the gold. He is discovered and beaten, but escapes and recovers. When he returns to confront the Rojos, he has a steel plate hidden under his poncho, which freaks out the Rojo leader who only shoots for the heart, and is killed as a result. The gunslinger probably gets the gold, or some of it. I don't remember.

I guess the reason that came to mind was because my odds would be improved if one of my adversaries were out of the picture. The Chinese had to stay because they were the only ones I had a remote chance of actually selling the Britany-Swindol sparks to and luring the Kurac into a confrontation. After the fiasco in the Weehawken tunnel, I was pretty sure the Chinese would have had enough theatrics and might meet. Ten million was a bargain, after all. If they didn't make the drop, I could pull the plug and vanish. Regroup, maybe fly off and then come back for the sparks. Or just let the fire hose inspector have them. Fucket, the sparks and the mission weren't worth my life. At least I hoped not.

Serbs would be in the game until the FBI took them out. Both were waiting for the sparks to show before they made a move. If one was in, so was the other.

If I was extremely lucky, the Chinese would show up at JFK just before the others. I had to plan for all three to make the scene, and use that to my advantage.

The wall behind me jarred, and I went back to the peephole.

One of the muscle-T Kuracs with snakeskin shoes was standing to one side of the open door to the other room. He was watching the hallway, one hand playing with an unlit cigarette.

I checked Tito's watch. It had taken them about an hour and a half to locate me through my credit card swipe at the front desk. A little less for the FBI.

A moment later two Chinese in leather sport coats appeared at the end of the hallway and froze.

My mind immediately went to work on where I could hide so that the flying bullets wouldn't tear through the walls and into me. Bathroom: the tile would help stop the bullets. Or I could curl up in the tub.

Vugovic was standing in the doorway to the other room, pointing at the Chinese.

"Get your boss, we need to talk."

The Chinese pulled cell phones slowly from their belts while shrinking back around the corner, out of sight.

Vugovic turned back into the room, and I could hear the Kurac talking and rummaging around, stripping the sheets off the bed. I'm not sure what they hoped to find—I would have thought it seemed pretty obvious that I wasn't in the room long enough to have left anything that would tell them where I was going next.

The two Chinese thugs appeared at the end of the hallway again. Two steps behind them was an older goon with black-framed, yellow-tinted glasses and a damaged complexion. They all had their hands in their jacket pockets. Slowly, chins up, they approached.

The Kurac guarding the door clucked his tongue, and Vugovic reappeared with a goon. It was good to get a closer look at Vugovic than before from the hill over the barn through binoculars. The streaked ponytail and close-cut hair to the sides looked the same, but from the peephole I could see that he had sort of a pinched, tucked-in jaw and bushy eyebrows over those flat, darting eyes. He looked like a major-league shitbag.

The Chinese stopped about ten feet back from Vugovic, the muscle parting so the boss could step forward.

"You have lost something, yes?" China Boss smiled, showing cruel teeth.

Vugovic cocked his head. "We will find what was misplaced."

"Not in there." China Boss pointed at the empty room. "Not at the beach. The search is not promising. For you."

"We are getting closer, he is getting tired and sloppy. He took a taxi here. What of the girl?"

"Our arrangements with Mr. Underwood and his woman are our affair."

"I was hoping we might combine resources."

China Boss snorted. "Why are we talking?"

"Because I do not think it does either of us any good to have a shootout. If you try to make an exchange with Underwood, it is likely we will show up, you know this?"

A shrug and another scary smile was China Boss's reply.

Vugovic kept trying. "If you recover the gems first, we can offer a finder's fee, avoid bloodshed."

China Boss's eyes widened briefly, and then he shook his head. "We know how the Kurac honor their agreements. They do not. While it is unfortunate that you have misplaced your belongings, your clumsiness is your own affair. I suggest you do not confront us. You only have a handful of men here in the States. We will smother you like a pillow on a grandmother's face. Then you lose the gems and your lives. Learn from your mistakes, Serbian. Go home, steal again. Just not from us." He turned and passed back between his men, who held their ground until China Boss was around the corner. Then they drifted backward around the corner, too.

Vugovic said something in Serbian to no one in particular, and by the tone I didn't need a translation. It may even have been Serbian for *douchebag*. What came through loud and clear was that he didn't think much of the Chinese.

Vugovic and his goons closed the door to the other room and walked right past my peephole and down the hall.

What had I learned? Nothing I didn't already suspect. JFK would likely turn into a gun battle. There was a good side to that, though. Confusion and mayhem make opponents slow to adjust to unexpected threats. Neither the Kurac nor the Chinese knew that the FBI was involved. Probably not, anyway.

It was another ten minutes before those two agents from the FBI showed up, went into the room, and came back out. My hunch was they'd left some sort of bug in there the first visit and had just come to retrieve it.

I fell back onto the bed, closed my eyes, and tried to think about taffy, tinkling ice, and my father's piano playing.

TWENTY-THREE

DCSNet 6000 Warrant Database
Transcript Cellular DCD
Peerless IP Network / Redhook Translation
Target: Loj Vugovic
Plaza Hotel Room / 13th Floor
Date: Monday, August 9, 2010
Time: 311–317 EDT

VUGOVIC: WE ARE GETTING CLOSER. THE SHOWER IS STILL WET. HE WAS HERE NO MORE THAN A HALF-HOUR AGO.

UNKNOWN: MAYBE HE IS STILL IN THE BUILDING. I WILL CALL DOWNSTAIRS TO THE MEN THERE TO WATCH THE DOOR CAREFULLY.

VUGOVIC: BAH. HE COULD BE ACROSS TOWN BY NOW, HE COULD BE ANYWHERE, SO REALLY WE ARE NO CLOSER. I SEE NO EVIDENCE OF THE GIRL. PERHAPS HE IS LEADING US AWAY FROM HER THE WAY A DUCK LEADS THE FOX AWAY FROM HER CHICKS.

UNKNOWN: PERHAPS SHE IS DEAD.

VUGOVIC: THAT COULD BE SO. I WOULD DEARLY LIKE TO DIS-COVER HER SITUATION ONE WAY OR THE OTHER. WITHOUT HER HIS TACTICS WILL BE MORE TRANSPARENT.

UNKNOWN: HIS SHIRT STINKS.

VUGOVIC: LET ME SMELL. IT IS SOMETIMES IMPORTANT TO KNOW A MAN BY HIS SMELL.

UNKNOWN: HE STINKS, SO WHAT?

VUGOVIC: YOU ARE YOUNG. EXPERIENCE WILL TELL YOU HOW TO READ A MAN BY HIS SMELL. HAVE YOU EVER NOTICED THE PARTICULAR SMELL OF A MAN AS HE IS BEING INTER-ROGATED? OR WHEN HE IS NEAR DEATH? OR WHEN HE IS ABOUT TO FIGHT OVER A WOMAN?

UNKNOWN: NO.

VUGOVIC: USE ALL YOUR SENSES. IT COULD SAVE YOUR LIFE.

UNKNOWN: WHAT DOES HIS SMELL ON THE SHIRT TELL YOU?

VUGOVIC: HE IS NOT AS AFRAID AS HE SHOULD BE, YET HE IS VERY TENSE AND EATING MOSTLY SUGAR AND STARCH FOR ENERGY. A LACK OF PROTEIN WILL MAKE HIS MIND WEAK.

UNKNOWN: YOU CAN SMELL ALL THAT?

VUGOVIC: AND MORE. I DO NOT DETECT THE SMELL OF A MAN PROTECTING A WOMAN.

OTHER: [UNINTELLIGIBLE]

UNKNOWN: WHAT'S THAT? CHINESE? IN THE HALLWAY.

[UNINTELLIGIBLE]

[BACKGROUND SOUND]

VUGOVIC: LET US SEE IF THE CHINESE WILL BE REASONABLE AND WEAK WHEN THEIR BOSS ARRIVES. STRIP THE BED.

UNKNOWN: IT IS STILL MADE.

VUGOVIC: STRIP IT. YOU NEVER KNOW WHAT YOU WILL FIND IF YOU DO NOT LOOK. I CAN SEE HE HAS CHANGED AT LEAST SOME OF HIS STINKING CLOTHES. NO LONGER ANY HAT.

UNKNOWN: THE CAB DRIVER SAID HE HAD WHITE HAIR.

VUGOVIC: YES, I COULD SMELL THE RESIDUE OF THE HAIR DYE IN THE SHOWER. SO HE IS NOW WITH WHITE HAIR, SAME PANTS, DIFFERENT SHIRT, NO HAT, PROBABLY WILL WEAR SUNGLASSES DURING THE DAY. IS THE WINDOW LOCKED?

UNKNOWN: LET ME SEE. YES. BUT WHERE WOULD HE GO OUT THERE?

VUGOVIC: HE GOT INTO THAT WORM'S APARTMENT TO STEAL OUR GEMS, DIDN'T HE? THIS SPIDER CRAWLS AROUND ON ROOFTOPS AND LEDGES WITH THE SAME EASE A DOG LICKS HIS BALLS. WHAT'S THIS IN THE SADDLE BAG?

UNKNOWN: I LOOKED. GUM WRAPPERS.

VUGOVIC: ALL OF THEM?

UNKNOWN: THEY SEEM TO BE ALL THE SAME.

VUGOVIC: IDIOT! DOES THIS LOOK LIKE A GUM WRAPPER?

UNKNOWN: LOOKS LIKE SOMETHING IS WRITTEN ON IT.

VUGOVIC: YES, IT DOES, DOESN'T IT? IT'S AN ADDRESS, IN MAN-HATTAN. DO YOU NOT SEE HOW YOUR INCOMPETENCE ALMOST LET THIS SLIP BY UNNOTICED? THIS COULD BE THE ADDRESS OF A MISTRESS OR CONCUBINE OR HOME OF A FRIEND WHERE HE INTENDS TO SLEEP.

OTHER: [UNINTELLIGIBLE]

UNKNOWN: CHINESE ARE BACK WITH A THIRD.

[UNINTELLIGIBLE]

[BACKGROUND NOISE]

[DOOR CLOSING]

END

SUCCESS IN WARFARE IS ACHIEVED BY ADOPTING THE ENEMY'S PURPOSE, AND BY STAYING CLOSE TO THE ENEMY'S FLANK. SUCCESS WILL IN TIME BE YOURS AT THE EXPENSE OF YOUR ENEMY IF YOU ACCOMPLISH THIS TWIN FEAT OF CUNNING.

—*Sun Tzu*, The Art of War

TWENTY-FOUR

IT WAS LIKE I had blinked. One moment I was lying atop the bed and it was dark. The next moment I was in the exact same position and it was light. The window glowed with early sunlight. The alarm clock said 6:05. I'd slept a little over two hours.

At first consciousness, I assumed I was at my apartment, and that the previous day had not happened, that Trudy was at her apartment getting ready for a day of work at A1 Gold Coast Realtors. It was Monday and the Screen Man had a whole day's worth of appointments. Sometimes we wake from a dream that seems so real that we have to force ourselves back to reality. It was only a dream, a nightmare, none of it happened. Then there are times when the reverse happens, when the nightmare is true, when you wake up in a hospital with no hands or upside down in an armored vehicle full of dead soldiers, and you have to force yourself to accept the new reality, that the simple life you had is no more.

It was made more chilling that morning by waking up in a strange room, the flood of Sunday's events overwhelming me to the point where I wondered if I just stayed in bed and went back to sleep maybe I would wake up back in that other reality where the nightmare wasn't true. Or maybe if I just lay there and didn't move, the Chinese and the Kurac and the FBI would blow through like a storm. If I just stayed where I was I could wait it out and emerge into the sunshine a free man.

There was a crash in the hallway.

I jumped to my feet and checked the peephole. Across the way room service was picking up a dropped tray.

Showers—I couldn't seem to get enough of them. I toweled off and dressed in the drab CVS shirt, the cargo pants, belly bag, straw trilby, and a large pair of sunglasses. As I exited the Plaza Hotel, a doorman in a stiff uniform bowed.

"Good morning, sir. Cab? Or are you out for breakfast?"

I was startled by the doorman's booming voice as much as by the fact that he was so cheerful. He didn't fit in with my new reality where everybody was trying to rip me off or kill me. When you consider my idiotic trilby hat, sunglasses, and shirt, it makes it even more surprising. Fucket: I looked like a douchebag. I guess when you pump twelve hundred dollars into a single night's stay at a hotel the staff can afford to be cheerful. When I looked at the guy's pink face and clear blue eyes, I realized he was just a guy, probably with a family and a small house in Queens, who liked going through life being happy, who realized that having enough is actually good enough. I used to feel that way sometimes at the beach house. There was a lot of contentment to be had in *enough*. Nobody would ever hunt him down or plot how to vivisect him.

"Good morning. Don't need a cab. I'm walking." I smiled, but my eyes were scanning the sidewalks for any lingerers, any Kurac or Chinese or FBI who might have been camped out waiting for me. I didn't see any. Maybe the storm had blown through.

"It's going to be a nice day, sir, not too hot, though we may have a storm in the late afternoon. We have umbrellas if you like. Are you here on business?"

"Passing through." The fountain in Grand Army Plaza gushed and cascaded before me, the smell of warm trees in the park tracing a light, undecided breeze. I walked down the steps and stopped, still looking.

"You don't seem in a hurry. I can recommend an excellent place for breakfast if you like. Just that way, on 56th."

"Do you eat there?"

He laughed. "No sir, on my salary I eat at the diner on Second Avenue. I would recommend that as well. But it's a walk."

The doorman's obliviousness to my situation, and his simple notions about the importance of weather and breakfast, somehow made me feel more whole, like there would be a corner I would turn someday and I, too, would be normal again. He gave me hope.

"Thanks."

"Enjoy your day and your stay."

I walked two blocks east through Midtown's canyon, checking my reflection in the store windows to make sure I wasn't being followed. I wasn't.

I thought about smoking a Winston. I didn't.

Under extreme stress people sometimes stop eating and find themselves disoriented or vulnerable as their system shifts into starvation mode. Under the current situation I was probably burning half again as many calories as I normally would be. For once, I could actually chow down without throwing on extra weight, the irony being I wasn't very hungry. I couldn't afford to be disoriented or vulnerable, but my impulse was to push myself and get more accomplished before allowing myself to rack up needed calories and nourishment.

Tito's watch told me it was going on seven, and the streets of Midtown were beginning to churn with early commuters and vendors prepping their newsstands and coffee carts for the approaching Monday workforce tidal wave. If I grabbed a cab then it would get me to LaGuardia pretty fast at that hour. But I wasn't sure Paramount Car Rental would be open that early. I had a little time.

Maybe it was dangerous, but I took a window booth at the Athens Diner and took off my hat and sunglasses. The doorman had made me want to be normal, if only for an hour or so before I went back to being hunted.

It was one of those enduring diners staffed by Greeks. The shapely waitress had lovely eyes, dark hair in a ponytail, and a large nose. Going through her normal routine, she, too, somehow made me feel hopeful, and normal, especially when she slid the coffee cup and saucer in front of me.

A normal breakfast for me was a bowl of seeds and twigs in skim milk. Coffee: black.

That wouldn't cut it.

"I'll have the Ulysses breakfast skillet."

TWENTY-FIVE

A YELLOW CAB RUMBLED me across the Triborough Bridge and through Astoria's mishmash of elevated trains and highways to LaGuardia Airport. The car rental places are on the lower arrivals level, which was just getting busy with flights moving business-people from other cities to New York. If the Serbs or the FBI or the Chinese or anybody else who might be looking for me happened to be watching the airports, they would be on the departures level above.

Rubin was a Hasid, the variety of Jew that wears only black trousers and white collared shirts with long curls at their temples. He ran the airport branch of Paramount Car Rentals, strictly a local operation that squeezed itself in at the end past Hertz. I'd used them before because they have a wide variety of fancy cars for rent and do a brisk business with hotshots who come to town, the kind that think showing up to a real estate deal in a Maserati or Jag would boost their mojo. The kind that like disposing of undeclared cash wherever they can. Unlike the national chains, Rubin accepted cash.

I bought a paper and sat for a while watching Paramount's rental desk, making sure nobody else was doing the same. It seemed unlikely that the Kurac or the FBI would have thought I would rent a car. Rentals usually only accept credit cards. If I used my credit card, bad guys would know exactly where I was, they had to know I knew that. The previous night's Plaza episode proved that. So they'd pretty much figure I'd take taxis and buses and trains.

It helped that Paramount wasn't that widely known at my level in the criminal world because thieves stole cars to do jobs. Paying for stuff was against their nature. To be honest, I don't know how to boost cars and driving a stolen car seems a liability to a successful operation. You have to cover the *what ifs* as much as you can in an operation, and *What if you get pulled over by a cop for a broken taillight?* is a deal breaker. That sort of thing happens all the time. The heat has an uncanny knack for blundering into an operation just when you least expect it. Like who would have expected that woman Florrie to call the cops on me back at the Garber place?

I'd rented an Escalade from Rubin a few years back for an operation that took me out to Long Island. I needed the room for a ladder, and an Escalade in Hampton Bays blends in. Had anybody tied the Escalade to lifting the sparks they might have jotted down the license plate and come to Rubin. But he's the consummate businessman and understands his customers' needs and what keeps them coming back. His customers highly value discretion. Especially when they tip him, which I did. I also sent him a card every Hanukkah and Passover. He was a good man to have on call.

Trudy and I never knew when we might need a secure exit from town.

There was a young Hasid working the Paramount counter. When their customer queue dried up, I approached. "Is Rubin in?"

"I can help you, sir."

"Rubin said anytime I came by I should see him personally."

"Of course. His office is right in there. Have a seat, I'll call him."

The small office was stacked with pink receipts, plastered with post-its with phone numbers without names. I sat in the plastic chair opposite the desk.

"Gill?"

He never forgot a name, so they said. The rumpled bald man in a yarmulke burst into the room, his eyes those of an insomniac.

"Rubin, good to see you. You look well."

"You don't. What's the matter?"

"Death in the family."

He clasped his face, the eyes wobbling. "I hate it when that happens. Not your mother, I hope?"

"She's been gone a long time. This was my aunt, not that close, but I'm executor. It's a pain in the ass."

"Should I even ask about the hair? You look like some kind of crazy rock star." Rubin flopped into his chair, pushing up on his white sleeves. Poor guy was so bald that his curls were mere wisps.

"Sometimes it's fun to change it up."

"A death in the family. That bites." He didn't believe a word of it, and he didn't have to, and knew he didn't need to. Those wild eyes told me he somehow enjoyed rubbing up against mysterious characters like me. He could fill in the blanks, though. Most people like doing something illegal so long as the risk of being caught is low.

"What do you need? I'd love to be more sociable, but it's Monday, and you know Mondays. All the shit that happens to people's rentals over the weekend? Puh! Don't get me started, 'kay?"

"Nothing fancy, Rubin. In fact, do you have any Toyotas, like a Corolla? I'm looking for the plainest car you have."

"I have plain coming out of my ass."

"Only thing is, I need to leave it for pick-up at JFK. I know you don't have a counter there. I can pay extra, of course."

"When is the pick-up?"

"I'll be done with it by ten tonight. I can leave it at short-term parking."

"Extra fifty. You can leave the keys and ticket with the parking space written on it with the attendants. I do this all the time, they work for me a little, you know? Just hand them the keys and tell them Rubin is coming to pick up, how's that?" He clapped his hands and stood.

I stood, too. "That works. Do I need to fill in paperwork?"

Rubin didn't bat an eye. "Hand me four hundred cash, I hand you the keys, and we're done, 'kay?"

I peeled off a thousand in hundreds and put it in his hand. "The rest is a deposit on damages, just in case."

Rubin pocketed the thousand and opened a desk drawer. He tossed me a key. "I don't even rent this car. It's just a courtesy loaner, or one my nephews use to run errands, like to pick up cars at JFK. Has a few scratches and a ton of miles, but it won't crap out on you. It's a Toyota sedan, plain as they come and reliable, parked in the very last spot on the right. If the car survives, leave some gas in it, 'kay?"

"Perfect. You're the best."

He clasped my hand and started off down the hall. "If I'm not the best, Hertz gets my business. I have no choice but to be the best, but thank you anyway." He turned. "Gill?"

I raised an eyebrow.

He wagged a finger. "Be careful. I expect that Hanukkah card."

"You got it."

The car was right where he said it would be, gray and weary, but the engine was strong and the transmission tight. The AC worked, too, and despite what the doorman said, Monday looked like it was going to cook up into a hot one on all accounts. It all just had to work ten or twelve hours more.

Tito's watch said nine forty-five.

TWENTY-SIX

DCSNet 6000 Warrant Database
Transcript Cell Phone Track and Trace
Peerless IP Network / Redhook Translation
Target: Dragan Spikic
Date: Monday, August 9, 2010
Time: 938–941 EDT

SPIKIC: TALK TO ME.

VUGOVIC: THE CHINESE HAVE A DEAL WITH UNDERWOOD FOR THE GEMS, AND IT GOES DOWN TODAY SOMETIME. WE WILL BE THERE.

SPIKIC: OUT OF MY MOTHER'S PUSSY! THE CHINESE!

VUGOVIC: FROM HONG KONG, THE ONES WE STOLE GEMS FROM, THEY ARE SETTLING THAT SCORE. WE WILL HAVE THE GEMS BY THE END OF THE DAY. YOU CAN TELL THE ISRAELIS WE WILL BE READY TO MAKE THE EXCHANGE WITH THEM TOMORROW MORNING.

SPIKIC: YOU SEEM PRETTY SURE OF YOURSELF, VUGO.

VUGOVIC: WE CAME VERY CLOSE TO CORNERING HIM AT THE PLAZA LAST NIGHT, WE WERE THERE BEFORE THE CHINESE, AND TOMORROW MORNING WE WILL HAVE A MAN ON THE INSIDE WITH THE CHINESE. UNDERWOOD WENT THERE IN A CAB. WE INTERROGATED THE CAB DRIVER. UNDERWOOD HAS COLORED HIS HAIR WHITE AND NO LONGER DRIVES THE MOTORCYCLE—THE POLICE AND THE CHINESE GAVE CHASE SO HE HAD TO ABANDON IT. SO HE TOOK A CAB TO THE PLAZA AND WAS IN A ROOM ON THE THIRTEENTH FLOOR, SHOWERED AND CHANGED. FROM HIS SMELL I CAN TELL HE IS WEAKENING, HE IS NOT EATING ENOUGH PROTEIN.

SPIKIC: WHO IS THIS CHINESE INSIDER YOU SAY YOU WILL HAVE TOMORROW MORNING?

VUGOVIC: A PUNK NAMED SHUI FU WING WHO CHASED AND SHOT AT UNDERWOOD. THE CHINESE ARE LETTING HIM COOL OFF IN JAIL. WE WILL BAIL HIM OUT, MAKE HIM OUR FRIEND.

SPIKIC: WHAT ABOUT THE WOMAN?

VUGOVIC: I THINK SHE MAY HAVE DIED. I DO NOT SMELL THAT HE IS PROTECTING HER ANY LONGER.

SPIKIC: WOULD HE HAVE SO EASILY ALLOWED HER TO EXPIRE?

VUGOVIC: I SPOKE WITH THE CUBAN, HE SAYS HE WOULD.

SPIKIC: ROBERTO?

VUGOVIC: YES.

SPIKIC: HE AGREED TO SPEAK WITH YOU?

VUGOVIC: HE WAS NOT HAPPY WE CHIMPED HIS MAN, THOUGH CLAIMED WE DID HIM A FAVOR.

SPIKIC: [LAUGHTER] THOSE SLEAZY CUBANS, THEY THINK THEY ARE SO CLEVER WHEN THEY ARE JUST WEAK AND USELESS SPICS.

VUGOVIC: HE ALSO SUGGESTED THAT HE KNEW YOU WERE WANTED BY THE HAGUE.

SPIKIC: AND WHAT DID YOU SAY?

VUGOVIC: I ASKED HIM WHO TOLD HIM THAT AND HE SAID HE WAS JUST GUESSING.

SPIKIC: YOU DON'T SUPPOSE HE IS PASSING INFORMATION TO THE CIA? I HEAR THAT THE CORPORATION STILL HAS CONNECTIONS.

VUGOVIC: I ASKED ABOUT THAT ALSO, BUT HE DENIED IT. TO GET ROBERTO'S COOPERATION I OF COURSE MADE EMPTY PROMISES IN EXCHANGE FOR INFORMATION.

SPIKIC: RELIABLE INFORMATION? CAN YOU BE SURE?

VUGOVIC: OF COURSE I CANNOT BE SURE, BUT I HAVE MET THE CHINESE SO KNOW THAT THEY ARE AFTER UNDERWOOD JUST AS ROBERTO SAID, SO DO NOT NEED TO KNOW ANY MORE THAN THAT.

SPIKIC: YOU MET THE CHINESE?

VUGOVIC: AT THE PLAZA, THEY SHOWED UP AFTER US AND DID NOT INSPECT THE ROOM.

SPIKIC: I WANT YOU TO DO WHATEVER IT TAKES, VUGO. ANY-BODY GETS IN THE WAY, MOW THEM DOWN, EVEN IF IT IS OUR OWN MEN. TAKE THE GEMS BACK AND DON'T LET THEM OUT OF YOUR SIGHT. I WILL CALL THE ISRAELIS ABOUT TO-MORROW AND SET IT UP

VUGOVIC: CONSIDER IT ACCOMPLISHED.

SPIKIC: FOR THE SAKE OF ALL MOTHERS AND THE RATS THAT IN-FEST THEIR PANTRY, IT HAD BETTER BE SO.

END

TWENTY-SEVEN

EUROPEAN ORGANIZED CRIME TASK FORCE
MEETING MINUTES
1100 EDT MONDAY AUGUST 9, 2010

ATTENDANCE: LOG ATTACHED

Re: Kurac gem theft conspiracy—recent developments re: G. Underwood

1. EOCTF Agents Brown and Acosta apprised superiors on tracing G. Underwood credit card in use to Plaza Hotel, 59th & 5th, Manhattan. Attempted intercept on 13th floor in advance of Kurac learning G. Underwood's whereabouts. Underwood had vacated the room just prior to arrival.

Room contained evidence of clothes change, discarded Jets hat, and shirt in garbage. Shower wet from bathing. Data collection device (DCD) planted in room behind television in anticipation of Kurac invasion of room. Observed Kurac enter lobby, followed shortly by members of Chinese Nee Fat Tong. Observed both groups leave premises shortly after. Returned to room to retrieve DCD. See transcript. Conversation between Kurac and Nee Fat Tong not collected, out of range.

2. Agents Kim and Bola of Intel Surveillance section reported tactical database intel. Nee Fat Tong, Hong Kong to intercept G. Underwood for Kurac gems. Details as yet unavailable, surveillance subsystems targeting, technical complications may indicate use of Taiwanese track-scrambled cell phones. Also report signal intercept from Weehawken Police with ID of expired license plate registered to Phillip Greene engaged in high-speed chase with SUV/Hummer registered to Ping Wong Grocery Distributors, Flushing, Queens—legal enterprise of Nee Fat Tong. Conclusion: Nee Fat Tong located G. Underwood, high-speed chase was result, local police attempted to intercede and detain. Shopping center security guard crashed into SUV/Hummer and ended up in river, driver swam to safety. G. Underwood on motorcycle slipped police gauntlet through Weehawken train tunnel. SUV/Hummer intercepted attempting to pursue. G. Underwood drove motorcycle into tunnel. Occupants: Shui Fu Wing, 26, male, Chinese national, U.S. legal resident; Pat Fong, 22, male, Chinese national, U.S. work permit; Tse Mo Shin, 22, male, Chinese national, illegal alien. All linked to Nee Fat

Tong. Dispatch to EOCTF Agents Brown and Acosta for field interrogation.

3. EOCTF Agents Brown and Acosta deployed to Weehawken PD with assist from interpreter from intel surveillance. Weehawken PD assisted with interrogation of detainees Shui Fu Wing, Pat Fong, and Tse Mo Shin in separate interviews. Wing and Fong nonresponsive. Shin—fearful of deportation—became cooperative, see transcript. Summary: Nee Fat Tong arranged to purchase Britany-Swindol gems from G. Underwood, arranged for drop of passports and tickets in advance, at which time Nee Fat Tong attempted to abduct G. Underwood, resulting in high-speed chase through pedestrian areas at riverfront. Exchange for gems scheduled to occur August 9th, status currently uncertain. Shin released on bond, currently implanted as informer within Nee Fat Tong, reporting to intel surveillance. Object: To learn of Nee Fat Tong possible exchange of gems with G. Underwood.

4. EOCTF Supervisor Palmer initiated discussion of current intentions of Kurac.

5. Agents Kim and Bola of Intel Surveillance section reported intercepts indicate Kurac plan to bail out Shui Fu Wing, in Hudson County jail for the reckless vehicular pursuit, and use him as informer within Nee Fat Tong to track plans for exchange with G. Underwood for Britany-Swindol gems.

6. EOCTF Supervisor Palmer initiated discussion of location of exchange, known or possible. No intel. Suggests that G. Underwood understands his predicament and needs a secure public place to perform the exchange from which he

can depart to the airport and leave the country undetected. Possibilities include an airport or train station where police, TSA, and National Guard are frequent and complicating factor to an attempted abduction. Discover which transit hub, scan departure manifests for G. Underwood, or possible aliases he may have used in the past. Press informer Shin for name on passports, flight, time, etc.

7. EOCTF Supervisor Palmer initiated discussion of injured T. Elwell condition, progress of search.

8. EOCTF Agents Brown and Acosta apprised superiors of increasing possibility she may already be dead. G. Underwood's continued mobility suggests he cannot be tending to an injured party, though it is possible she is not badly injured, or may have already departed the city to seek shelter elsewhere. Kurac intercepts indicate they also believe she may be dead. T. Elwell no longer seems germane to a study of G. Underwood's whereabouts or possibility of a safe house.

9. Intel Profiler Agent Laurenta provided input on G. Underwood M.O. based on previous observations and recent activity. Anticipated multilayered subterfuge not yet apparent but should not be discounted. Essential he does not discover FBI is a factor in blocking his escape and using him to draw the other parties together for the exchange. Based on his military applications of Sun Tzu text "Art of War" it should be anticipated that G. Underwood will use the Kurac and the Nee Fat Tong at cross purposes to help effect his escape. If it is suspected that G. Underwood is aware of the Justice Department involvement he will likely attempt to enact a

"cascade" in which each pursuer eliminates or paralyzes the other until there is only one pursuer. If this exchange takes place in a public arena such as an airport the situation could turn explosive, resulting in civilian casualties.

10. EOCTF Agents Brown and Acosta apprised superiors of G. Underwood "Screen Man" van impoundment and inventory—see attached for full inventory. Contents of van primarily related to making and repairing screens. Late-model Dell laptop computer discovered in compartment under driver's seat. Electronics forensic unit to report today on contents of hard drive, browser history, etc.

11. EOCTF Supervisor Palmer scheduled reconvene Monday 9th @ 1500 EDT.

********************MEETING ADJOURNED******************

TWENTY-EIGHT

I PARKED ON A Manhattan side street in the Twenties and made my way through busy sidewalks to the elevator bank in an old factory building on Broadway.

Removing my trilby, I exited the elevator directly into the fly shop. To my right by the windows: all kinds of specialty clothing and fly rods. Straight ahead: books and an island of cubbies filled with feathers tied on small hooks. Left: outerwear, boots, waders, fly-tying tools, and supplies. Farther left: "May I help you?"

It was a young guy in a purple Patagonia pullover, ponytail, and sandals. Stray feathers dotted his clothing.

"I'm going to take a trip to the Bahamas and learn how to fly fish."

His eyes widened, his head bobbing. "We can help you with that! When were you thinking of going?"

"Pretty much now. See, I just got laid off and got a nice settlement package, thought this was as good a time as ever to take a few months off and do something just for me."

"Stupendous! Good time to go, off season. Let's go look at the catalog, and then I'll make some calls, how's that?"

"I already have a lodge that I want to go to. Bernard's Cay Bonefish Lodge. An old friend operates it. I sent Tim an email last night saying I was coming—can you contact her and confirm?"

"I think Bernard's Cay would be perfect. And you know Tim: she's a certified casting instructor. I'll shoot her an email and confirm."

"Let's go with that. Two weeks. Then we'll see where I should head next, how's that?"

"Dude, I am *so* jealous, you're going to have an awesome trip." He eagerly jabbed a finger at the laptop.

I wandered off into the store. If you've never been to a fly shop—I hadn't—it's sort of like a golf, climbing, or ski emporium. There was a lot of designer outdoorsy clothing that was like it was from an L.L. Bean catalog. It ranged from tropical wear for Ecuador to parkas for Tierra del Fuego. I flipped a few price tags and rolled my eyes—they were about four times what I would ever pay for clothes. My idea of a shirt is one that costs under forty dollars. Under twenty even better.

At the fishing rod rack, the price tags were equally eye-rolling. They were all six hundred dollars and up. So were the reels. Just the line that went on the reels was pushing a hundred. Walk into a ski or golf shop and I guess you'd find pretty much the same level of pricey merchandising.

The lures they sold—flies—could either be fuzzy specks or fluffy pink birds that fit in your hand, all with a single hook to match. Many were tied with feathers, while others were constructed from plastic foam, wire, and hair. Some looked like something you'd stomp on if you saw it in your bathroom, or swat with a newspaper on the kitchen counter. Others looked like cat toys. They had eyes and looked like frogs and fish and mice and maybe even squid; I couldn't be sure what they were all supposed to be. Most were tucked neatly into about a jillion cup-sized cubbies built into the top of a wooden desk. Below, the desk drawers held dozens of plastic boxes with more flies. A wall rack of plastic drawers held still more. The sheer volume of flies suggested a huge knowledge base and was a little intimidating. There were thousands of different kinds. How could you possibly know which fly you were supposed to use? In golf, all the balls are the same size, and aside from color, very much the same. Were fish really this choosy? I guessed people were pretty particular with what they eat, so why not fish?

There was an entire wall of the components used to tie flies should a guy want to make them himself. I guess some people have a lot of time on their hands.

Farther along, I found racks of rubber pants and boots for walking around in rivers and staying dry. I was hoping I wouldn't need any of those, and from the pictures I'd seen I didn't think I would. In the tropics, I'd roast like a pork shoulder in those things. Confirming my suspicion was a rack of neoprene hi-tops for walking in the ocean, which from a display I could see were worn with flimsy, quick-drying pants. Very expensive flimsy, quick-drying pants.

The luggage section of the store displayed an array of special padded cases for fishing rods of every dimension, some that were tubes, and others that were more like briefcases. It seemed the rods themselves came apart into two or four sections. One of the cases drew my attention. It was perfect not only to transport fly fishing equipment but also sparks. It was a soft-sided duffel on wheels that had room for rods and numerous nooks for reels and other equipment, definitely the deluxe travel case for the hardcore angler who planned to check his equipment. While I would have preferred to keep my valuables close, I didn't dare subject my carry-on baggage to close scrutiny. If for any reason they went through the bag, they would be sure to find that I was transporting a substantial sum of cash and jewelry. That would not be good. In this piece of luggage I could layer the cash behind the padding and intermingle the sparks with the reels so that the scanners wouldn't notice them as being separate from the metal of the equipment.

"Okay, Bernard's Cay is expecting you day after tomorrow!"

"I need to book the flights. Through Nassau?"

"Yup, you'd have to fly into Nassau tomorrow, then catch the morning flight to Bernard's the following day. Can't do it all in one day, have to stay over in Nassau for a night."

"No flights out tonight?"

"No way. No flights to the Bahamas after, like, noon."

"Can I arrange the flight through your shop?"

"We can recommend a travel agent we work with for our group trips."

"Let me put it this way … what's your name?"

"Josh."

"Josh, I need you to be my full-service fly-fishing guy, and help me out with the travel agent to get my tickets. Since I'm new to this, I also need you to help me out because I have none of the stuff." I waved my hand around the shop. "Tell me what I need, I'll buy it."

The kid practically wet himself with excitement. "Whoa! You have nothing? Not even a rod?"

I set my trilby on the counter and pulled a thick wad of hundreds from my pocket. "So you'll book me the tickets, too? I need to pay for all this in cash, if that's okay. I just sold my car and would rather use up that cash than deposit it only to spend it, if you know what I mean."

He gulped. "Let me call my boss, but I'm sure that'll be fine, dude."

What businessman doesn't like large influxes of cash?

I dropped ten grand and change in that store. When I left two hours later, a miniature fly shop was all packed into that rolling duffel and a shoulder bag. That was the good news.

The bad news was that the soonest flight I could book to Nassau was early Tuesday morning. I needed to stay one more night without my pursuers knowing about it.

TWENTY-NINE

The tackle safely stowed in the Toyota's trunk, I left the car where it was and entered the subway at 23rd and Lex, bought a fare card, and headed uptown to Grand Central Station. It was the best place I could think of to make a phone call to Vugovic. I had his number from Tito's phone.

What made Grand Central an ideal location was lots of cops and a sprinkling of National Guard roaming around—it's not the kind of place people come to do abductions. Also, it's a transportation hub. I could go practically anywhere locally by dozens of different trains, including upstate. Once they pinged my phone there, they wouldn't bother to come looking. And neither would the FBI. The Plaza was as near as I cared to come to these dirtbags until that evening at the exchange. I didn't want to chance any close encounters that weren't completely necessary. I suppose I could have called from a diner on 23rd Street and been fine. I was being extra, extra careful in the home stretch.

I stood just to the side of an entrance off of 42nd Street, brass doors churning pedestrians in and out of the station next to me. Forty feet from me, watching the entrance, were two National Guardsmen with machine guns. My own personal bodyguards, for the moment.

"Yes?"

"It's Underwood. We should talk."

There was a long pause, during which he probably wanted to ask how I got his number but thought better of it.

"So, the mouse taunts the cat, hmm?"

"I've been thinking, Vugo, and I hope you have, too. There's a better way to do this. Right now you and the Chinese are set up for a gun battle when I try to make the exchange. That's not good for anybody, most of all, me, because I won't get my ten million."

"Is that your price? Ten million?"

"Firm. Two in cash, the rest in Guatemalan bearer bonds. After all this hassle, I would think it would be worth your while to just pay it to me yourself and cut out the Chinese."

"I hear the Chinese did not deal to you from the top of the deck. You did not expect us to, either, or you would have tried to return what was stolen. Why now?"

"Like I said, I think you're probably gearing up for a big gun battle in which the timing will be very tricky. You may mow down the entire Tong, and me, but that doesn't mean you'll put your hands on the Britany-Swindol sparks. I'm smart enough to know that if you capture me I'm dead no matter what, so handing over the sparks at that point means squat."

"We might let you die more quickly if you turn over the gems."

"Look, Vugo, I'm giving you this one opportunity to do this on the up and up. I don't want to wait around any longer. I have to get Trudy out of here, now. This way you get the gems, one hundred percent certain. The other way is a crap shoot."

"I suppose you think I can snap my fingers and magically make ten million in cash and Guat bonds appear."

"Spikic should be able to arrange that through the Russians."

"You seem to forget who you are dealing with, Underwood. We are a people who do not make terms. We make enemies and then kill them. We will do what it takes to find you."

"Nice speech, but how does that get your boss the hundred and fifty million from the Israelis? It won't. Look, I get that you're a soldier, you're all about killing and winning. Is that all that matters to your boss? I'd make sure, if I were you."

"I do not make terms, ever."

"I guess this was a mistake. Fine. I'm just going to skip town and get Trudy to a doctor, worry about the sparks sometime down the road. Bye."

I hung up. But I left the phone on.

Predictably, my phone rang, and it was Vugo.

"Underwood, you are too hasty. Americans are always in haste. Why don't you let us get you a doctor for Trudy."

"Is this why you called me? Look, I'm at Grand Central right now. Be here in two hours with the money, and I'll give you the sparks. Call this number when you get here."

I hung up but still kept the phone on to see if he would call back.

He didn't.

Somebody else did.

"Mr. Underwood?" It was a woman's voice.

"Yes?"

"We have a solution to your problem."

"Who is this?"

"Agent Brown, Federal Bureau of Investigation."

One Mississippi, two Mississippi...

"So what's the FBI's solution to my problem?"

"For one thing, we can sequester Trudy in a hospital under a false name and save her life."

"And then prosecute her, great."

"I think we can work a deal, here, where you both get probation for helping us recover the Britany-Swindol gems and secure a conviction of the Kurac. You just have to set it up. You're already at Grand Central."

"Doesn't mean I've pitched a tent here."

"All you have to do is go through with whatever you're going to do to make the exchange, and we'll do the rest. But you have to make the exchange, the money for the gems. No double cross or we all lose."

"So I don't get the ten million?"

"No. The ten million is evidence."

"We get probation and I get Trudy well, that's the bargain. Probation that can be revoked permanently if I get a parking ticket or Trudy jaywalks."

"You might as well take it, Mr. Underwood. Better to be alive than dead. None of these people, not the Chinese or the Serbians, are going to give you ten million dollars. No matter what kind of bargain it may seem to you, they steal, they don't pay, and that's who they are, and they will steal these gems from you and kill you.

Didn't you get that from your conversation with Vugovic just now? And how do you hope to set up any exchange with us listening to your every word? Any deal you try to arrange, we'll know about it and be there anyway. And as you said to Vugovic, the alternative is a gun battle at LaGuardia in which you still won't get your ten million, much less escape with Trudy."

Did she expect me to correct her about the airport, or confirm it?

"LaGuardia is a big place." Maybe she'd buy it, maybe not.

"What's your choice?"

I let another couple long *Mississippi*s slip by, like I was in anguish.

"You guys screw me over and I won't testify."

"We're the good guys, Underwood. We don't screw people over."

"I have a huge scar on my stomach that reminds me every day that there are no good guys."

"See you in two hours."

She hung up. I disabled Phone #2.

The two National Guardsmen were looking at me, and I didn't feel very safe anymore.

THIRTY

EUROPEAN ORGANIZED CRIME TASK FORCE
MEMORANDUM
MONDAY AUGUST 9, 2010

TO: EOCTF SUPERVISOR PALMER
FROM: INTEL PROFILER AGENT LAURENTA
RE: G. UNDERWOOD MILITARY PSYCHOLOGICAL PROFILE

I conducted a review of G. Underwood's military and medical records to develop a tighter understanding of his past in hopes of anticipating how he will behave in the future. Full records are available in the file. Salient observations:

- Underwood was injured during a Naval operation of his own design in the Gulf. While the exact nature of the operation is classified, hospital interviews reveal that the operation was designed to capitalize on the enemy's expectations, which in "Art of War" theory are a weakness for opposing forces. However, Underwood's interpretation of events indicate that unbeknownst to him, his superiors used his operation as a feint to distract the enemy from another front, to the extent that his superiors intentionally revealed the operation's unfolding to the enemy in advance. The result was that the compromised mission went badly, with multiple fatalities, and Underwood critically injured. According to Underwood, his operation was used as a decoy for another that failed to deploy adequately due to a clerical error.

- Contrary to surveillance information received August 8th in a conversation between Roberto Guarrez and Loj Vugovic, G. Underwood met T. Elwell at the psychiatric ward of Portsmouth Naval Medical Center in the summer of 2002 and participated in interpersonal psychotherapy (IPT) as part of treatment for post-traumatic stress disorder (PTSD). The role-transition stage of IPT was conducted as behavior therapy designed to correct behavioral deficits. Roleplaying in which the patient re-centers their skill sets on a vocation divorced from the one in which the stress disorder originated was used so that behavioral disorders are not propagated. Others in the group chose to direct their military skill set toward occupations such as advertising, police work, real estate, and woodworking. Underwood's choice for his roleplay was jewel thief. Attending physicians thought this an interesting choice and one that needed to be explored rather than discouraged in as much as PTSD has been linked to changes in cognition such as perceived threats, vigilantism, indifference to the law because of prior abuse by authority figures. Resultant psycho-physiological arousal often manifests itself in hyper-vigilance and diminished empathy associated with criminal behavior. After a series of structured interviews, coaching, and behavioral assessments, Underwood seemed to acquire the reinforcers to lessen his life punishment and changed his roleplay to window washer. Upon discharge from the hospital, outpatient coaching to prevent relapse was recommended. Underwood never returned to Portsmouth, and it is unknown if he ever received outpatient coaching.

- Conclusions: Underwood's criminal behavior is the result of unresolved behavioral disorders cultivated during service and subsequent PTSD. In essence, he has re-created in a criminal environment the military environment that harmed him. He has taken his tactical training and experience in the Middle East and applied it to the logistics of stealing gems. Comparative elements include allies with shifting alliances (fellow criminals, organized crime), authority figures (police, security guards), codes of conduct ("The Clause"), and comrade in arms (T. Elwell.) He believes his tactical theories failed when applied in the Gulf because his operation was undermined by authority figures which resulted in the death of the entire squad with which he was embedded. As a jewel thief, his tactical theories have been applied and he now undermines authority by his success. In effect, by successfully stealing gems, he is reversing the emotionally crushing consequences of his failed military career.

- Application: Understanding Underwood's behavioral disorder and relationship to authority should assist federal agents in predicting his future actions and in apprehending him. Of primary consideration is that surrendering to authority is not an option. Knowing that he will always defy and attempt to divert agents from his actual intent using tactics is crucial to anticipating his actions. Of secondary consideration is the stability of his current mental state. If T. Elwell dies, it could trigger a complete PTSD relapse in as much as her death would have been as a direct result of his tactical theories gone awry, which would mirror the loss of the squad in the Gulf. In that event, it is prudent to anticipate this relapse would express itself as either avoidance (he would simply isolate himself and drop out of sight) or hyperarousal (anger and violence). Even if T. Elwell is already dead, the PTSD relapse could express itself as delayed onset and occur at any time.

THIRTY-ONE

INVESTIGATIVE DATA WAREHOUSE
SPT SUBSYSTEM

SSA EMPLOYMENT BIO:

**UNDERWOOD, GILL # 842-00-1010 DOB AUGUST 23, 1971,
BETHESDA, MD**

1987—1989 RITEWAY VOLKSWAGEN REPAIR, CLIFTON, NJ

1989—1993 MOUNTAIN SPORTS, MADISON, NJ

1989—1993 FAIRLEIGH DICKINSON UNIVERSITY LIBRARY, MADI-
SON, NJ

1993—2004 US NAVY, WASHINGTON, DC

2004—2005 MANHATTAN WINDOW CLEANING, NEW YORK, NY
2005 *DECEASED*

SSA EMPLOYMENT BIO:

**ELWELL, TRUDY # 078-05-1120 DOB MARCH 17, 1974, SCARS-
DALE, NY**
1987—1991 FICAS INDUSTRIES, WHITE PLAINS, NY
1992—2004 US NAVY, WASHINGTON, DC
2005—2010 A1 GOLD COAST REALTORS, FORT LEE, NJ

THIRTY-TWO

DCSNet 6000 Warrant Database
Transcript Cell Phone Track and Trace
Peerless IP Network / Redhook Translation
Target: Tito Raykovic
Date: Monday, August 9, 2010
Time: 1206–1207 EDT

TITO: IDI?

IDI: WHAT IS IT?

TITO: YOU HAVE NOT BEEN HOME SINCE SATURDAY NIGHT.

IDI: I KNOW.

TITO: [UNINTELLIGIBLE] WHAT AM I TO THINK?

IDI: I NEED SOME TIME TO MYSELF, THAT'S ALL.

TITO: WHERE ARE YOU?

IDI: AT A VERY NICE HOTEL IN MANHATTAN.

TITO: IN MANHATTAN?

IDI: OF COURSE.

TITO: MOTHER OF GOD, HOW MUCH IS THAT COSTING ME A NIGHT?

IDI: YOU'RE NOT PAYING FOR IT.

TITO: WHO IS?

IDI: MR. SPIKIC WAS KIND ENOUGH TO GET ME A ROOM. IT HAS BEEN QUITE AN ORDEAL TO HAVE MY THINGS PAWED THROUGH BY STRANGERS, TO HAVE HAD ALL MY JEWELRY STOLEN.

TITO: WHY DON'T YOU COME HOME?

IDI: I LIKE IT HERE. I WILL COME HOME WHEN I FEEL LIKE IT.

TITO: ARE YOU SLEEPING WITH THIS MAN?

IDI: HE IS A GENTLEMAN. HE KNOWS HOW TO TREAT A LADY AND DOESN'T YELL AT ME ABOUT MONEY BECAUSE, UNLIKE YOU, HE HAS IT.

TITO: I AM TRYING NOT TO BE ANGRY. I AM TRYING NOT TO BE JEALOUS. YOU ARE MY WIFE AND I WOULD LIKE YOU TO COME HOME. IT IS NOT RIGHT FOR YOU TO BE STAYING AT A HOTEL THAT ANOTHER MAN PAYS FOR.

IDI: IT WAS NOT RIGHT TO HAVE BEEN ROBBED, IT WAS NOT RIGHT TO HAVE A CARELESS HUSBAND. IT WAS NOT RIGHT THAT—

TITO: I AM COMING TO GET YOU!

IDI: [LAUGHTER] SO YOU THINK YOU ARE MAN ENOUGH TO GO UP AGAINST DRAGAN? HM? HELLO? IDIOT HUNG UP ON ME, JUST [UNINTELLIGIBLE]

END.

THIRTY-THREE

I TOOK THE CROSSTOWN shuttle to Times Square and switched trains to the Downtown 1 train to 23rd Street. I walked toward the Toyota, stopping briefly for a slice of pizza and a Pepsi. At the car I lit up Phone #3 for the first time and called directory assistance. It took me a little squabbling with the operator, but I found a messenger service on 8th near 23rd Street. At a CVS on the corner I looked for a box of some kind. Didn't have to be anything special, just had to have a little weight. I settled on a boxed set of old-fashioned glasses. I also bought a gift bag and a fancy bow. When I was done it looked like a birthday present. Forgot the card, but I think the message I was sending was clear enough without it.

I walked into Chelsea Messengers. "Hi."

The Middle Eastern guy at the counter smiled. "Can I help you?"

"Yes. See, I need this delivered to a special friend at four o'clock, at the Banana Republic at Grand Central. It's his birthday. I'd take it, but I have to catch a flight."

"Certainly. Do you have an account?"

"No. I have a credit card, but I just sold my car and I'm trying to unload cash. Is that all right?"

"Certainly." He slid a form in front of me.

I filled it out, handed him the gift and a hundred dollar bill.

He scrutinized the form. "Vugovic?"

"Yes. Deliver to Vugovic at the returns counter at Banana Republic at four. He works there."

"We need a last name."

"He only has one. He's Serbian."

"They only have one name?"

I shrugged. "Weird, huh?"

He handed me my change and said, "Have a nice day."

"You too."

Back at the car I used Phone #3 to call directory assistance for western New Jersey, out in the sticks near Pennsylvania.

"Yeah?"

"It's Gill Underwood."

"Jesus. Gill Underwood. Well, how the hell are ya, Gill? I haven't seen you since Portsmouth Medical."

"I know, it's been awhile. This is sort of out of the blue."

"Man. So how you been?"

"I've been better."

"Whoa. What's up? You having relapse?"

"Sort of."

"Have you been going to therapy?"

179

"No, I haven't. I've been with Trudy."

"Trudy Elwell? From IPT?"

"Yup, same Trudy."

"Holy shit. No kidding. Tell her I said hi."

"Can I come out for a visit, Larry? I need to talk."

"You mean right now?"

"Yeah, right now. I can be there in an hour or so, depending on the traffic."

"You okay to drive, Gill?"

"Yes. I haven't been drinking, no drugs or anything."

"I'll have to move a few things around. I refinish furniture now—funny, huh? Ordinance disposal to woodworking. I know, I know, woodworking is what I chose for interpersonal therapy, but I found I liked it. Sanding and scraping wood is like grinding all the shit out of my brains. What about you? Hell, you're not a jewel thief or anything, are you? Ha! I sometimes thought about you and that whole role-transition thing with you as a jewel thief."

"Got directions?"

"Sure, come west on I-80, head north on Route 15 to 206, make a left at Fratelli's Italian toward Dingman's Ferry Bridge. In Layton, make a right at the old red schoolhouse, and I'm all the way at the end by the creek with the green pickup."

"Leaving now."

"Well, it's good to hear your voice, Gill, and I look forward to seeing you. I hope I can help."

"You told me to call anytime, for any reason."

"Ha! That sounds like something I might say. But I meant it. We go back, and that was hard stuff we did. See you soon."

As you drive west on I-80, the housing developments thin a little though the shopping malls don't thin much at all, at least up until you veer off and north on Route 15, where New Jersey gradually becomes hilly and densely wooded. Trudy and I once did a picnic hike into the hilltops of Stokes State Forest, which open up to sweeping valley views. To the north, you see the Delaware River Valley and the Catskills and Kittatinny Range. To the south, you see woodland diced with occasional farms all the way to the Watchung Range, I-80 and a less wild corridor leading back to the city. We saw a bear that day, with her cubs, angling through a blueberry hollow. The mom didn't look at us, just lifted her nose over her shoulder to give us a sniff as she retreated, the cubs bounding in front of her. That was a good day. A jillion years ago.

When I saw the park entrance on my right, I pulled in, paid the entrance fee, and wound around the curves of the forested road toward the overlook. Every mile or so there's a pull-out for a trailhead. Where trees thinned, glimpses of the scenic view flashed until the road split and I drove right up a steep road to a parking lot. Only one other car was there. Monday midday in August wasn't that popular a time for Stokes State Forest, I guessed.

It is only a short walk along a well-worn path to the view. The pavilion there looks like a log cabin without any walls, its timbers carved with the names of countless visitors. The summer skies were hazy, not as they'd been in the fall when Trudy and I were there, but you could still make out the Catskills, and the cut of the Delaware Valley. Other people there were on a bench, a middle-aged couple curled up like teenagers. I wondered if they were married, or if they were cheating.

A warm breeze rose from the valley floor, and buzzards skated and roller-coastered on the thermals across the face of the escarpment.

A path led down to a more secluded spot, to a bench and a view off to the southeast. I hiked down and took a seat.

The smell of warm pine and goldenrod washed over me, as did the touch of Trudy's hand to my face.

"I'm sorry, Gill."

"I know, sugar, I know, I know. I'm sorry. It's not your fault."

It wasn't her fault she was dead—it was mine.

My vision swam, and not just with tears; my breathing was rapid and I couldn't seem to get enough air. My hands trembled when I held them out, and when I tried to stand I lost my balance and lurched toward the edge of the cliff. I fell to my side at the ledge, and kicked my feet to push myself away from tipping over into a seven-hundred-foot tumble. The world was darkening, shadows of the buzzards plunging me into darkness, the sound of their wings crackling on the thermals like death's snicker, laughing not because I was going to die, but because I was going to live. Because I was going to be the one to survive. Again. I smelled diesel fuel leaking from the upturned transport. A dim shaft of sunlight. Lifeless soldiers bundled in gear. The clutter of guns and ammunition and binoculars and maps.

Cupping my hands over my mouth, I restricted the air to my lungs, and crawled on my elbows and knees back to the bench. I had to stop hyperventilating. I had to stop the panic attack. I focused on being a child in bed by the night-light, the sound of my parents downstairs, the murmur of their voices, the tinkle of ice, a piano and a whiff of tobacco.

"Whoa! Buddy, you okay?"

There was a hand on my shoulder. I couldn't answer.

"Let's get him up."

"He could be injured, we might hurt him." It was a woman's voice.

"I don't see any blood, and we saw him walk down here. I think he's having a seizure or something. He could roll right off that edge. Help me."

I felt myself being dragged, and when I opened my eyes the people standing over me were the couple from the bench.

"Are you all right?" she asked.

"I will be."

"Should we call you an EMT?" he asked.

"No, it's passing."

"Are you epileptic?" she asked. "You shouldn't come to places like this if you're epileptic. You could have a fit and fall right off."

I took my hands away from my mouth and breathed deep and long through my mouth. A vulture was eyeing me from a nearby tree. The couple was just as intent, and so I tried a smile. "Thank you for helping me. I'm not sure what happened. Memories. Too many all at once."

"Let us drive you to the hospital," she said.

"Can you walk?" he asked.

"If you'd walk me back to my car that would be a big help. I need to shake it off. There's nothing they can do for me at a hospital."

I stood and they took my arms.

"Is it mental?" she asked.

We turned and began the climb back to the pavilion.

"Honey, you can't ask the man that."

"He as much as said so."

"Yes, it's mental," I said. "But it comes and goes, hasn't happened in a long time. I'll be all right, and fine to drive."

"Are you sure?"

Back at the car I did some deep knee bends and breathing exercises. "Thanks again for helping me."

"You sure you're okay?" she asked.

"Yes, I'm sure."

"Stay away from high places for a while," she said.

"Honey, you can't tell a man what to do. He knows he almost died."

"I can't very well let him drive off and then fall off some other cliff, can I?"

I opened the car door. "Thanks again. You were both very nice to help like that. A lot of people wouldn't have, and I hope I didn't ruin your day."

"Go see a doctor," she said.

He rolled his eyes and led her toward their car.

THE ABLE WARRIORS OF OLD FIRST SITUATED THEMSELVES BEYOND THE POSSIBILITY OF DEFEAT, AND THEN WAITED FOR AN OPPORTUNITY OF DEFEATING THE ENEMY. TO SECURE AGAINST DEFEAT IS IN YOUR POWER, BUT THE OPPORTUNITY OF DEFEATING THE ENEMY IS PROVIDED BY THE ENEMY HIMSELF. THUS THE ABLE WARRIOR IS ABLE TO SECURE HIMSELF AGAINST DEFEAT,

BUT CANNOT MAKE CERTAIN OF DEFEATING THE ENEMY. THUS IT IS SAID: ONE MAY KNOW HOW TO CONQUER WITHOUT BEING ABLE TO DO IT.

—*Sun Tzu*, The Art of War

THIRTY-FOUR

LAYTON IS JUST AN auto mechanic, a post office, a deli, and a bar.

I followed the directions and turned at the schoolhouse, and after the last turn the road turned into gravel that got thinner and thinner until finally a white clapboard house with porch and large barn appeared between the trees. In coveralls, Larry was out front, a yellow mutt hard by his side, a shotgun tucked under one arm lazily.

We both registered surprise—me over his long beard and him over my white hair.

I parked at a worn spot by the barn and got out.

"Larry, have you gone native or what?"

His cheeks went rosy—he was the kind of guy who blushed all the time. Larry lost his hands back in Kuwait, replaced with articulated hooks. He extended one, and I shook it, and he pulled me in for a bear hug.

"Look who's talking! What's with the white hair? Lost weight. You look like Billy Idol or something. I hardly recognize you."

"Long story. What's with the shotgun?"

"It goes with the beard and overalls, don't you think?"

"Let's not forget the dog."

"That's my bitch, Marianna."

The dog panted lazily, with the kind of sleepy contentment you only seem to see in farm dogs.

Larry cocked an eye at me. "Let me show you around." The barn was a fully fitted workshop with an array of antiques—dressers, rockers, bureaus, highboys, lowboys, end tables—in various states of repair. There was a dust-free room for drying final finishes, and another that was an office strewn with invoices and empty coffee cups. A small stream ran behind the house and barn, and he'd built a bridge over it to a small clearing and a bench. Sun dappled a gravestone in the middle of the grass clearing. The engraving read: *All the Shit That Doesn't Matter.*

I smiled at the gravestone. "Nice."

"This is my place, this is where I come to re-center myself." He sank into the bench, Marianna flopping down in the grass next to him. "So what shit matters to you, Gill?"

I settled in next to him, my jaw tightening.

"Okay if I open up here a minute?"

"That's why you came, that's why I waited."

"Here it is in a nutshell. I'm a jewel thief, and so was Trudy. We stole from Gold Coast high-rise apartments from people who flashed it around, you know, not only the gems but the cars, the furs, all that. Not a justification, but these people wouldn't know what that gravestone meant. Maybe there was a little revenge in it, I'm not sure. You know, getting back at all the people who create that shit that doesn't matter."

"Wow, that's kinda cool, even if it may not have been the most healthy life. You said you *are* or *were* a jewel thief?"

I leaned forward, elbows on knees, staring at the grass.

"I'm not sure what I am now."

"And Trudy?"

"She died."

"When?"

"Night before last. In my arms. Shot. During an operation."

"Damn. As we used to say in the service, life really sucks sometimes. Gill. I am so sorry."

I couldn't speak for another five minutes, so lit a Winston. Larry began to hum a slow version of "Amazing Grace." I could hear him slowly flexing his hooks. But he stopped when I spoke again.

"There's a lot to regret, and a lot of healing that I need to do. But I have something to do before I can start that."

"You want to stay here for a while?"

"I have to accomplish something."

"No, I don't think you do, Gill. Revenge isn't the answer."

"It isn't revenge. I need to know she didn't die for nothing."

"So what is it you have in mind?"

"This operation: we stole from the wrong people, by accident."

Larry leaned forward. "Which wrong people? Not the Russians."

"Worse."

"The Serbs?"

"Yup."

"Woo boy." He leaned back again. "I assume you've been very tactical?"

"I wouldn't have come if I hadn't been, I wouldn't draw them here. In fact, I'd already be chopped up if I hadn't been careful, especially with the phones. I've been using prepaids. They have a hard time listening to those, and I turn them off so they can't ping them. I've been on the move almost constantly."

"If anybody can stay a step ahead, I guess it would be you. How much you steal?"

"There's about a hundred and fifty's worth."

"Thousand?"

"Million."

"Million? Holy cow. That's too much, Gill. The goons will go apeshit and do anything to get that stuff back. Just walk away. Get out of here."

"I thought about that option, believe me. But I've got to complete the operation. I can't let it end in failure and death."

"Operation? That sounds like spook speak, must have picked that up from those CIA types you worked with."

"Well, I don't know what else to call it, and it's just as complicated as any mission I ever devised. The Chinese want to take it off my hands for ten, or nothing if they can figure a way."

"Ten million. Man."

"And I can't count out the Cubans. I'm on friendly terms with them, but there's an understanding that everybody is out for their own interests, part of the rules of engagement."

"Mind if I do a little head shrinking, Gill?"

"Have at it."

"You realize that the world you created as a jewel thief to re-place the military is exactly the same, don't you? I mean, you hear yourself, right? *Operations, rules of engagement.* The idea was to create a new persona for yourself, one divorced of the past."

"I realize all that. Now."

"So let me get this straight. You have the Serbs, the Tong, and the Corporation after you? Have you left anybody out?"

"Feds."

"Damn, you don't do anything halfway, do you, Gill? Which ones?"

"FBI has been following the action through surveillance. I'm guessing they've been following the Serbs trying to make a bust, and then suddenly I came along and fouled everything up. Now of course they want me to turn for them, with the usual assurances."

"You and me have had a belly full of those assurances. How on earth do you think you can make the exchange with all these parties involved?"

I grinned, with little enthusiasm. "I have a few ideas, but it's going to be dicey."

"You didn't come here just to talk, did you?"

"I did. Mostly."

"You need something diversionary, in a small package."

"Yup. I need a diversion and I need a hot tamale."

"I'm not sure I should help you, because I'm not sure it will. I think it might just make things a lot worse."

I met his eye. "How exactly could it be worse?"

He frowned and stared at the gravestone.

"I don't do that stuff anymore, Gill. People get hurt."

"The same way I don't do that stuff anymore?"

"It's fireworks. I think of it as fireworks."

"Can you make me some fireworks that I can detonate with a cell phone?"

Larry stood and walked around the gravestone. "You don't need to do this, Gill, you can just walk away. It won't bring her back."

"Nobody needed to shoot her. She didn't have a gun, she was on a bicycle, pedaling up the road. Just say no and that's that, no regrets. I can make do on my own. Though I can't guarantee what I come up with will be as controlled as what you would."

"You knew being a jewel thief was dangerous. You took your chances and now there are consequences."

"We had an exit strategy, and I still do. Trudy would want us to get away with what we took. If for nothing else, she'd hate the Kurac that did it to her. I have a place to go to recover and leave all this behind once and for all. I've lost too many people I cared about. I can't do it anymore. I realize that. Now."

"Have you ever heard of synchronicity, Gill?"

I shook my head.

"Life is made up of events that sometimes happen at the same time as other events and create a result or outcome that was unanticipated."

"You mean the fact that Trudy and I happened to target this guy's apartment just when the Serbs were storing gems there? You're not going to dive into some sort of space-time continuum crap, are you?"

"Would it make it easier to call it the collective unconscious?"

"Either way, what does this have to do with my exit strategy?"

"*Destiny, not fate.* These things that have happened and what will happen next may have a life of their own, are destined, and

191

there may be some other event or person you can't even anticipate that will change the game. But your destiny does not have to be your fate. What I'm saying is, don't turn this into a suicide mission to take out the people who killed Trudy. Trudy wouldn't want that, would she? She would want you to get away."

"I didn't have in mind a suicide mission."

"You may not know what you really intended. What sort of device you come up with if I didn't help you?"

"Nitrates and fuel oil, what else?"

"And the hot tamale?"

"Kerosene and benzene."

"What's the incendiary tamale for?"

"Destroying evidence."

"What kind of evidence?"

"A car."

"And your detonators?"

"Model rocket engines, battery pack, remote control toy."

"Going all Radio Shack here, I see." Larry grimaced. "Do you even have any idea how much you need to first blow out one car and then burn the other one to the ground?"

I shook my head.

"Benzene and kerosene? Where's your oxidizer?" He stood, and locked his hooks behind his back. "You have to promise me there will be no innocent bystanders killed or injured. That kind of bad karma sticks a lifetime. On you and on me."

"Promise."

Larry walked through the patches of sunlight to the bridge, Marianna trotting behind, and me a few steps behind her. We crossed the creek, past the barn, around back of the house to where a rusty steel shipping container stood. Opening the back doors of the container revealed a wall of what looked like old chairs, banisters, dressers that had been salvaged for parts. He pulled away two chairs, pushed aside a dresser, and revealed a concealed metal door. A key on a long chain from his overalls unlocked the door. He shoved it open, and pulled the chain on a battery-operated light.

"This is my lab. You have a phone you want to use?"

I handed him Phone #3 and we both sat at a workbench surrounded by hand-operated hobby tools like awls and coping saws and files. There were rolls of wire, plastic drawers, and large Tupperware along the surrounding walls. The place smelled like linseed oil and hydrogen peroxide. I had no idea why.

Larry opened a drawer and handed me a set of small screwdrivers. "Remove the back of the phone."

While I did that, he turned on a battery-powered soldering iron. He reached into an insulated drink cooler. From it he came up with what looked like a brick of shrink-wrapped white cheddar and set it on the counter. He opened a few plastic trays and picked out small lengths of wire and what looked like what would be the blasting cap. From a large drawer he selected a battery holder and six AA batteries. On a shelf he found a cigar box.

"Got it open?" Larry held a pair of pliers.

I handed over the phone, back removed. He glanced it over, found the counterweight that made it vibrate, and rolled it into the housing. Then snapped off a piece of the outer casing on the side where the counterweight could be accessed. "Put it back together."

While I did that, he mixed some epoxy, and glued the block of cheese into the right corner of the cigar box, and the battery pack into the center. I handed him the reassembled phone and he glued that into the left corner.

"Anybody have the number to this phone other than you?"

"You're the only one I called on it. Except for directory assistance."

"Good. I'm setting it for vibrate and then making sure it's off. Don't turn it on until you're ready to arm it. And make sure it is still on vibrate, otherwise it won't work."

"Got it."

Larry wired and soldered the batteries into a circuit that would connect the batteries to the hot detonator. The trigger was a small plug with two wire ends extending from the end. He pointed to it.

"When the phone vibrates, the counterweight spins and connects these two wire ends, completing the circuit."

He used a circuit tester to check that the circuit was hot before removing a battery and setting it inside the box.

"Here's what you do. Step one: turn on the phone. Wait to make sure that there are no messages or anything from the service provider that will make it vibrate and blow you up. Step two: plug the trigger into the hole in the side of the phone—about like this. Step three: insert the battery into the power pack. Step four: attach the alligator clips to the cap, holding it away from the charge in case it goes off because of some unforeseen change in the setup. Step five: insert the cap into the charge, place the cigar box where you want it, and get away from it."

"How powerful is it?"

"It'll demolish that car of yours, likely kill anybody inside if it's under the front seat or on the back seat, likely injure anybody standing near it."

"That's some firework."

"Something tells me you're going to need a sizeable distraction if you plan to get away. You ever hear of a Mark 77?"

"The new napalm bombs." Technically they weren't napalm, but they amounted to the same thing, and were dropped from F-18s.

"Mm-hm. Hot tamales made with kerosene and benzene, but they have an oxidizer, thermite, and a touch of white phosphorus, just for fun. Melts the snow and ice off my driveway in February but quick." Larry stood and dragged a heavy, white pickle bucket from the corner. "In the Gulf, ground troops liked to flush out caves with the stuff, only it wasn't regular issue, was only supposed to be used from the air. Seems someone figured it wasn't PC to kill the enemy that way, even if it meant it put the good guys in harm's way. So we sometimes helped out the infantry on the sly."

He pried open the pickle bucket. It was filled with water. It was also filled with olive-drab cylinders about the size of a submarine sandwich. Larry lifted one out with both hooks and dried it on his coveralls. One hook tapped at a cap on one end of the cylinder. "There are four notches. Each one is five seconds. Turn it all the way, that's twenty seconds before it goes off. Then you pull the cotter pin out of this hole and get away."

"Burn a car to the ground?"

"The engine block won't burn completely."

"I can't thank you enough." I stood.

"You can thank me by taking out the bastards that killed Trudy and getting your ass out of town and into recovery." He stood too, and guided me out of the container. "Drop me a postcard so I can have some satisfaction that I've done the right thing, because I fear I haven't. At the same time I see you'd try to pull the escape using crap ordinance, and if you didn't make it, and bystanders got hurt, I'd feel it was partially my fault. You had me over a barrel and you knew it."

"I didn't think of it that way, Larry, and now I feel bad." We stopped next to my car.

"Don't feel bad, just get the hell out with the goods and drop me a postcard." He pointed a hook at me. "Repeat the five steps for the cell phone."

"Turn on the phone, make sure there are no messages that will vibrate the phone. Insert the trigger. Insert the battery. Attach the gator clips, hope the cap doesn't burn. Insert cap into the charge and place under seat and get away from the car."

"If you blow yourself up, or injure any innocent bystanders, I'm really gonna feel like a dirtbag for helping you."

I gave him a hug. "Wait for that postcard."

As I drove up the gravel driveway, Larry, Marianna, and the shotgun were in my rearview mirror exactly as I had seen them when I arrived.

Tito's watch. Two o'clock: time to call Vugovic and get the show on the road. I raced along the interstate back toward the city.

THIRTY-FIVE

EUROPEAN ORGANIZED CRIME TASK FORCE
MEETING MINUTES
1500 EDT MONDAY AUGUST 9, 2010

ATTENDANCE: LOG ATTACHED

Re: Kurac gem theft ring—recent developments re: G. Underwood

1. Agent Hurtado of forensics reported that Dell laptop (Vostro 1000) recovered from the Screen Man van contained mostly invoicing, accounting, and scheduling software commonly used by small businesses (see handout for complete list of hard drive contents). Browser history had been deleted, but cached data revealed searches on the residence (phone

number, occupant identity and bio, Google Earth) of 11M at the Grand Excelsior belonging to T. Raykovic, the residence that G. Underwood burgled. Word documents limited to a handful of short poems, many of which had been deleted but were cached. Also included was an incomplete letter to an aunt in California dated in 2009 that included only the header and no text.

2. Intel Profiler Agent Laurenta noted that the poems were not included in the handout and asked that a copy be provided for circulation.

3. EOCTF Agents Brown and Acosta apprised superiors on contact with G. Underwood for exchange at Grand Central Terminal with Kurac. See transcript. Cooperation agreed in exchange for immediate medical attention for T. Elwell and probation for both. Time of exchange contingent on call from G. Underwood to Vugovic. Agents in place at station under cover and await alert and instruction of exchange location. Assuming exchange will be requested as one-on-one and that Kurac will pepper station with their people to apprehend G. Underwood and recover the cash/bond payment (ten million dollars). Agents in field equipped with lethal and non-lethal (Tasers) weapons to subdue Vugovic and G. Underwood and any Kurac operatives necessary or possible and to avoid any possible collateral damage to bystanders. Coordination with National Guard and NYPD initiated. Grand Central effectively netted for capture.

4. Intel Profiler Agent Laurenta provided input on G. Underwood M.O. Based on previous observations and meeting

from same morning, Intel Profiler warned against contact with G. Underwood, as multilayered subterfuge not yet apparent but should not be discounted. Agent Laurenta repeated that it should be anticipated that G. Underwood will use the Kurac and the FBI at cross-purposes to help effect his escape. As before, if it is suspected that G. Underwood is aware of the Justice Department involvement, he will likely attempt to enact a "cascade" in which each pursuer eliminates or paralyzes the other until there is only one pursuer.

5. Agents Kim and Bola of Intel Surveillance section reported data mining of Social Security records indicate that G. Underwood #842-00-1010 DOB August 23, 1971, Clifton, New Jersey is registered as deceased as of August 2005. Death certificate indicates accidental death. G. Underwood was a window cleaner who fell twenty stories to his death in downtown Manhattan. The identity of G. Underwood therefore is in question.

6. EOCTF Supervisor Palmer asked why this information was not available previously on August 9, 2010.

7. Agents Kim and Bola of Intel Surveillance section reported that the Social Security data center servers were down for Sunday maintenance.

8. EOCTF Supervisor Palmer asked EOCTF Agents Brown and Acosta if a fingerprint check was run on G. Underwood from his apartment.

9. Agents Brown and Acosta confirmed that they had no reason to believe G. Underwood was not G. Underwood.

DNA hair samples were collected and sent to lab August 8th, results not expected for at least a week from the NSA.

10. EOCTF Supervisor Palmer instructed Agents Brown and Acosta to gather the fingerprint check immediately on "G. Underwood" from his apartment. In addition, requested Intel Profiler's assessment of G. Underwood's actual identity.

11. Intel Profiler Agent Laurenta suggested that G. Underwood could still be the actual G. Underwood "ghosting" through identity theft.

12. Agents Kim and Bola of Intel Surveillance section reported surveillance subsystems targeting Nee Fat Tong have been successful in cell phone intercepts with the help of Tse Mo Shin, 22, male, Chinese national, illegal alien, who turned informer. Agent Kang of intel surveillance, his handler, obtained his cell phone number and service provider and subscripts of all numbers he calls leading to matrix of Nee Fat Tong cell phones. All phones being monitored for G. Underwood transmission.

13. EOCTF Supervisor Palmer initiated discussion of G. Underwood's options. He can exchange with the Kurac or he can exchange with Nee Fat Tong. With the Kurac he obtains FBI blanket medical for T. Elwell and safety for both. With the Nee Fat Tong he obtains ten million dollars and possible escape. Which is his most likely course of action?

14. Intel Profiler Agent Laurenta suggested that G. Underwood had engineered the double exchange option as a way of dividing his enemies' forces. FBI was lured into making contact with him so that he could use them to intercept

the Kurac and make way for his exchange with the Nee Fat Tong. T. Elwell has been used as false indicator of his motivation and likely dead or already out of the state/country. Reference made to Intel Profiler's memorandum of August 9th regarding the psychological profile of G. Underwood. Agents should recognize that G. Underwood is emotionally unstable and prone to PTSD relapse at any time. This could manifest itself in uncharacteristically violent behavior. G. Underwood is also highly resistant to authority figures. This combination could prove dangerous when he is apprehended.

15. EOCTF Agents Brown and Acosta suggested that the FBI obtains goals either way. If G. Underwood does not show at Grand Central Terminal, surveillance and informer with Nee Fat Tong will afford an intercept if he attempts to exchange with them.

16. EOCTF Supervisor Palmer advised extreme caution at Grand Central Terminal to ensure that the Kurac are not apprehended prematurely and that gunplay in a transportation hub is avoided at all cost. Intercepts indicate the Kurac have obtained fully automatic weapons from the New Jersey Russian syndicate. Coordinate with NYPD.

17. Agents Kim and Bola of Intel Surveillance section reported intercepts coming through currently in real time from G. Underwood to Vugovic, stand by for speaker phone:

TRANSCRIPT OF SPEAKER PHONE

- YES?
- IT'S UNDERWOOD.
- SO LET'S DO THIS, UNDERWOOD.

- FOUR O'CLOCK. IN THE BANANA REPUBLIC, EN-TRANCE ON 42ND STREET. JUST YOU AND YOUR BRIEFCASE, TWO MILLION CASH IN HUNDREDS, STANDARD 10K BUNDLES IN STANDARD ISSUE MUS-TARD BANDS. THE REST: EIGHT MILLION IN GUAT BONDS. I'LL MEET YOU AT THE RETURNS DESK. THERE ARE COPS RIGHT OUTSIDE THAT LOCATION ON 42ND STREET ALL THE TIME, SO DON'T TRY ANY-THING CUTE. AND REMEMBER, THERE ARE A LOT OF INNOCENT BYSTANDERS AROUND THERE.
- NOBODY IS INNOCENT.
- FOUR O'CLOCK.

END

18. EOCTF Supervisor Palmer advised agents to ping and in-tercept G. Underwood's cell phone. Deploys Grand Cen-tral intercept, reminding agents to advise all operatives of extreme caution and no preemptive action. Next meeting scheduled for Tuesday August 10, 2010, time: 900 EDT.

******************MEETING ADJOURNED*******************

THIRTY-SIX

DCSNet 6000 Warrant Database
Transcript Cell Phone Track and Trace
Peerless IP Network / Redhook Translation
Target: Dragan Spikic
Date: Monday, August 9, 2010
Time: 1532–1533 EDT

SPIKIC: TALK TO ME, VUGO.

VUGOVIC: UNDERWOOD CALLED. HE IS AFRAID OF THE CHINESE
NOW AND WANTS TO HURRY TO ESCAPE TO SAVE THE LIFE
OF HIS WOMAN. HE ASKED THAT I MEET HIM AT THE GRAND
CENTRAL BANANA REPUBLIC WITH THE TEN MILLION DOL-
LARS, ALONE.

SPIKIC: WHAT TEN MILLION DOLLARS?

VUGOVIC: WE'VE PUT A LITTLE SURPRISE IN THE BRIEFCASE IN-STEAD OF THE TEN MILLION DOLLARS. WE WILL APPREHEND HIM AND THE GEMS AND THEN DISEMBOWEL HIM WITH POWER TOOLS.

SPIKIC: SEE, I TOLD YOU, HE IS A COMMON THIEF, A STUPID CROOK.

VUGOVIC: IS IT SET WITH THE ISRAELIS TOMORROW?

SPIKIC: YES. MAKE SURE THERE ARE NONE OF THIS WORM'S GUTS ON THE GEMS. I WANT THEM TO LOOK NICE FOR THE JEWS. CALL ME WHEN YOU HAVE THEM. BUT YOU MUST HAVE THEM TONIGHT OR WE HAVE SERIOUS PROBLEMS.

VUGOVIC: PROBLEMS?

SPIKIC: I HAVE A BOSS, TOO.

VUGOVIC: HE MUST UNDERSTAND—

SPIKIC: WHAT MUST HE UNDERSTAND EXCEPT WE HAVE FAILED AND ARE WEAK?

VUGOVIC: WE ARE DOING ALL WE CAN. THERE IS ONLY SO MUCH THAT—

SPIKIC: YOU HAVE TO ANSWER FOR FAILURE; I HAVE TO ANSWER FOR FAILURE. DO YOU UNDERSTAND ME?

VUGOVIC: AS YOU SAY.

END

THIRTY-SEVEN

I STOPPED IN FORT Lee, just before the George Washington Bridge, and parked behind Tip Top Gym. That was my other gym, another place where I kept a change of clothes and a toiletry kit and could stash sparks. In my locker I had a can of tennis balls. I emptied it, filled it with water, and slid in the incendiary grenade. Common practice is to store them in water just in case the canister develops a leak. The phosphorus inside bursts into flame anytime it comes into contact with oxygen. I didn't like the idea of driving around with that thing in the trunk or carrying it around. A healthy respect for explosives is healthy, as Larry used to say.

Phoning was getting too dangerous—every time I turned on the phone I had to expect that my location was being mapped by somebody unfriendly. Or worse: listened to. I knew that it was difficult to monitor calls on prepaid phones, but that didn't mean it was impossible. I couldn't risk letting anybody know my next move. So instead of calling Doc I just drove to Queens through afternoon traffic thick with trucks.

I looked at Tito's watch: 4:00. I would have loved to have been able to sit across 42nd Street at the outdoor café with a beer and watch the shit storm at Banana Republic, but I needed to take advantage of the FBI and the Kurac being distracted at the same time.

Parked on Union Street, I opened the car trunk. My new two-tone fly-fishing duffel and matching dual-rod case made me smile. Imagine me, fly fishing? Imagine me out of this mess zooming across the Bahamian shallows through mangrove channels, emerging into the expanse of blue bays and crystal-clear flats? I wanted to inhale that crisp ocean air and have it blow through my hair, making it thick with salt.

Zipping open the handsome duffel, I pulled out fly-fishing clothes, snapping off a jillion tags in the process. I changed in the back seat. The solid blue shirt and khaki pants looked like tropical safari gear, very lightweight and vented, with huge pockets, which was good because I had wads of cash I wanted to keep close. The legs zipped off so you could make shorts, kind of like convertible pants. Bright white running shoes went on my feet. I used some Pepsi to slick back my white hair, and put on a fresh pair of cheap CVS shades with amber lenses. A regular fashion plate.

I slid the cigar box out from under the seat and armed the explosive in exactly the way I had been instructed and slid it under the seat again. I put Phone #3's number into the speed dial of Phone #2.

At the corner I dumped my CVS shirt, cargo pants, and straw trilby into a trash can and turned the corner toward Main Street. I didn't see anybody unusual standing around the entrance to East

Trading Jewelers, so I walked in. There was an Asian woman at the counter—a slim one this time, with long hair.

"Hi, I need to see Doc. She's expecting me."

"She not here."

"Call her. It's very important, and I know she wants to see me immediately. My name is Gill. I'll be at the Burger King."

One thing about fast food places is that they are crowded at all hours, especially on Main Street, which has a jillion buses and subways. The sidewalks are always packed with people like it was Coney Island on the Fourth of July.

There were so many Asians milling around on the sidewalk that it was impossible to tell if the Tong had Doc's place staked out. My hunch was that Doc wanted this deal to actually go through and may have talked sense into the Hong Kong friends, who in turn would probably not stake out her place but wait for a call.

I sat in the corner of the Burger King, away from the windows, and waited. In five minutes Doc came through the doors in a tan pantsuit.

"You want a burger or something?"

"That's okay, Doc, I try not to eat this stuff."

She squeezed between rows of students and old-timers to my table and sat across from me.

"Gill, I apologize for last night, and so do the Hong Kong friends. The guy driving the Hummer, Tse Mo Shin, was the same one you bounced around at the motel, and he was pissed off."

"Yeah, well, it doesn't exactly make me trust you guys more or anything."

"The volleyball had the paper and the tickets inside, didn't it?"

"That's the only reason I'm here."

"How is Trudy?"

"Hanging in there, thanks to the voodoo stuff from Mr. Zim."

"Good to hear. You know, the Kurac would have filled the volleyball with scorpions. You dyed your hair—has that helped stay clear of the Kurac? I don't like you with white hair. You look like a punk."

I didn't like the way Doc was being so chit-chatty. It made me feel like we were being listened to, that she was wired and trying to tell the Hong Kong friends that I had changed my look.

"So, Doc, can we go ahead and do this thing, no screwing around?"

"There's the Kurac and then there's the FBI. After that chase last night, the cops—"

"Did the Hummer and train smash into each other?"

"Thankfully, no, but the cops grabbed the three men inside the Hummer, and tried to turn one of our guys, Shin, into an informant for the FBI. He's been passing only the information we want to go back to the Fed."

"Yes, I got wind the FBI are snooping around. But you don't have to worry about them or the Kurac for a few hours, as long as Shin doesn't flip for real."

"How do you mean?"

"I mean right now the Kurac and the FBI think I'm handing over the sparks at Grand Central Station. They're otherwise occupied. We don't have a lot of time, though. I'm not sure how long that will keep those guys tied up. Can your Hong Kong friends deliver right now so we can get this over with? I'm beat."

She pulled out a cell phone. "You should have called. I could already have it arranged."

"Your friends knew we were doing this today; they should have the cash and bonds ready. Using my phone has become too dangerous—and if I were you I'd be careful with your phone. The FBI have the Kurac totally wired, know everything they say, and I've got to believe they can ping and intercept anything you say when you call your friends."

"These phones we use are protected." Doc pushed a speed dial number and listened. "They are Taiwanese. All calls go overseas first and are encrypted."

"Maybe the Kurac think that their phones are protected, too. You know that the FBI can actually turn on the microphone on some phones even when they're turned off? I'd say as little as possible. Send one guy with the money in even packets. You, me, and him will go get the sparks and then part ways. Nice and easy."

Doc began speaking into the phone in Chinese.

"Doc, in English, so I know what you're saying."

She put a hand over the phone. "They don't speak English, Gill."

"Well, don't fuck me over, Doc, or we're all liable to end up in the hospital, or worse. I mean it, I have fail-safes in place, tell them that. They mess around and everybody loses. They play it straight, we all win. Tell them that."

She spoke rapidly into the phone, shielding her mouth, eyes darting toward the front of the restaurant. After a few moments she snapped the phone shut.

"They'll be here in a few minutes."

"They?"

"I meant 'they' in the sense that the Hong Kong friends are sending someone over with the cash."

"You verify the sparks, I verify the cash."

"Exactly. Where are we going to get the sparks?"

"You'll know when we get there."

"You have to tell us when we get in the car anyway, so we can know where to go. You tell me, I'm sitting here with you: how are they going to know until they get here?"

"Cute, Doc, but you could be wired."

"Gill, you're paranoid."

"Paranoid and still alive. I have respect enough for your friends to know that they will pull anything they can to hold onto that cash. Don't look insulted—I have no doubt you'd like to see this deal go through no matter what. Their motives are their own. And if they wanted you to wear a wire, you'd do it, you wouldn't have a choice."

"You sure you don't want a burger or something while we wait?"

"I'd rather go around the corner for string beans with minced pork."

"We could do that."

"But I'm not exactly hungry at the moment."

"You don't look so good, Gill."

"I know, I look like Billy Idol."

"The stress of this situation is taking a toll."

"Under the white hair there are a few gray ones creeping in as we speak, Doc. The only thing I can do about it is exactly nothing except to stay focused and keep moving forward. Let's wait out front."

We waded through the other patrons and out the door, standing in front of the Burger King plate-glass windows. I matched a

Winston and scanned the masses, but it was impossible to tell if any scouts had been deployed to trail us. I had to assume they had.

Then I saw him. It was China Boss, the one from the Plaza hallway with black-framed yellow sunglasses, damaged complexion, and oversized sport coat. In his hand was a small red suitcase.

How big a pile is two million dollars? I'd spent some time thinking about that, playing with the wad of cash I had. The math was made a little easier having fifty thousand in hundreds on me, which was about two inches thick. So I was estimating that a million in one stack of hundreds would be forty inches tall, Divide that into four stacks bunched together, and the pile would be about five or six inches wide by a foot long by ten inches high. China Boss's little red suitcase could easily hold two million, plus the bearer bonds. Might also hold a Tech 9 and bad intentions.

I stomped out my smoke as China Boss came to a stop in front of us, his eyes trained on mine. He mumbled in Chinese to Doc.

"What did he say, Doc?"

"He said you look tired."

"Tired of people telling me I look tired. Let's go, I have a car. He drives."

China Boss took the driver's seat, Doc riding shotgun, me in back with the suitcase.

"Doc, I want you to reach under the driver's seat. Take out what you find."

A moment later Doc was holding the cigar box, her brow knit.

"Open it."

She did, and both her and China Boss recoiled.

I held up Phone #2.

"Any cute stuff and the deal is over with a wave of my thumb. Tell him, Doc."

Doc rattled off some Chinese.

"Close it and hand it to me."

I took it from Doc and set it on the seat next to me.

"I'm going to count the money now and make sure we're not taking a trip for no reason. Doc, tell him that, and tell him to not even think about pulling one of his guns. It won't work."

While Doc translated to China Boss, I zipped open the little red suitcase. Sure enough, a dense pack of stacked hundreds with mustard bands: ten thousand dollars each. Since I had the cell phone in one hand, I had to feel through the cash for Monopoly money one-handed. Random stacks were pure green and random bills from those packs all had the security stripe. From my belly bag I pulled the currency marker and checked out random bills. There was a manila envelope under the money, and it contained the rest of the haul: eight million in Guat bonds in two hundred thousand dollar denominations.

A movie I saw in the hospital came to mind, one of those spaghetti Westerns. Clint Eastwood was in it, and in the end there was a three-way showdown in a cemetery over a treasure buried in a grave. Clint was the only one who knew the name on the grave, and he wrote the name of the grave on the bottom of a rock. The survivor of the shootout would turn over the rock and be rich, while presumably the other two would be dead. But Clint had an advantage. Only he knew one of his opponent's guns was unloaded, and only he knew that he hadn't written anything on the bottom of the rock. Why would he? If he didn't win the shootout, why let his enemy have the treasure?

"Doc, tell him it all looks good, and if he just plays it straight and easy, we'll both have what we want with nobody getting killed." I stuffed four bundles of cash and ten of the Guat bonds from the suitcase in the belly bag for pocket money. You never knew in a situation like that when you might have to make a run for it. "He can drive now. Toward the Grand Central Parkway, heading west."

"Airport?"

"No guessing."

While China Boss took a few turns toward College Point Boulevard, I reached into the cigar box and pulled the trigger out of the cell phone. It scared the hell out of me that some chucklehead might dial a wrong number, or that AT&T would send a text message trying to sell me crap I didn't want. The odds were long, but that's the kind of thing that happens in an operation. The unexpected.

THIRTY-EIGHT

EUROPEAN ORGANIZED CRIME TASK FORCE
MEMORANDUM
1630 EDT MONDAY AUGUST 9, 2010

TO: EOCTF SUPERVISOR PALMER
FROM: EOCTF AGENTS BROWN AND ACOSTA
RE: G. UNDERWOOD/KURAC EXCHANGE, GRAND CENTRAL
TERMINAL

Details of the exchange: With the cooperation of New York City police and managers of the Banana Republic at Grand Central, EOCTF Agents Cox and Farnsworth were stationed inside the Banana Republic posing as return desk employees with two members of the New York City organized crime task force concealed in the changing room nearby and two others posing as customers. Surveillance cameras were installed to cover the interior of the store. EOCTF Agents Brown and Acosta were stationed outside the Banana Republic and witnessed two known Kurac operatives identified as Moti Rulov and Hig Junopic enter the Grand Central Banana Republic at approximately 4:00 p.m. Rulov carried a brown briefcase. At the returns desk, Rulov and Junopic inquired whether a friend had been waiting for them. Before EOCTF Agent Cox could reply, a slender unidentified man in a bicycle helmet entered the store carrying a gift bag and announced he had a delivery for "Vugovic." Rulov and Junopic approached the man and asked if he was Gill Underwood. He answered that he was a messenger and asked if Rulov was Vugovic. Rulov said he was and took receipt of the gift bag. The messenger asked for a signature. While Junopic signed the messenger's receipt, Rulov examined the contents of the gift bag and tossed it aside. They departed the Banana Republic at approximately 4:05 p.m., EOCTF Agents Brown and Acosta tracking them back to the lobby of the Plaza Hotel, where they were witnessed meeting with Loj Vugovic briefly before all departing and walking east on East 58th Street. Along the way the brown briefcase was deposited in a trash receptacle. New York City Organized Crime Task Force were alerted to isolate and retrieve the briefcase. Vugovic, Junopic, and Rulov stopped into the Old Stand Pub on Second Avenue and met three other Kurac. They emerged from the bar and departed in three Audi sedans parked on Second Avenue. EOCTF agents and New York City Organized Crime Task Force members detained and questioned the messenger, Thomas Forini, of Chelsea Messengers. The gift bag contents were examined and identified as a set of double old-fashioned glasses purchased from CVS. The package was retained for forensics to examine. EOCTF agents and New York City Organized Crime Task Force members returned with Thomas Forini to Chelsea Messengers to interview staff and review security video.

Interim conclusions: The false exchange may have been a diversion for an actual exchange taking place elsewhere, possibly with the Nee Fat Tong. The Kurac possibly sensed the exchange was false, and in any case did not bring the agreed fee in cash and Guat bonds, but instead a brown briefcase (recovered by the NYPD) was found to contain a large pit viper, the exact type as yet unknown. Agents Kim and Bola of Intel Surveillance section report they have lost touch with Tse Mo Shin, 22, male, Chinese national, illegal alien, who turned informer. Surveillance subsystems targeting Nee Fat Tong cell phones no longer functional. Surveillance section suggests the informer may have been uncovered.

Suggested course of action: 1) Contact G. Underwood by phone and attempt to coerce his cooperation, possibly with the assistance of an FBI tactical negotiator. 2) Intel surveillance section needs to re-establish data mining of Nee Fat Tong to determine if an exchange has taken place with Gill Underwood.

THIRTY-NINE

China Boss's eyes were constantly on me in the rearview mirror as the Toyota bolted down the Van Wyck Expressway.

I was both nervous and tired. My mind kept wandering as the world zipped by outside. For some reason I found myself remembering the day Phil Greene fell. We were on a scaffold thirty-seven floors up cleaning windows on an office building. He was an ex-con, one who'd actually held onto a job and left crime behind. When I'd applied for the job the boss tossed my resume back at me, said I had no experience and he wasn't in the business of training window cleaners. Phil was in the shop at the time and overheard. He approached and asked me what my last job was. I told him, and I told him I'd been in the hospital after being wounded. Greene stepped up to his boss and said he'd train me. The boss agreed, but said he wouldn't cut Phil any slack on his quotas, either. So I went to work with Phil, and he literally showed me the ropes, the locking and loading of the scaffolds, the safety harness procedures.

"Accidents happen when you don't respect the odds," Phil used to say. The odds caught up with him when he unhooked briefly to adjust a roller bearing on the underside of the scaffold. He didn't realize there was a kink in the cable that untwisted suddenly and dropped his side of the scaffold two feet. I fell to my side, dangling from my hitch, and when I got my feet under me Phil was gone.

By the time I got to him there were already police there and an ambulance arriving. I pushed through the crowd, but a cop grabbed me by the arm.

"Not so fast," he said, jerking me back.

"I'm his partner."

"Name?"

"Phil Greene."

He let me go and I knelt next to Phil. Dead. His head was shattered, but still together more or less. The rest of him looked crumpled. The cop and his partner came up behind me.

"Phil: what happened?"

I turned and told them about the twist in the cable.

"Who is he, Phil?"

I blinked.

"That's Gill Underwood."

They misunderstood me. I could have corrected them. But I didn't. Opportunities to change up my identity didn't come along that often, and this one was a gift. Phil was single, similar age and build as me, no family.

Here was Phil, a criminal who'd gone straight, done well for himself, and in an instant all that adds up to is a shattered corpse. How long before I was a schmuck like Phil face down on the pavement? All for what? No better time to embrace my inner jewel thief.

I knelt back down and slid out Phil's wallet. With my back to the cops, I wiped the blood off Phil's wallet onto my own wallet, and handed my Gill Underwood wallet to the cop. The EMT guys nudged me out of the way and I never saw Phil again. I handed in his resignation, and obviously passed on the funeral that our boss paid for. It was closed casket so nobody was the wiser.

"Here? Hello?"

Doc was waving a hand in front of my face.

"Yes, here. Turn here. Short-term parking."

We entered the short-term parking garage at JFK, each of us searching our surrounding carefully. We were probably all looking for the same thing: China friends or Kurac or both. I didn't see any. My guess was that China Boss's people would be there soon enough, but that I had a window of opportunity to make the exchange and slip out before they arrived. I could only hope the failed exchange at the Banana Republic had the Kurac a furlong behind and wouldn't place.

"Go to the top floor of the garage. Doc? I'm going to ask one last time: please make this go smoothly. All kinds of really bad stuff could happen here, or we could all walk away rich. Let's not have anybody get greedy."

Doc gave me a wink and a nod.

I checked Phone #3 and no calls had come in that might make it vibrate. I re-seated the trigger.

"Park over there," I held Phone #3 up where my pals could see my thumb hanging over the speed dial. "Park next to the stairs." There were almost no vehicles in that back part of the garage, just a beat-up pickup truck catty corner to us at the stairway. I guessed it might belong to an employee, free parking, but out of the prime spots near the airport entrance. I looked at Tito's watch; it was going on five thirty. Perhaps that employee worked an odd shift and wouldn't happen to stumble upon our exchange.

China Boss turned off the car, keys in the ignition, and looked at me and stared at the phone in the mirror.

"I'm getting out, you two stay in."

I opened my door.

China Boss opened his and skipped ten feet away, a silver automatic pistol in his hand. A black suppressor the size of a stick of dynamite was fixed to the end of the barrel.

I glanced at my phone. It had timed out the speed dial feature. China Boss must have seen that in the mirror.

Doc was out of her side of the car, her head jerking back and forth between me and China Boss. "Gill, don't do anything stupid! Let me talk to him!"

China Boss barked at me, cruel teeth flashing, and fired a shot into the passenger window of the car, the suppressor doing little to silence the blast of the pistol. Safety glass rained like a cascade of rice onto the garage floor, the thwack of the shot echoing through the other levels of the garage.

I put my hands up. "Tell him I have no weapon, Doc."

Doc came around the front of the Toyota, the Chinese coming out of her rapid fire.

China Boss snarled.

Doc gulped. "Take us to the sparks, Gill. Show us where they are."

I nodded toward the stairwell, and China Boss motioned us both with the gun barrel. We all slowly stepped in that direction, with Doc going through the door first.

The landing was a little cramped for all of us, so China Boss stood in the doorway, his foot propping the door open.

"It's in the fire hose box, Doc. In back."

Doc's trembling hands fumbled with the door to the box, got it open, then she struggled to move the hose, first one way, then the other.

China Boss barked at her and she barked back. The hose jerked loose and swung out. The black plastic wrench box fell out of the cubby onto the floor.

We all hesitated.

"That's it, Doc. The sparks are in that box."

She picked the box up and struggled with the clasps. I stepped forward to help, but China Boss objected with a swing of his gun barrel. It caught me on the shoulder instead of behind the ear, and I wheeled away from Doc and against the stair railing.

Doc made a complaining sound, and China Boss came back with a slithery remark that made Doc stop and spit at him.

China Boss leveled the gun in front of me and the barrel popped like a nail gun: a bullet thwacked into Doc's throat, high where the base of the tongue would be. She dropped the box, mouth agape and red, eyes filled with rage. China Boss fired again into her forehead, and it was like a red party favor burst out the back of her skull. She jerked left, then right, blinking rapidly, but still standing. I don't know what she did next because my fist was tight on that black suppressor.

There's only one way to disarm someone holding a pistol: brutally and by the barrel. When you grab a pistol by the barrel you have a lot of leverage to peel it out of the attacker's hand. Force it up and relentlessly toward the attacker's head, with everything you've got because you may not have anything at all if you don't. Keep your center of gravity and head low, surge upward. True, this also tends to force the attacker to grip the gun harder, and to sometimes squeeze off a shot or two into the air. All good. Fewer bullets in the gun is a good thing. Also, there's a decent chance that any given automatic will jam if the ejector side of the gun is obstructed or turned upward. The suppressor had lengthened the gun barrel, to my advantage. More leverage.

For good measure, it never hurts to kick your assailant in the nuts. I missed, but a sharp blow to the shin was almost as good.

China Boss reeled back against the stairwell wall and out of the doorway, his eyes wild behind the yellow sunglasses. I was bigger, heavier, and he tried to twist farther to the side. The door to the stairwell slammed shut just as a shot from the gun burst off into the ceiling. Another thing about suppressors: they don't get as hot as the barrel, so I was able to maintain my grip. He tried jerking the other way, from under me, but that rolled the barrel under his right ear. I heaved, jamming him into the corner, and the pistol went off again, splattering the corner behind the door with blood and probably his ear canals. After a violent twitch, he went limp immediately, air groaning out of his lungs.

I stepped back, my vision swimming, adrenaline frothing my brain.

There's an animal rage you have when engaged in hand-to-hand combat that isn't easy to shake off. You're in kill mode, all switches turned toward brutality. I began kicking dead China Boss, cursing him, then pulled away and crouched at the railing, eyes shut, trying to restore normal breathing. As my heart rate came down I felt sick, my stomach knotting up and trying to crawl into my chest. Killing someone wasn't exactly routine for me. I'd only done it twice, both after the squad was killed and before I was rescued. Both of those guys were smaller, too, but they had AK-47s, which was actually better because it was harder for them to turn the barrel on me at close quarters. They both smelled really bad, and the one kept spitting on me for some reason. One begged for mercy. But once I started to kill it made it easier to keep doing so no matter what. I didn't regret having done it—like China Boss, each of them was trying to kill me. Yet I hated how I felt afterward. Aside from the nausea, there's a feeling something like the day after you get drunk at a party and embarrass yourself. You don't remember everything that happened, just flashes of the worst moments, and those stay with you. I had hoped to never do it again. But who was I kidding?

I was lucky China Boss's people weren't there yet or I would have been a dead man because I was so shaky I couldn't have run if I tried.

I opened my eyes and looked down the stairwell. Doc lay flat out on the next landing, lips and fingers twitching. I staggered to my feet and looked through the door's window. People in the distance, but no commotion. How much time had passed from the first shot, I wasn't sure. Could have been only thirty seconds. If anybody had heard it, they couldn't have been sure it wasn't a hammer or nail gun or a door slam.

I unzipped the legs on my pants and put them on my hands like mittens.

The pistol was on the floor behind me. I picked it up by the suppressor. Sure enough, the last shell had jammed in the ejector as that side of the gun was pressed against China Boss's chest when it went off.

Down the stairs, I wrapped Doc's right hand around the pistol's blood-misted handle, unscrewed the suppressor with my prints on it and put it in my pocket. I lifted the pistol by the trigger guard and the back of my index finger, went up the steps, and placed it at the top landing. I checked to make sure I didn't step in any blood, which was localized to the wall and pools under both of the dead. For Doc and China Boss to have killed each other, one would have had to survive longer than the other, and I was counting on forensics to show Doc lived longer, so must have had the gun last to have killed China Boss. That's why her prints needed to be on the gun. True, they might find traces of fiberglass from the suppressor in some of the wounds, but I couldn't wipe down the bloody suppressor and not have that look very suspicious. The only clean part of the gun the part closest to the wound? No way.

I put the black plastic wrench under my arm and leaned again against the railing, trying to smooth out my breathing. Voices.

Carefully, I peered out at the car.

China friends, five of them. They were examining the Toyota's broken glass, peering into the car, at my money case and at the cigar box. I turned on Phone #2 and found the speed dial. How I hated to lose that money. Then again, I could take all five hoods out, leave a pile of burned money, and let the police draw their own conclusions about what happened between the car and the stairwell, not to mention the brand-new fishing tackle in the trunk. Probably take them weeks of head scratching even with the FBI involved. A nice explosion would give me a diversion to dash down the stairs and slip away. I did still have a hundred and fifty million dollars in sparks under my arm, and a million in Guat bonds, plus maybe five inches in hundreds.

Bad people and bad luck don't always cancel each other out, but it's nice when they do. Three Audis came squealing around the corner of the parking garage. The Chinese took notice, and a couple of them looked toward where I was in the stairwell, maybe thinking about running. Of course there was no way to lock the door and I didn't have anything to wedge it shut with.

It didn't matter, because there wasn't any time to do much of anything: the Kurac pointed their machine guns out the Audi windows and raked the Chinese. Slugs wumped into the metal door next to me and shattered the wired glass.

Just a little bit closer.

I should have been running at that point.

Then again, if there was a chance to take out a bunch of those Serbs, and Vugovic, it was worth it to press my luck and have them out of circulation. That was mission critical.

There was the sound of shell casings tinkling on concrete and the squeal of breaks.

One Mississippi, two Mississippi...

Car doors opened.

I jockeyed my eye at the edge of the shattered door glass, moving to erase the blur of broken glass with a clear view.

The Chinese were splayed around on the ground next to the Toyota.

225

Audis behind them, doors open, the Kurac approached the splayed, bloody Chinese. Vugovic swaggered from the far side of the nearest Audi, chin out and clearly pleased with his handiwork.

I pressed the redial, and rolled away from the door glass.

One Mississippi, two Mississippi …

A pressure wave hit my body.

The explosion: *FWOOMP—BOOM.*

A burst of shredded metal and windshield slammed the door, the glass window cracking, a billowing cloud of smoke rampaging through the garage.

I didn't take another look.

Leaping whole flights of stairs I hit the ground floor, the shockwave of the explosion still vibrating in my body, my ears still ringing.

I looked through the wired door glass into the first-floor parking lot and saw red flashing lights race into the parking lot entrance. I had to wait long enough for the cops to get past me and upstairs but not so long that they locked down the garage or possibly even the entire airport.

First things first.

I used my pant legs to quickly wipe myself down. No doubt there was blood on me somewhere, but I had to make sure there was nothing obvious. I even took off my shirt and checked the back. I was clean, except for the white running shoes, which were speckled with blood.

Wiping down the suppressor I wrapped it in one pant leg with Phone #2 and beat it against the cinder brick wall, just to make sure the phone was completely dead, and because I was still angry at the phone for timing out on me. I don't like technology making bad decisions—that's what humans are supposed to do.

Through the glass I could see a street drain close by, so I opened the door.

A ginger-toned black guy—the kind with red hair and freckles—ran right into me: "Whoa!"

I blurted: "Some bad shit up there, man!"

"What happened? I heard this huge … what happened?"

His jumpsuit had "Gunny" scripted over the breast pocket. His cologne was the faint smell of vodka. Not sure why people think vodka has no smell and they can get away with drinking it on the job.

"Must have been a car bomb! I was just coming down from the second level when there was this BOOM on an upper level …"

"And I just started my shift! Shit! My truck! I gotta see."

He raced past me into the stairwell, headed up.

Gunny was in for a nasty surprise.

The pant legs with the phone and suppressor went into that drain, and I went toward the parking lot exit, black plastic box in hand, the air filled with sirens and the acrid smell of oxidized nitrates from the explosives. There were a lot more cars at that lower level, and businesspeople with roller luggage trotted nervously toward their cars. Nobody except me knew what happened, of course, but it was in the air, people just knew something really bad went down.

I jogged across the access road and curved back toward where the taxi stands were at arrivals. From the distance I could already see cops locking down the roads.

A Hertz jitney rattled by and I waved it down. The driver didn't want to stop but I stood in the road so she had no choice.

"Thanks for stopping." I smiled as she opened the door.

"Not supposed to pick nobody up from out here."

"Something crazy happened, an explosion. They wouldn't let me go to the bus stop. I need to get my rental." I clambered up into the bus. There were a lot of people with big, scared eyes. They were dwarfed by walls of multicolored luggage.

I sat in the last open seat, surrounded by what looked like a cheerleading squad or church group: the girls were all various shades of blond with very white, straight teeth—the girl-next-door. Next to me was the girls' chaperone, a mid-forties woman in stretch pants, blue eyeliner, and an orange pageboy. She whispered: "Did you see what happened?"

The entire bus leaned in to hear.

I whispered back: "I just heard the explosion, and saw flames coming out of the parking garage. Probably a car bomb, I dunno. I just want to get out of here, you know, before something else happens."

There was a collective blond gasp.

Pageboy scowled. "Fucking Muslims!"

Maybe they weren't from a church group. I hoped not.

IN ALL BATTLE, THE DIRECT METHOD MAY BE USED FOR WAGING WAR, BUT INDIRECT TACTICS WILL BE NEEDED IN ORDER TO ENSURE VICTORY.

INDIRECT TACTICS, CAREFULLY APPLIED, ARE INEXHAUSTIBLE AS HEAVEN AND EARTH, UNENDING AS THE FLOW OF RIVERS AND STREAMS; LIKE THE SUN AND MOON, THEY END BUT TO BEGIN ANEW; LIKE THE FOUR SEASONS, THEY DEPART TO RETURN AGAIN.

THERE ARE FIVE MUSICAL NOTES, YET THE COMBINATIONS OF THESE FIVE RESULT IN MORE MELODIES THAN CAN EVER BE HEARD.

THERE ARE FIVE PRIMARY COLORS (BLUE, YELLOW, RED, WHITE, AND BLACK), YET IN COMBINATION THEY RESULT IN MORE HUES THAN CAN EVER BE SEEN.

THERE ARE FIVE CARDINAL TASTES (SOUR, ACRID, SALT, SWEET, BITTER), YET COMBINATIONS OF THEM RESULT IN MORE FLAVORS THAN CAN EVER BE TASTED.

IN BATTLE, THERE ARE TWO METHODS OF ATTACK—THE DIRECT AND THE INDIRECT; YET THESE TWO IN COMBINATION RESULT IN AN ENDLESS SERIES OF MANEUVERS.

—*Sun Tzu*, The Art of War

FORTY

EUROPEAN ORGANIZED CRIME TASK FORCE
MEMORANDUM
1830 EDT MONDAY AUGUST 9, 2010

TO: EOCTF SUPERVISOR PALMER
FROM: AGENTS KIM AND BOLA, INTEL SURVEILLANCE
SECTION

Re: G. Underwood investigation—ghosting

1. Surveillance subsystems targeting Nee Fat Tong cell phone intercepts were restored at approximately 1600 EDT. Transcripts reveal Nee Fat Tong aware that Kurac made bail at Hudson County court for Tong operative Shui Fu Wing at

approximately 1000 EDT with the object of using him as an informer.

2. Ping and intercept G. Underwood's cell phone detected locations variously. 1505 EDT Flushing, New York, traveling, destination JFK airport, ending 1623 EDT.

3. G. Underwood DNA hair samples were collected and sent to NSA lab August 8th, results not expected for at least seven to ten days. Print check on "G. Underwood" from his apartment match US Navy file for G. Underwood #842-00-1010 DOB August 23, 1971, Clifton, New Jersey. Death certificate of August 2005 reports accidental death from fall of twenty stories. Y3 SPT Subsystem data mining of comparative information suggests identity of person who fell to death was Phillip Greene, SS# 181-11-9898 DOB March 3, 1970, a fellow employee of G. Underwood, and that G. Underwood likely co-opted Greene's identity at the time of death. G. Underwood licensed his business "The Screen Man" using Phillip Greene's Social Security number and to file taxes and to obtain a driver's license and passport. G. Underwood continued to use his actual identity socially.

4. Homeland Security advised to add G. Underwood and Phillip Greene to No Fly List, apprehend and detain.

FORTY-ONE

VORTEX 5 SATELLITE

LOCATION: THE CAUCUS RESTAURANT, 401 9TH STREET NW
WASHINGTON, DC 20004
DATE: MONDAY, AUGUST 9, 2010
TIME: 1936 EDT
DEPUTY DIR. EOCTF SUPERVISOR PALMER (SP)
DEFENSE INTEL. AGENCY DIR. LEE (DL)

SP: Bill, good seeing you. Glad you could meet me on short notice like this.

DL: Anytime you're buying, I'm here for you.

WAITER: Can I get you gentlemen something from the bar?

SP: Yes, a sidecar for me.

DL: Ketel One martini, up, dry, dirty, twist.

WAITER: Very well. Do you want to see menus?

SP: Later. Maybe.

WAITER: Very well. I'll be back shortly with your cocktails.

DL: So, Tom, how you liking EOCTF?

SP: To be honest I think I preferred being a liaison at DIA. It was easier, I'll tell you that. I wasn't working all these crazy hours, weekends, all that. Delores is not a happy camper. She's basically raising our girls herself.

DL: Well, it's a rung to better places maybe. Think of it that way.

SP: How about yourself?

DL: Can't complain. It's not hectic, and the SIGINT programs make data collection so much easier. We're buried under data, though.

SP: I hear the NSA has programs that do the analysis as well as the collection.

DL: Hm, yes, well, that scares me not just a little. Pretty soon you have a machine making the calls, dispatching covert Tile 50 teams to assassinate despots.

SP: Hasn't stopped 381 from doing the same. Soon as they find Bin Laden, he's a dead man.

DL: I'm not so sure machines can make the distinction between enemy combatants and a senator on the IC trying to cut their budget.

SP: Just the same, is there anybody who doesn't think 381 doesn't still do X50 covert ops?

DL: Tom, you're getting paranoid.

WAITER: Here you go.

DL: Thanks.

SP: Thank you very much.

WAITER: You're very welcome, and I'll stop back in a bit to see if you want menus.

SP: Cautious, not paranoid.

DL: If they were targeting a satellite at this table, you don't think that the CIA could figure out that when you say "381" you mean them? And frankly, even I don't really believe they do those X50 covert ops, not after they got caught.

SP: You've been in this business a lot longer than me. Don't you ever just sort of get a sense that 381 is somehow monitoring what we do? Maybe not all the time, but sometimes? And have you ever had a project that had some odd details that make you think 381 was somehow involved and just slipped out just before you got there?

DL: The case you told me about, the Serb gem-theft ring?

SP: That's the one.

DL: As I recall, night before you were going to spring the trap, the Serbs had the gems stolen from them?

SP: Except now it turns out this thief is ghosting, and he's ex-Navy intel.

DL: Hm, yes, that does sound a little spooky. Whopper of a coincidence he stole the gems when he did.

SP: And this thief worked out of a Cuban mob over in New Jersey.

DL: Spookier still. All this and the Serbs.

SP: Why are the Serbs spooky?

DL: Bosnian conflict. The CIA was a little slow to report atrocities they collected intel on. They had egg on their face when it leaked.

SP: Not sure how that could be connected to a gem-theft ring. I have little doubt these Serbs have blood on their hands from the conflict, especially the older ones, but what would the connection with 381 be?

DL: [laugh] Didn't you just recount the feeling you get when you're on a project and it feels like the CIA has somehow already been there? I can't tell you why the CIA would want to steal these gems and ruin your party, but as you say this is spooky from enough angles to warrant looking into.

SP: Your sources see deep enough into the data pool for this?

DL: Deep enough.

WAITER: Gentlemen, another drink, or are you ready for menus?

DL: I'd better go, Tom. My marriage needs me.

SP: Just the check. Thanks, Bill. Call you tomorrow?

DL: Tomorrow. Be well.

END

FORTY-TWO

THE BATON-TWIRLING SQUAD FROM Minnesota was nice enough to give me a ride in their van to Jersey City on their way to Montclair for a jamboree or something. I told them Hertz lost my reservation, and Cheryl, the girls' coach with the blue eye shadow and orange hair, offered to help me out. It was a short ride made long by Cheryl's chatty prying. She wanted to know who I was and what I did and where I'd been. My lack of sleep was impairing my ability to fictionalize, and Cheryl was pushing my brain to the absolute limits. I started with the story that I had just returned from visiting my aunt in Florida. That made the rental car complicated, so I just said my car was in the shop, and I needed a car for a few days.

"Don't you have any friends who you could borrow a car from?"

"Not at the moment."

"Don't you have any family?"

"I do, but they need their cars."

"What's wrong with your car?"

"Um, the brakes."

"That's a one-day job, they should give you your car back."

"The brakes are special order, we're waiting for parts."

"What kind of car?"

"A, uh, Maserati."

"You drive a Maserati?"

"Yes, I drive a Maserati."

"That doesn't sound very sensible for an everyday car. You should buy another car."

"I don't want to carry double insurance."

"What's your insurance company?"

"Allstate."

"Have you tried Geico?"

"Yes. I tried Geico."

"How much was that a month?"

And on and on and on. I felt like just saying:

"Look, Cheryl, I'm a jewel thief, and in this box is a hundred and fifty million dollars in sparks, and I went to the airport to detonate a car bomb and blow up a Chinese tong and a Serbian smuggling ring. But first I made a man shoot himself in the head."

Imagine how many questions THAT would have created.

My brain throbbed from the weight of all the lies I'd packed into forty minutes as I began to walk north and away from the Holland Tunnel's entrance. Tito's watch told me it was 7:11.

Twenty minutes later I was at my gym in Hoboken, the one where I'd stashed the sparks in the tennis balls. I opened my locker; stuffed my belly bag, sparks, and clothes under the track-suit and on top of the tennis racket; and tromped to the showers.

The hot water jetting onto my skull helped ease the brain throb and relax my neck, which was rock hard from the tension of the exchange and killing. It was hard to believe it went down like that. Doc getting popped in the neck and head was gruesome, and I liked her; I thought she was on the up and up even if her friends weren't. Reliving the struggle with China Boss made me feel brutal and mean and want to go back to kicking a dead man, so I tried to pretend I saw it in a movie.

Worse was reliving my clumsiness right at the most critical moment. I should have just gotten out of the car and not announced that my companions should stay in the car. In fact, I should have told them to get out with me. China Boss had to believe that my plan was probably to detonate the car and kill them once I was a safe distance from the car. And why not? That way I could walk with the ten million and the Britany-Swindol sparks. At the same time, China Boss saw my phone had timed out and that my threat to detonate was empty. Believing that my intentions were not to follow through with the exchange, his decision to turn the tables was well calculated. I should have checked the phone periodically to make sure the speed dial was locked in and ready, but more importantly I failed to adequately know my enemy. Understanding the enemy's perspective and interests was critical.

I went from the shower to the whirlpool and from there to the sauna. I think I slept a little in both places, or passed out.

Laid out on my back on the wood bench in the sauna, I was jolted awake by two men in towels who sat across from me.

The bald and bearded one said: "The TV is saying it wasn't terrorists."

"Then who?" The other had a beak-like nose. "Who else would blow up a car at the airport?"

"I'm only saying what they are saying. What about Timothy McVeigh?"

"Who?"

"Guy who blew up that building in Ohio."

"Oklahoma bomber?"

"Oklahoma, Ohio, Iowa, whatever. That's the guy. He was a white guy, just pissed off about paying taxes."

"Yeah, yeah. He blew up the IRS or some shit. That makes sense."

"Maybe this makes sense, too, an angry employee. The bomb went off at a remote part of the garage. And they have a picture of a guy they're looking for, you see that?"

"Yeah, yeah. Looked like Billy Idol. A Muslim can dye his hair."

They glanced at me and my white hair. I said:

"Hey, I have an alibi."

They laughed, and Bald Bearded said: "Maybe you better choose a new hair color, amigo. Every cop out there is looking for a guy like you with white hair."

"You're shitting me. Really?"

"Yeah, yeah," Beak Nose said.

I made an effort at a convincing laugh, and gestured at Bald Bearded. "I guess maybe I better shave my head."

"Don't knock it 'til you tried it," he winked.

"I always wanted to try it, and now I have my chance. I go out there like this and everybody will be calling the cops every which way."

"Yeah, yeah."

I pulled my towel over my face and lay back down. So, the FBI figured they'd just haul me in the good old-fashioned way. Not a bad move on their part. Since I stiffed them at Grand Central and instead blew up a car at JFK, I guessed they were done playing games and issued a composite, maybe a security still. It would follow that Gill Underwood would be on the No Fly List at that point, and it was likely Phil Greene was on there, too. I still had the Michael Thomas passport I got from the Chinese, and that's the name that was on my ticket for Nassau. How would the FBI know about the new identity? It seemed farfetched that any of the captured Chinese would say much of anything that might implicate themselves in the exchange, much less provide details on my passport, if they even knew any. Showing my face at LaGuardia the next morning might be hairy. My options beyond that would be to drive, to take a bus, or to take a train. Cars make a lot of sense for versatility, but fugitives always seem to get pulled over by troopers or fingered by motel managers. Greyhound? I'd sooner have gone to prison than take a long-haul bus filled with Axe body spray, Hardee's wrappers, and quiet desperation. Trains were nice. Big seats. I could sleep.

As much as I would have liked to come in out of the cold with Tim in the Bahamas, that was seeming like a low-percentage play. Could I really see myself going back to the fly shop and saying: "I lost all the stuff you sold me yesterday. Hit me again."

My next move? Obvious. Shave my head with the razor in my toiletry kit, put on the tracksuit and old Pumas. That outfit was so common in New Jersey that it was practically a uniform. Trenton should have named the striped tracksuit the official state fashion. Bald and in a tracksuit, I would blend with the populace well enough.

Then what? Was my part done, had I really killed Vugovic and his goons, possibly even the dirtbag who shot Trudy? Probably. They were all standing close enough to the car that they were at least severely injured. Vugovic was a few paces behind his men. He might have survived, but he'd be in the hospital for sure and I had to imagine the FBI would hang onto him and charge him with conspiracy and smuggling. There might be some other stray Kurac goons around but nobody to tell them what to do. Yet Vugovic's boss was still at large, and I knew that was the real mission. No doubt Spikic didn't want to dirty his hands and run me down himself, especially if he was in hiding from The Hague. Then again, with a hundred and fifty million at stake, he might well, especially if encouraged. That was the point, and had been all along, That was the mission that nobody told me, the mission I was expected to figure out.

Two down, one to go: the FBI. Even if they managed to get their hands on me I wouldn't be sliced and diced like if the Kurac bagged me. Just the same, the FBI wouldn't pay me for the sparks and I would be prison-bound. A poor result, all in all. The only way to get out from under the Bureau was to give them what they wanted: the sparks and me. Or let them think they got what they wanted. That's where the incendiary grenade could come in handy. Maybe.

Traveling with the Britany-Swindol sparks wasn't a good idea. I didn't dare try to take them past customs. The idea of just letting them go, of dropping them at a police station, was a disservice to Trudy, even if it might take some of the heat off. So far I'd only squeezed one million forty thousand dollars out of them. True: handing them over to the FBI had the potential to buy me some leniency should they catch me. I was probably dreaming if I thought handing over the sparks would inspire the FBI to turn a blind eye to my escape, that they wouldn't try to hunt me down in the Bahamas. Especially after the car explosion at JFK. They may not have known I caused it, but it would make them pissed off enough not to be in a forgiving mood.

I took the towel off my face and sat up.

I waved at Bald Bearded and Beak Nose. "See you guys."

"Yeah," they said in unison.

In a bathroom stall I did the first pass of going bald with a small scissors. The second pass was with a razor in front of a mirror, both times trying to avoid witnesses. Plucking my eyebrows softened the look of my eyes. I shaped up my stubble so that it resembled a beard and mustache.

Billy Idol was gone, and I looked radically different. Fortunately, I had slicked back my hair for the Mike Thomas passport photo, so I was still a close enough match for the passport photo, if not my Phil Greene driver's license. The beard and mustache would have to go when I traveled, to help match the photo.

The freaky part about seeing your head naked for the first time is that there are contours you never knew were there. There were dents and dings, too, and I could only account for one or two; the rest were mysteries. Clearly my head wasn't meant to be bald. I never knew it before but I didn't have a very attractive scalp.

Dressed in the official New Jersey state uniform, I looked at myself in the mirror. My own mother wouldn't have known me. Trudy would have laughed her ass off, and I smiled imagining her reaction. Then I gulped, my eyes watering. Those scumbags had to shoot her, didn't they? I looked away from the mirror. I couldn't allow self-pity and regret to interfere. I had to earn that luxury by making the operation a success.

Back in a bathroom stall, I took everything out of my pants and my belly bag. Time to do inventory and condense and lighten my load. No need for those tickets to Iceland, or for Trudy's passport, though I tore out the picture and saved that. It was the only picture I had of her, and I wanted to remember. Needed to remember. I had about six inches in cash totaling a hundred and sixteen thousand dollars. The five Guatemalan bearer bonds stayed, folded in quarters—I hoped they were good, but it would be idiotic to toss a possible million-plus. If they were genuine there'd be eight-and-a-half percent interest when they matured, eighty-five thousand dollars. My Phil Greene passport and license were worthless and a liability. Better to have no ID than that one. From now on I had to be Mike Thomas. The credit cards: way too hot to use now. Pack of gum: still could come in handy, if nothing else to keep my breath fresh. Airline tickets to Nassau: too early to toss those. I wanted to be on that flight in the morning in the worst way. Yet I knew a train to Canada would be much safer.

Next I had to get rid of the socket wrench box that held the sparks. Laying the gems out flat inside the tennis racket cover might work. So I placed the socket wrench box on my knees and opened it.

The socket wrench box had toilet paper in it.

And nothing else.

Empty. The sparks were gone.

The spinning planet ground to a screeching halt, my brain buzzing, ears thrumming, eyes swimming with the vision of tissue paper and nothing else.

On the street daytime was fading, and the cooler August night on my bald head made me shiver at first. I matched a Winston and walked north and found a bar and grill where there was a spot at the bar in front of the TV. My order was coffee, a salad, and a steak. I wanted bourbon. Instead, I asked the barmaid to switch the TV to 12, the New Jersey news channel, and I stared blankly at the talking heads.

Empty.

When? How? Who? It was crazy. And yet it simplified my life not having the sparks on me. They'd been a curse the last two days, a magnet for trouble and near death. Now that part of my predicament was null and void. There was nothing left to leverage for cash, nothing to negotiate with. Did that mean the mission was scrubbed, that I was basically free to go? Who was I kidding.

My brain whipped back to the haunting questions: When? How? Who? There's a point where you're so stunned that you can hardly try to answer questions; all you can do is repeat the questions.

At the top of the hour and halfway through my Caesar salad, a news break came on about the JFK car bombing.

The FBI and NYPD had decided to shape it up for the media as a drug deal gone bad between rival gangs, with one trying to double cross the other. Close enough. Eleven dead, two critically injured. Then they put up my picture, one taken from an airport security camera. It was me in zip-off shorts, blue shirt, and white hair exiting the garage after the explosion, crossing the access road. Fuzzy and distant, they put next to that picture my Phil Greene driver's license photo. They'd Photoshopped Phil's hair white. I snuck a look around me at the other bar patrons, the top of my naked head hot. Nobody was staring at me, even though I felt they should be with my picture on the TV. The newscasters said the police were looking for the man in the picture, who may be traveling under the name Gill or Phil or an alias and may have gotten a ride from JFK to Jersey City. Cheryl, the girls' coach from Minnesota, must have seen my picture on the news and fingered me. Poor cops. I could only imagine how long that interview lasted.

Nothing like your picture and name on TV to make you break a sweat. I needed those Britany-Swindol sparks to get me out of this and lure Spikic to the surface. The FBI wouldn't let me slip unless I turned them over, and even then it would be a tight squeeze to avoid capture. Unless they thought I was dead.

Eleven dead: that's the five Chinese, plus the two in the stairwell, plus four out of six Kurac. The math: two Serbs survived. I hardly had to guess if one of them was Vugovic. That bastard had probably survived a jillion tight spots, and would grimly cling to a life of depraved indifference far beyond when—by all rights—he should have been cinders in a corner of hell. He was that type, one of the bad ones that never die, an agent of Satan that has his middle finger before the nose of God. Divine justice? Fucket. Not for Vugovic.

There's a movie where a gunslinger comes to a western town about to be brutalized by approaching outlaws. The gunslinger agrees to help the gutless townspeople organize to fight off the invaders. Only the gunslinger ends up taking advantage of the situation to brutalize and plunder the town himself, because in a former life they had betrayed him when he was their sheriff. He even makes them paint the town red and post a new sign declaring the town's name as Hell. Then the outlaws come anyway and brutalize the town and the gutless people who live there. Of course the gunslinger kills and torments the outlaws, but not before the town is burned to the ground. Off rides the gunslinger from the charred ruins of the town, vanishing into a heat shimmer.

Empty.

Could have been anybody. Maybe someone just nosing around the airport stairwell. Who does that? What were the odds? Slimmer than slim. I played the slim odds and lost. Likely it was an amateur, who will just as likely get caught as soon as he shows one of the hot sparks to a jeweler. I tried to imagine what would have happened in that stairwell had China Boss not shot Doc. Doc would have opened the box and it would have been empty and China Boss may have shot me for trying to rip him off. So in a weird way it was good that the exchange turned sour. Bad for Doc, of course. The whole time she really didn't seem to realize what a dangerous spot she was putting herself in. Guess all she could see were dollar signs. Or maybe blinded by *yuanfen*.

The barmaid was shaking a martini on the other side of the bar; then she opened the shaker and poured the contents into a stemmed glass. I could smell the vodka.

I pushed the remainder of my salad away and sipped my coffee.

Vodka.

Gunny.

Gunny, the maintenance guy at the bottom of the JFK stairwell, smelled like vodka. When I put the sparks in the fire hose cubby there was an almost empty pint of vodka. I assumed it was garbage someone stuffed in there, but it was probably Gunny's stash.

Something told me Gunny's burning concern for his truck may have had something to do with the sparks being under the seat.

Half my steak stayed on the bar, and the rest I didn't taste. I asked the barmaid to call me a cab.

Tito's watch said it was going on nine.

Unless they thought I was dead.

FORTY-THREE

DCSNet 6000 Warrant Database
Transcript Landline Track and Trace
Havana Social Club Jukebox
Peerless IP Network
Target: Roberto Guarrez
Date: Monday, August 9, 2010
Time: 2104–2114 EDT

GUARREZ: CLOSE THE DOOR, MIGUEL. WELL, THIS IS A SURPRISE. A DANGEROUS ONE. YOU SHOULD NOT HAVE COME.

UNDERWOOD: EVERYTHING I DO NOW IS DANGEROUS.

GUARREZ: THAT HAS BECOME OBVIOUS TO THE CHINESE AND THE KURAC. YOU HAVE CHOSEN A GOOD DISGUISE. THEY SAY THERE'S NO BETTER MIRROR THAN THE FACE OF AN OLD FRIEND. I HOPE NOT. YOU DON'T LOOK WELL.

UNDERWOOD: WOULD YOU EXPECT ME TO LOOK WELL?

GUARREZ: HOW IS TRUDY?

UNDERWOOD: BETTER BUT NOT GREAT. IT'S TIME FOR US TO GET OUT OF HERE.

GUARREZ: SO YOU SOLD THE SPARKS TO THE CHINESE?

UNDERWOOD: DIDN'T HAVE A CHANCE. THEY TRIED TO DOUBLE CROSS ME JUST WHEN VUGOVIC AND HIS BOYS SHOWED UP, GUNS BLAZING, AND THE WHOLE THING WENT INTO A TAILSPIN. I DID MANAGE TO UNLOAD A FEW PIECES HERE AND THERE INDIVIDUALLY TO HELP PAY EXPENSES ALONG THE WAY, AT STUPID LOW PRICES. BUT WHAT WAS I SUPPOSED TO DO? ABOUT HALF OF THE BRITANY-SWINDOL SPARKS ARE LEFT.

GUARREZ: I HOPE YOU ARE NOT THINKING THAT I WILL BUY THE REMAINDER. GILL, THOSE SPARKS ARE TOO HOT TO HANDLE NOW. I WOULD ALSO HAVE TO GIVE YOU NEXT TO NOTHING.

UNDERWOOD: I KNOW. THAT'S WHY I NEED TO TAKE THEM AND GET OUT.

GUARREZ: WHICH IS WHAT YOU COULD HAVE DONE TWO DAYS AGO.

UNDERWOOD: POSSIBLY. EXCEPT HERE I KNOW PEOPLE. ON THE OUTSIDE I'LL HAVE TO UNLOAD THEM SLOWLY, STONE BY STONE, WHICH MEANS HOLDING ONTO THE EVIDENCE, MAYBE FOR YEARS. THAT'S BAD PROCEDURE.

GUARREZ: I HOPE YOU ARE NOT THINKING ABOUT TRYING TO FLY OUT OF HERE. EVEN AS YOU ARE.

UNDERWOOD: I NEED A PLAIN JANE, RELIABLE, LATE-MODEL TOYOTA MAYBE, WITH TINTED WINDOWS EVEN BETTER.

GUARREZ: YOU WANT THIS FROM ME?

UNDERWOOD: YOU OWN A COUPLE CAR DEALERSHIPS. I WAS HOPING YOU COULD MAKE A CALL.

GUARREZ: WHY SHOULD I DO THIS?

UNDERWOOD: I CAN PAY YOU, OR BARTER. I STILL HAVE SOME MILITARY-GRADE INCENDIARIES ALONG WITH THE EXPLOSIVES I USED AT THE AIRPORT. I HAD A CACHE OF THE STUFF BURIED UPSTATE. HARD TO COME BY. I WON'T BE NEEDING THEM. WOULD RATHER NOT DRIVE TO MEXICO WITH A TRUNK FULL OF EXPLOSIVES AND TOO DANGEROUS TO LEAVE LYING AROUND.

GUARREZ: I HAVE NO NEED OF EXPLOSIVES, AND DO NOT KNOW ANYONE WHO DOES. BUT I WILL ARRANGE THE CAR. FOR TRUDY'S SAKE.

UNDERWOOD: IS THAT YOUR WAY OF SAYING YOU'RE A ROMANTIC?

GUARREZ: TELL ME WHAT COMPANY YOU KEEP, AND I WILL TELL YOU WHO YOU ARE. THAT'S MY WAY OF SAYING I HOPE YOU SEND ME THAT BLANK POSTCARD. WHEN DO YOU WANT THIS CAR?

UNDERWOOD: LET ME SEE, IT'S NOW … AFTER NINE. HOW ABOUT ONE A.M.?

GUARREZ: [LAUGHS] THEY SAY THERE IS NO SUCH THING AS A SIMPLE FAVOR. I BELIEVE THEY ARE RIGHT.

UNDERWOOD: CAN THEY PARK IT IN A HANDICAP SPACE IN THE BOTTOM-LEVEL GARAGE AT THE EXCELSIOR? AND HANG FUZZY DICE FROM THE MIRROR SO I'LL KNOW WHICH CAR?

GUARREZ: MIGUEL, ARE YOU TAKING THIS DOWN? HE WANTS HIS CAR AT THE BOTTOM LEVEL OF THE EXCELSIOR'S GARAGE. AND HE MUST HAVE FUZZY DICE. ANYTHING ELSE, GILL? A MAP TO THE TREASURE OF THE INCAS, PERHAPS?

UNDERWOOD: NOTHING ELSE EXCEPT THANK YOU. JUST A CAR AT THE BOTTOM-LEVEL GARAGE AT THE EXCELSIOR. NEEDS TO BE THAT LEVEL BECAUSE THAT'S THE WAY WE'RE COMING IN TO GET THE CAR.

GUARREZ: FROM THE CLIFFSIDE?

UNDERWOOD: WE HAVE IT ALL WORKED OUT. RATHER NOT COME IN THE FRONT DOOR. I REALLY APPRECIATE THIS, ROBERTO.

GUARREZ: IF I SAID 'YOU'RE WELCOME' I'D BE A LIAR. IF I SEE YOUR FACE AGAIN I'LL TURN YOU IN TO THE FBI. DOING THEM FAVORS HAS THE POSSIBILITY OF PAYING OFF.

UNDERWOOD: I WOULD EXPECT NOTHING LESS. WHAT WAS IT YOU ONCE TOLD ME, ONE OF YOUR CUBAN SAYINGS? SOME-THING ABOUT NOT OWING MONEY TO A RICH MAN, OR OWING FAVORS TO A POOR ONE?

GUARREZ: [LAUGHS] GO.

[UNINTELLIGIBLE]

[BACKGROUND NOISE]

GUARREZ: YOU HEAR THAT, FBI? YES, YOU IN THE JUKEBOX. I HAVE GIVEN YOU GILL UNDERWOOD AND THE BRITANY-SWINDOL SPARKS LIKE A BOY GIVES A GIRL A FLOWER. IT IS UP TO YOU TO PLUCK THE PETALS. I GAVE YOU VUGOVIC AND THE KURAC, TOO. I AM AN HONEST BUSINESSMAN BUT THESE PEOPLE COME TO ME AS A COMMUNITY LEADER. I DO NOT KNOW WHY THE FBI SEEMS TO THINK OTHERWISE BY PUT-TING LITTLE MICROPHONES IN THIS MACHINE, BUT I HOPE IT DEMONSTRATES I SPEAK THE TRUTH. WE ARE RECORDING THESE CONVERSATIONS AS WELL. SO GO IN PEACE, AND LET THIS SIMPLE CUBAN IMMIGRANT CONTINUE TO LIVE THE AMERICAN DREAM. LET'S GO, MIGUEL.

END

FORTY-FOUR

I WALKED DOWN TO Boulevard East from the Havana Social Club and stood at the parapet. Manhattan glistened on the water. Wakes from ferries and barges drew dark, sparkling streaks on the Hudson's surface. Fishing for the pack of Winstons in my belly bag, I came up with the large pack of gum, the one with Mr. Zim's gum mixed in with the Wrigley's. Looked like I probably wouldn't have to take that way out. I smiled. There was comfort in that deadly gum; I had ready access to that hard edge where worries and heartache begin and end. That gum was the brink that I approached, a horizon of failure that I'd managed to avoid, of the struggle I was determined to win for Trudy.

There were footsteps behind me.

I turned.

Miguel stepped aside, and Roberto came alongside me at the parapet, lighting a cigar.

"Let's hope our fish swallows the bait."

"Did your people have any trouble with Gunny?"

Roberto squinted at the end of his cigar, then scanned Manhattan's mountain of light. "We have the gems."

I put my gum away and found the Winstons. "Our bargain still stands?"

Roberto grinned, eyeing me sidelong. The Clause clearly states that it's everybody for themselves, that honor among thieves is optional.

"I will honor our arrangement, but for my own reasons, and for the mission."

"Which reasons?" I lit a smoke.

"Nobody comes to my town and kills one of my men and escapes. I don't care if the victim was a rat. It's bad for morale. My people have to know that our justice may not be immediate but it comes. Unlike the clumsy Russians, the hot-headed Italians, and these psychotic Kurac, we know how to use time to our advantage, to work with the unfolding events to our purpose. Imagine: when you first came to me after stealing the gems, I could easily have taken them from you. I did not. Why?"

"You let me take all the heat and sort things out so you could waltz in at the end and get the gems anyway." I laughed. "That's beautiful."

Roberto tipped an ash over the parapet, the sparks flittering down into the darkness. "It was a long shot betting on you, Gill. True, I only get half the gems this way, but I get them clean. Had I taken all the gems from you ten of my men would be dead battling the Kurac and the Chinese, maybe more, maybe a car dealership firebombed, and the Feds and local and state police would be all over me."

"Brilliant. But you knew I'd go after Spikic. That was the point."

Roberto just smiled to himself. "You knew the mission when you saw it. I'm sorry about Trudy, Gill."

His eyes told me he knew she was dead.

I looked away. "That … that wasn't part of the mission, was it? Shooting her?"

"Not *my* mission."

I cleared my throat. "Well, I'm happy to have Vugovic out of the picture."

"You had better hope the FBI hold him tight, my friend. The car is ready. It has red fuzzy dice hanging from the rearview mirror and is parked two blocks up on Boulevard East, right-hand side. Miguel?"

Miguel stepped forward and handed me a car key.

"I better get going, Roberto."

"Mind a little advice?"

I took a deep breath and he continued.

"Watch your back. And I don't just mean for Kurac."

I studied his dark eyes, and he mine.

I nodded. "I'll see to it."

I walked north along the parapet and found the car. It was a Toyota, dark green, with almost two hundred thousand on the odometer, half tank of gas. I got in and felt dizzy, my hands trembling, but I drove and the attack passed.

FORTY-FIVE

BENITO'S WAS EMPTY EXCEPT for busboys and the bartender in a red vest. Tito was at the dark-wood bar. It didn't look like he was too far gone, which was both surprising and good. He stood when he saw me.

"Again?"

"Tito, relax."

"You are going to get us both killed!" he hissed, eyes on his surroundings.

"Your wife come home?"

Tito sank onto his barstool, "She is with that Kurac pig." His face burned crimson with rage.

"I have a proposition."

The bartender approached. I said, "Coffee."

Tito said nothing.

"Tito, what if I told you that you could even the score with that guy?"

"I should find them both and kill them, that's what I should do!"

"Shhh! Look, Tito, let's be smart about this. There's another way. But you've got to get a hold of yourself. You've got to go to the Plaza Hotel and tell this guy ... what's his name?"

"Dragan Spikic," he spat.

"Go to Spikic and tell him that I'll give him the Britany-Swindol stuff back for two hundred thousand dollars. The condition is he has to come tonight at one in the morning to the Excelsior upper garage's handicap spot. And he has to bring your wife—Idi, right?"

Tito looked confused. "What is this to me? Why are you tormenting me?"

"Focus, Tito, focus. In this handicap spot will be a car with red fuzzy dice on the rearview mirror and instructions on where to drive to meet me. He has to bring Idi so I know he won't try anything—if he did she might get harmed if there was any rough stuff or double-crosses."

"You're mad! Crazy! He is Kurac, he doesn't care about Idi."

"He doesn't know I know that. But he's got to have her come with him or it's no deal."

"Why do I care about this?"

I leaned in. "You want them dead?"

His jaw muscles flexed but he couldn't get the words out.

"Of course you do. This way that will happen, and you won't take the blame."

"How?"

"It's better you don't know all the details. But if you do as I say they won't see the sun rise."

"Why should I believe you?"

"Why the hell not? Did I have to come to you to help me? No. Have I lied to you? No. Look, I felt bad for all the crap you've had to put up with because of what happened the other night."

"What happened the other night was that you stole from me and ruined my life!" Tito was fumbling for his gun again.

"Tito, shooting me won't change what happened. I didn't do this to you on purpose. You have to think about the future, and about how you're going to move on. Move on without Idi, without a messy divorce and paying her every month to keep that dog in luxury."

He palmed his silver pistol under the bar, pointing it at me. "Or I could just bring you to him."

"What good would that do?"

"It would get me off the hook with the Kurac."

"He's about the last one standing, Tito. When he's gone, your problem is gone. When Idi is gone, your other problem is gone. You'll be a free man."

He squinted. "Why should I trust you? The man who stole my gems and then my cell phone!"

"Let's be fair. The gems were an accident that I couldn't undo, and the cell phone I returned."

"How can I be sure you're not playing me for a fool?"

"Tito, I'm giving you a golden opportunity. Tell him he has to show up with two hundred grand and that Idi has to come with him. They have to come get the car and follow directions on where to meet."

"Two hundred grand." His eyes were far away. "I'd love to have two hundred grand, that would solve other problems."

"Well, you'll never have two hundred grand paying for facials for that dog every week."

He slid the pistol back into his pocket, and a calm came over him as he mumbled to himself.

"Tito, will you do it?"

He seemed to awaken from a dream state: "Yes, I'll go now."

The bartender placed a hot coffee in front of me. "Milk and sugar?"

"This is fine the way it is. Will you call a cab for Tito?"

He nodded, and picked up the phone.

I put a hand on Tito's shoulder. "You got it straight, right? Red fuzzy dice …"

He nodded. "… handicap space in Excelsior upper garage, instructions on the windshield, bring two hundred grand and Idi."

I zipped through half a cup of coffee worrying about Tito, who for him seemed unusually calm.

"Cab." The bartender pointed out the front windows toward a taxi at the curb. I threw a five on the bar and walked Tito out to the car. He was almost smiling: "And you say they won't see sun-up if they follow the instructions?"

"Not if they do what we tell them to."

"What if they don't follow the instructions?"

"Then they will see the sun come up."

Tito slid into the cab, which did a U-turn and sailed south on Boulevard East.

I found my Toyota with the red fuzzy dice and drove to Fort Lee and Tip Top Gym.

THE ART OF WAR INSTRUCTS US TO DEPEND NOT ON THE PROBABILITY OF THE ENEMY'S NOT COMING, BUT ON OUR OWN PREPAREDNESS TO RECEIVE HIM; NOT ON THE POSSIBILITY OF HIS NOT ATTACKING, BUT RATHER THAT WE HAVE MADE OUR POSITION UNASSAILABLE.

—*Sun Tzu*, The Art of War

FORTY-SIX

THE HOT TAMALE WAS under the back seat of the Toyota and set for a twenty-second delay. The handicap spot was near the elevators and a straight shot to the garage exit. The grenade's pin was pulled most of the way out. When Spikic released the hand brake, it would pull fishing line threaded under the carpet that would pull the pin the rest of the way out, starting the timer.

Half the Britany-Swindol take was in the gas tank. When the car went up in flames, the gas tank and fuel would actually protect the gems from being incinerated. It would take awhile before the tank blew, and when it did it would burn at a much lower temperature than the Mark 77 fuel in the grenade, and probably the force of the explosion would force the tank away from the car body. I was counting on the gems being blown out onto the pavement and recoverable.

I was also counting on two bodies being almost completely immolated in the car fire. One male, one female. One me, one Trudy. I had no doubt they might have some way of figuring out the two bodies were not us, eventually, after some pretty serious lab work on what little remained of the bodies. At first, though, they would have to believe it was us, what with the gems and the story Roberto and I fed them through the jukebox.

I had to make sure this all went down the way it was supposed to, so I had to be onsite but out of sight. Across from the Excelsior was a five-story brick apartment building. Slipping the locks on the building's foyer was about as easy as it gets, and at the top of the stairwell the door to the roof was unlocked. I was in position on the roof by eleven thirty, and the car was in the handicap space in the Excelsior garage across the street.

My timing was good. The FBI started to show up at quarter to midnight. A large van with tinted windows and a phony magnetic sign for restaurant supply rolled gently to the curb opposite the Excelsior's driveway. Nobody got out.

Then a fake cable TV truck arrived and parked just north of the driveway at a hydrant.

The black and Hispanic agents I saw at the Plaza strolled arm and arm and sat on a bench at a bus stop. They checked their watches. After ten minutes they stood and strolled into the lobby of the Excelsior and did not come out.

A sedan with tinted windows showed up and parked just south of the driveway at the bus stop.

They had the place pretty well bottled up from all angles by twelve thirty. I'm sure they were hoping to catch us arriving at the lower level.

Was it possible not to smoke a jillion cigarettes waiting for this show to start? This was the culminating moment. My success and my escape depended on them believing at least for a while that I was dead, or at least that someone else had the gems and that most of them were destroyed in the fire.

I smoked and chewed Wrigley's, careful to avoid the two sticks at the end.

"Hey."

I turned.

"Hello."

"Your wife not let you smoke inside either?" My new friend was also in a tracksuit, but he was fat with long black hair and yellow slippers on his feet. "Haven't seen you up here before."

"I'm visiting."

"What floor?" He flashed a huge flame from a lighter at a cigarette.

"First."

"Then how come you came all the way up? You coulda stepped out onto the stoop to smoke." He exhaled a cloud of smoke.

I pointed at a wedge of Manhattan between the Excelsior's towers. "The view."

"Not from around here. If you were, you'd get used to that. Where you from?"

Second time in the same day I had to run into people that ran off at the mouth. I wanted to be left alone with my nervous tension and daydreams about the Bahamas.

"Clifton."

"Oh yeah? I know people from Clifton. You know Peter Dremmer?"

I glanced at the street and saw Tito walking fast toward the Excelsior lobby.

"No, never heard of him."

"What school you go to?"

"Fairleigh Dickinson."

Tito went into the lobby.

"No, I mean high school."

"Clifton High."

"I knew a guy once who went there. What year?"

A yellow cab—the kind they have in Manhattan—pulled up to the curb across the street.

"Um, eighty-nine."

"I went to high school in Weehawken. What are you looking at?"

"Me? Just people. I like to watch people."

Wrapped in a white fur coat, Idi and a runt in a leather trench coat headed from the cab toward the lobby. Spikic was practically dragging her, and I could hear her whining.

My companion pointed at Idi and Spikic. "Heh, look at those two! Just the type that live at the Excelsior."

"Is it fancy over there?"

"Fancy but no class. Lotta foreigners, Russians, that sort of thing, and they throw their money around." He flicked an ash over the edge of the building. "I'm Fabio."

I shook his hand, and it was moist. "I'm Ralph."

"Ralph? Like Ralph Kramden?"

I shook out another smoke.

"Here." Fabio pointed his flame thrower my direction and almost burned off my eyebrows while lighting my cigarette. "So who is it on the first floor? What apartment?"

"Huh?" I was riveted on the garage exit. What was Tito doing there? Sure, he lived there, but he should have had sense to be elsewhere, and with an alibi.

"Who are you visiting, Ralph?"

Three gunshots sounded from across the street, from the garage.

Fabio leaned on the building parapet. "What was that?"

Three more shots.

"I don't know, Fabio. Were those gunshots?"

That idiot: Tito.

Two men in FBI jackets emerged from the sedan and jogged toward the garage entrance.

"Lookit, Ralph. It's like on TV. The FBI!"

Fuzzy dice swaying in the window, the Toyota lurched from the garage, narrowly missing the two agents. It was hard to make Tito out behind the wheel as street light twisted through the car, but his silver pistol flashed, clasped to the steering wheel. Idi was easy to make out in the white fur coat in the passenger side—she was screaming hysterically. He cut the wheel hard and drove across the sidewalk, sideswiping a tree.

The cable TV van zipped forward and blocked Tito's path, so he pulled a squealing U-turn that took him up on the sidewalk directly below me.

I leaned back. I didn't want my eyebrows singed a second time that night.

The fake restaurant supply truck made a U-turn at the same time as Tito and slammed the Toyota's front fender and wheel. The ball joint collapsed and the wheel splayed out sideways. The Toyota came to a stop in the middle of Boulevard East.

Agents from the cable truck were already jogging across the pavement toward the Toyota, guns drawn.

The black and Hispanic agents raced from the Excelsior lobby.

Doors to the fake restaurant truck opened.

One Mississippi, two Mississippi…

It looked like a camera flash went off in the back seat of the Toyota, then a blob of light grew like a balloon and burst into a white hot gas. Fire that hot doesn't look like fire. It almost looks like a plume of glowing, roaring milk.

"Holy bejesus!" Fabio shouted, turning away from the searing white light.

I ducked my head, momentarily blinded. "Dammit, Tito."

"Holy *fucking* bejesus!" Fabio shouted again.

Agents reeled away from the Toyota shielding their eyes. The safety glass vaporized; the tires burst and melted into crackling puddles. The hissing chassis thudded to the pavement and the shriveled driver's door swung open. Tito was a glowing white cinder behind the skeleton of the steering wheel.

I had to give Tito credit. His idea wasn't really a bad one even if it was crazed. Kill Spikic and take the two hundred grand and don't follow the instructions, just take the car and run. The cops would likely think I did it. He had no idea the car was rigged with a hot tamale. I guessed the result was the same, more or less, as long as Spikic was dead. Tito's empty revolver should have taken care of that. First three shots probably dropped him, the next three shots used to finish him off, probably shots at the head.

The bad part of the plan was taking Idi with him. When will men learn that you can't force a woman to love you?

For my purposes, I was glad he had done that. One man and one woman. Me and Trudy.

Fabio had his phone out. "I'm calling 911!"

The black van managed to back away from the Toyota's volcanic roar, the paint on its hood smoking from the heat. Local cops arrived lights flashing and barricaded the street in either direction. Fire engines wailed in the distance.

As the chassis buckled, the trunk popped open and gas from the tank leaked onto the pavement, bursting into flames on its way to the gutters. Local police ran forward with fire extinguishers to put out the flaming fuel. People don't realize that it takes a lot to make a gas tank explode. You can't just fire a bullet into it and make it go off. The fuel itself needs air to burn, so even a flaming leak from the tank will only ignite what leaks out, not the rest of the tank. Fumes in the tank above the fuel have to ignite to blow out the tank, and that takes a lot of heat, but preferably a spark. I've seen car fires on the side of the highway blacken cars whole and the gas tank never goes off, probably because the brunt of the heat produced by the fire rises. The heat from this Mark 77 fire might be different, and the agents and police seemed to realize this and back away from the fireball. Fire engines roared to the scene, positioning themselves at the hydrants.

"Well, Fabio, I'd better get downstairs and make sure people aren't near the windows. If the gas tank goes off…"

POOM! A mushroom cloud of yellow and orange fire rose from the Toyota's trunk.

Fabio's eyes were wide. "Wow!"

I slid past him and into the stairwell.

Downstairs on the sidewalk there was a crowd. They'd spilled out of the apartments to watch the fire. In their shadow I walked north and around the bend. Ambulances blooping their sirens raced past me. I walked down the cliff to River Road to the Port Imperial Ferry terminal. Taxis were always waiting there for ferry passengers, and they stood outside their vehicles looking up at the dimming glow of the Toyota atop the cliff. Flashing red lights from all the emergency vehicles spun on the Excelsior like it was a disco. The incendiary would run out of fuel soon enough unless it caught the asphalt road surface on fire. The fire department's hoses would likely prevent that.

I had a cab stop at an all-night liquor store on the way to the Days Inn in Edgewater. I arranged a wakeup call for five and a cab to the airport for six. Old Crow bottle on the nightstand, I sipped bourbon in front of the TV and watched an old Western. Henry Fonda was a gunslinger trying to retire, but there was some punk pestering him to shoot it out one last time with a hundred men for some reason. I couldn't figure out if it was a comedy or not, and didn't make it to the end.

I didn't dream.

FORTY-SEVEN

VORTEX 5 SATELLITE
LOCATION: OLD EBBITT GRILL, 675 15TH STREET NW
DEPUTY DIR. EOCTF SUPERVISOR PALMER (SP)
DEFENSE INTEL. AGENCY DIR. LEE (DL)
DATE: TUESDAY AUGUST 10, 2010
TIME: 1721 EDT

SP: I hope I'm not single-handedly ruining your marriage, Bill.
    Making you go out for a drink every night after work...

DL: I could get used to this, Tom!

BARTENDER: Gentlemen?

SP: A sidecar for me.

DL: Ketel One martini, up, dry, dirty, twist.

SP: So have we gotten any spookier, or am I just paranoid?

DL: Like a haunted house. Your man Spikic? His real name is Major Zoran Radmatic, the "Butcher of Pov," massacred a couple thousand defenseless Bosniaks in 1995. CIA had pictures. Nobody ever saw them.

SP: How is Spikic's alias not in the Y3 SPT database? We should have been informed. 381 receives our departmental briefings, they know what we're working on.

DL: Why do you think?

BARTENDER: Gentlemen.

SP: Thanks.

DL: Perfect, thanks.

SP: Take it out of here. I'm not sure what to think, Bill. Except maybe the worst.

DL: Word is that the CIA sanctioned the Pov massacres and many others. They even encouraged Radmatic to destroy that village and mow down all the people. Women, old people, children …

SP: Not personally, not verbally …

DL: Verbally.

SP: Why would they do such a thing?

DL: Bosniaks were Islamists. Not all of them from Bosnia.

SP: Mujahideen?

DL: There was a battalion: El Mujahid. Bad guys were in it, al-Qaeda, to include some of the 1993 World Trade plotters, so the thinking went.

SP: But to kill a whole village...

DL: People seem to forget that even before 9/11, and particularly after 1993, al-Qaeda has been on the radar as a serious threat. They wanted as many of them dead as possible. And by "them" I mean not only the Mujahid but their future: their families, the families of those who would support them.

SP: Bartender? Another? Bill, I think I'm going to need a lot more than two drinks to choke this down.

DL: Tom, you have to admit, for the CIA, the genocidal Serbs were a blessing. No U.S. boots on the ground, and people like Radmatic and General Mladic to do the dirty work of wiping out a generation of terrorists. Not as noble as what we did in Afghanistan against the Russians, perhaps, but a means to an end. And the feeling was that the Bosniaks had been warned not to invite the Mujahid to come fight. They knew they were a liability but fought with them anyway. Their mistake.

SP: So now all these years later we have Radmatic posing as Spikic running a global gem-theft syndicate. We're about to grab him. So 381 sends in a man to stop us? What do they care?

DL: I heard what happened last night.

SP: You mean about Spikic? Yes, he's dead. Shot three times in the chest, three in the face.

DL: Imagine if you grabbed Radmatic. Imagine you were set to prosecute him. Do you think he wouldn't try to use what he knows about the CIA's complicity in Bosnian atrocities to save his skin?

SP: So if you're 381, why not just assassinate Radmatic?

DL: My guess is they couldn't find him, or that they were waiting for you to find him for them. When you had pulled him in close, they sent a man in to flush him out into the open. How much were the gems worth?

SP: One hundred fifty million.

DL: One hundred and fifty million is good rat bait. I'm sure they'd just as soon do the same with General Mladic except the Serb military has him tucked away. You can be sure that if he's ever turned over alive it won't be until he's so old and feeble his mind is gone.

SP: Why didn't Milosevic spill the beans? Surely he knew.

DL: You'll note he happened to die while on trial. Perhaps he intended to. People that have the capacity to seriously compromise the CIA have a way of dying at convenient junctures.

SP: So this means that Gill Underwood is a CIA handyman?

DL: Is that your jewel thief? Yes, he was probably a contractor. Maybe the Cubans were running him for the CIA, as a buffer. The CIA has gotten a lot better at keeping their distance, about maintaining plausible deniability. I've heard that with handymen they don't even explicitly tell them what they're supposed to do. They're just supposed to figure it out. In this case I'm sure the target was obvious enough.

SP: But this man Underwood was a career Navy intel officer, injured in action. And then a career jewel thief. What kind of handyman is that?

DL: Fits the profile. CIA often recruits disaffected troops, even at hospitals where they are recovering from PTSD, many lost souls looking for some sort of direction, any direction. Think about it: if you're the CIA, you don't have to pay this Underwood character, you just have to let him steal. There's no money changing hands; you're not even telling him exactly what to do. You just put him in the situation and have him take care of it. No money trail, no communication trail. More often than not they switch out their identities with dead men, so they're ghosts. In this case, you have someone who is skilled at breaking and entering and stealing. Better him than someone with a Langley building pass. If he gets caught by the local flatfoots, so what? If he starts in about a connection to the CIA, who's going to believe a common thief?

SP: Only thing is … the only thing I don't get is that Underwood's woman got shot when he stole the gems. Underwood has been making a lot of noise like she's still alive, but we think she may be dead and that he's using her to make us and the Kurac mis-anticipate his motives. But what bugs me is that she was shot by one of the Kurac five hundred feet away. That's a hell of a shot for a goon. Maybe she wasn't shot? Maybe Underwood wanted us to think she was? Or maybe Underwood shot her?

DL: [laughter] That's hard to say. You can be sure there's some trickery attached to it. Or, just as likely, it was a function of The Clause. You know The Clause?

SP: Not in this context.

DL: Supposedly, there's an unwritten rule in the CIA, and it's called The Clause. It all has to do with protecting the mission, of covering the CIA's trail of witnesses and mistakes, of closing the door and turning out the lights. No matter the cost.

SP: Cost. In money?

DL: [laughter] That, too, I suppose, but I was referring to human lives. The fine print in The Clause is that *everybody* is expendable.

SP: And what about us?

DL: Hm?

SP: You and me. What does 381 do about us? Are we expendable?

DL: I'm sure they think this all went completely over your head, Tom. They're used to thinking the Bureau is comprised of lesser beings.

SP: If they record all calls, then they know I called you.

DL: A subsystem would have to flag a call like that, and why should such a call be flagged?

SP: If they were looking to see if I'd reach out to another source, they might.

DL: Now you're making me want another drink. But I won't, because I'm going to resist your paranoia. You should know by now what happens to snoops, to complainers, to might-be whistle blowers within the intelligence community.

SP: They get promoted, or reassigned.

DL: Precisely. They don't pry out the bent nails in the FBI; they hammer them flat and move on. On that note, I'm driving back to Reston, safe in the knowledge that at the very worst I might be reassigned to Huntsville, Alabama.

SP: Thanks for the history lesson, Bill.

DL: You're not going to follow up on this, are you? Let it go, Tom. There's nothing you can do, especially now that the deed is done.

SP: I don't like being the inferior being.

DL: Perhaps you'll find some solace knowing that in the end, we're all—even the CIA—inferior beings to the NSA.

SP: [laughter] Good night, Bill.

DL: Safe home.

SP: You too.

FORTY-EIGHT

EUROPEAN ORGANIZED CRIME TASK FORCE
MEETING MINUTES
900 EDT WEDNESDAY AUGUST 11, 2010

ATTENDANCE: LOG ATTACHED
RE: KURAC GEM THEFT RING—RECENT DEVELOPMENTS
RE: G. UNDERWOOD

1. EOCTF Agents Brown and Acosta apprised superiors on Monday evening's operations. Grand Central Banana Republic exchange of Britany-Swindol gems a feint by G. Underwood, who attempted the actual exchange with the Nee Fat Tong at JFK airport one hour later. Intel Surveillance

Section was unable to provide adequate data to indicate there was another exchange planned at approximately the same time. The result of the second exchange was a shoot-out between the Kurac and the Nee Fat Tong and car explosion. Intercepts indicate G. Underwood was in possession of military-grade explosives that forensics say were used in the explosion. It is believed G. Underwood used the car explosion to escape. Britany-Swindol gems not recovered at that time. Only two survivors of the car explosion and shootout, both Kurac, both at Queens County Hospital under guard. See attached list of dead and injured. One lookout was arrested and detained, Bobo Dismic, armed with a SIG Sauer P229. He was on the Homeland Security special interrogation list by the CIA and transferred to their authority.

2. Agents Kim and Bola of Intel Surveillance countered the assertion that their section was unable to provide adequate data. The Kurac were pinged after the feint exchange at Grand Central and could have been followed. A cell phone intercept from approximately 1600 EDT was posted indicating jeweler Doc Huang placed a call to Nee Fat Tong underboss Jimmy Kong requesting a meeting in Flushing to "finalize the deal" and also asked if his men were ready to follow and intercede. Had operations checked the posted data at that time they could have acted appropriately. Agent Kim referred to previous meeting in which Intel Profiler warned of a possible feint.

3. Intel Profiler Agent Laurenta confirmed that in previous meeting she had advised of the possibility that G. Underwood

would engineer the double exchange option as a way of dividing his enemy's forces.

4. EOCTF Agents Brown and Acosta apprised superiors that the coordination protocols with NYPD task force and National Guard at Grand Central delayed operations following the feint exchange, to include securing a briefcase discarded by the Kurac that posed a significant danger to the public. Records indicate the posted information was accessed at approximately 1630 and operations team was en route to the airport when reports of JFK car explosion were broadcast. The car explosion overloaded the agency's resources coordinating with counterterrorism forces convinced explosion was terrorist act. Emergency protocols enacted by Homeland Security diverted operations forces to counterterrorism duties. Underwood escaped the failed JFK exchange due to Port Authority police unable to enact their emergency protocols completely and in timely manner.

5. EOCTF Supervisor Palmer advised agents that a review of operations and surveillance procedures would be enacted by internal review section to determine how future operations might function more efficiently and what personnel assignments need to be adjusted.

6. EOCTF Supervisor Palmer requested update on events of Wednesday, August 11th at 100 EDT in Hudson County, New Jersey.

7. EOCTF Agents Brown and Acosta apprised superiors that that morning's operations in Hudson County, New Jersey, successfully recovered a portion of the Britany-Swindol

gems. Intercepts indicated G. Underwood and T. Elwell had arranged with Roberto Guarrez, reputed Cuban syndicate chief, for a car to be delivered for their use in flight to Mexico with the gems. Operations mobilized and were in place well in advance. An attempt was made to intercept the targets before they drove out with the car from a parking garage, but data posted by Intel Surveillance was in error as to the location of the target vehicle—it was on the upper level of the garage, not the lower level.

8. Agents Kim and Bola of Intel Surveillance section countered the assertion that their section was unable to provide accurate data. A review of the records indicate the transcripts were correct regarding what was said between G. Underwood and R. Guarrez regarding the location of the car.

9. EOCTF Agents Brown and Acosta apprised superiors that contingency measures were enacted to seal off all vehicular exits from the building. At approximately 100 EDT gunshots were heard inside the garage on the upper level. Two agents were deployed to investigate, when the target vehicle exited the garage at a high rate of speed almost injuring the two agents. Undercover vehicles boxed in the car and disabled it according to standard procedures. Agents began an approach to the vehicle when an incendiary device ignited within the vehicle before the occupants of the dark car could be identified positively.

10. Agents Kim and Bola of Intel Surveillance referred to their transcripts indicating that G. Underwood intercepts suggest that he had a "trunk full" of military-grade ordinance.

11. EOCTF Agents Brown and Acosta indicated that the immolation function of the ordinance precluded standard field tests, but that observations at the time of ignition suggest male and female occupants in the vehicle, age and identity still unconfirmed, contents of vehicle unconfirmed. An unregistered .38 caliber nickel-plated handgun was recovered from the wreckage. Ballistics confirm that this weapon was discharged just prior to the exit from the garage, where the body of a male victim was located. The victim was identified as Dragan Spikic, suspected leader of a Kurac syndicate trying to exchange stolen Britany-Swindol gems with the Israelis. On his person was a M70 handgun. It is assumed that G. Underwood arranged a last-minute exchange and the deal went bad. Circumstances suggest that G. Underwood shot and killed D. Spikic with the nickel-plated handgun found in the remains of the burned vehicle. The gems recovered were in the fuel tank and thus not destroyed by extreme heat. Presumably they were in the gas tank for the purposes of smuggling them to Mexico.

12. Intel Profile Agent Laurenta suggested that the circumstances may have been carefully engineered by G. Underwood. Of concern is the reason for both the type and use of incendiary ordinance.

13. EOCTF Agents Brown and Acosta indicated that briefings by Intel Profiler Agent Laurenta suggested that G. Underwood was unstable and might act violently. Agents Kim and Bola of Intel Surveillance had posted data suggesting that G. Underwood was in possession of military ordinance of this type and was unable to dispose of it before

his departure. Operations were using available information provided by other departments in accordance with procedure. Suicide is listed under guidelines as possible function of violent behavior prior to capture. Operations enacted standard protocol to apprehend G. Underwood but did not have the opportunity to intercede in his suicide.

14. EOCTF Supervisor Palmer asked why Tito Raykovic's wife was accompanying D. Spikic to an exchange, and if so, what became of her.

15. Agents Kim and Bola of Intel Surveillance section referred to intercepts indicating that she had left her husband after the theft of the Britany-Swindol gems from T. Raykovic and had taken up residence with D. Spikic at the Plaza Hotel. Intercepts with T. Raykovic indicate the couple was estranged.

16. EOCTF Supervisor Palmer rephrased his question as to whether she was at the exchange, specifically, noting that criminals don't commonly bring their girlfriends to exchanges.

17. EOCTF Agents Brown and Acosta indicated that it was possible she was along as insurance that things would not turn violent. I. Raykovic was witnessed entering the building with D. Spikic. The garage surveillance camera system had been sabotaged and did not capture data of the actual encounter with G. Underwood or where I. Raykovic went after the encounter. Other area surveillance data might reveal her escape. Pings on her phone are nonresponsive.

18. Intel Profiler Agent Laurenta suggested the possibility that G. Underwood attempted to coerce D. Spikic and I. Raykovic to drive from the garage in a car rigged to explode with an incendiary and half the gems. The incendiary would make identifying the bodies difficult except that they matched male and female like G. Underwood and T. Elwell. The original intent was to have them drive the car out and make it look like G. Underwood and T. Elwell were dead, and that instead G. Underwood and T. Elwell may have escaped.

19. EOCTF Agents Brown and Acosta posed the question that if G. Underwood did not drive the car out of the garage, then who did, and why?

20. EOCTF Supervisor Palmer tabled the discussion until such time as forensics delivers more information on the car and its occupants. In the meantime the file on G. Underwood will remain inactive and prosecution against the two Kurac by the Justice Department should be initiated once the suspects are deemed medically fit to stand trial or extradited under warrants posted by other countries.

21. EOCTF Agents Brown and Acosta cited an instance in which a prisoner extradited abroad had found European security lacking and managed to escape and return to the U.S. to commit more crimes.

22. Before adjourning the meeting, EOCTF Supervisor Palmer announced that he had accepted a promotion effectively immediately, and that an acting supervisor would soon be installed to head the EOCTF.

******************MEETING ADJOURNED******************

FORTY-NINE

FairfaxAdvance.com
Wednesday, August 11, 2010

Crash Kills Local Man
    by Kerry Wells, Staff Writer
Police responded last night to reports of a vehicle that had gone off
Ridge Road and flipped. The driver, William Lee, was returning to
his home on Laurel Lane in Reston when apparently he lost control. The impact of the crash proved fatal. Investigators confirmed
that he had a single drink with a friend just prior to the accident.
While Mr. Lee was apparently not impaired, police speculate that
he may have fallen asleep at the wheel. Mr. Lee was a career intelligence director with the Defense Intelligence Agency, a Rotarian,
and a longtime resident of Reston. He leaves behind a wife and five
sons.

FIFTY

FISHING FOR BONEFISH IS a little like golf except the holes move. The course is what's called a flat, a vast expanse of ocean often no more than calf deep, or less. The caddy is the guide who tends the tackle, spots the approaching fish, and advises the angler on how to make casts. The cart is the boat that takes the angler from place to place looking for bonefish, poled from a raised rear platform by the guide. Unlike golf, casts are sometimes made from the boat as it drifts mile after mile over the flats. Other times you wade.

The fish themselves are really nothing much to look at. With olive backs, mildly striped mirror-like sides, and white bottoms, they have downturned mouths like a sucker or a carp. Their small-ish eyes are set on either side of a pointy snout. These fish travel in groups, the size depending on the size of the fish. Larger fish the size of a forearm—or larger—travel singly or in groups of three. Smaller fish sometimes school by the thousands.

I had never heard of a flat, and when I saw how big, sunny, and uniform they were, they reminded me of some deserts in the Middle East. The impression was reinforced by headgear anglers wear. Many hats have shrouds or cowls that cover the neck and face. I wore a bandana under my hat and across the lower half of my face. The rest of the outfit was light in both weight and color; the shirts and pants are made of quick-drying materials with a lot of pockets for gear. Flats boots are neoprene tennis shoes with thick soles made specifically for protecting anglers' feet from sharp shells or coral heads.

Some flats are covered in drab turtle grass that looks like camouflage through the rippled water surface. Others are sharp brown coral heads. But mostly the bottoms are clean, almost featureless sand where small crustaceans live on what the tides bring. Of course, the tides also bring bonefish nosing the bottom, eating the shrimp and crabs. The fish shove their noses into the sand and blow to scare up their prey, leaving telltale blowholes in the sand bottom over large areas.

The cycle of life on a flat doesn't stop there. A lemon shark's favorite meal is a bonefish, and so they prowl the flats a little like the coyote after the roadrunner. Bonefish are fast, and when you hook one you have to let them run. Eventually the pull of the line and the bend of the rod slows a bonefish down, and you can play the fish out and land it before letting it go. If a lemon shark is around at that time it will chase down the bonefish and rip it in half. You have to keep an eye out for the sharks when you release bonefish—they'll take them right out of your hand, and possibly take your hand, too. Wading can also attract them because the plumes of sand from your footprints look to sharks like bonefish blowing holes in the bottom.

One of the guides told me that the last thing you want to do is try to run from lemon sharks. The thrashing sounds like bonefish spooking, and the sharks target the commotion. He once saw someone bit on the ankle running from a shark on the flats, and it was lucky there was a boat nearby. The splashing and blood in the water would have drawn sharks from a quarter-mile radius in a matter of seconds. Most are only maybe three or four feet long. If you slap your rod on the water near them they will shoot away. Still, I wouldn't want to be on a flat with a bloody nose. Like any other shark, they smell blood from a distance, and if you have a fish that's bleeding when you release it, that bonefish is lunch.

People are sometimes floored that the bonefish are all released. Yet golfing is not about eating golf balls. True to their name, bonefish are so bony that the meat has to be completely picked through by hand before being made into cakes, and the taste is mild and unremarkable.

The tactics of bonefishing involve the angler or his guide spotting the fish and then determining where the fish are, how many there are, and what direction they are traveling. With some experience, the angler can see the fish once they come within casting range, and he can attempt to cast his shrimp-like fly three or four feet ahead of the lead fish.

I have no doubt that any guide would say the number one mistake anglers make with bonefish is how they hook them. The fish is following the fly, you strip, strip, strip—tug. That little tug should be answered with a long strip to hook the fish. The temptation is to raise the rod to hook the fish, but that doesn't work for some reason. I've had guides explain that it is because of the way the fish's mouth is angled down. I don't get that.

Once the fish is hooked the angler has about two seconds to get ready for the fish to rocket across the flats. At first hooking, the fish runs some tight circles, which is the time when the angler needs to ready his line. Because reels are not used in the retrieve of the fly, there's a lot of loose fly line on the deck of the boat or on the water. When a fish takes and zooms away, that line jumps into the air and races through the rod's guides after the quarry. The angler has to manage how fast the line travels and in what direction so that it doesn't wrap around the reel and halt. When that happens, the fish breaks off. Once the loose line whips through the guides, the angler lowers the rod and lets line peel off the reel. Now the angler is fishing from the reel, which has the capacity to put the brakes on a racing fish by controlling how fast it lets the line roll off the reel.

Then there are those sharks that will follow and seek out bonefish in ankle-deep water. When you see one chasing your fish the guide will usually tell you to lower your rod and let the fish run from the shark. That usually doesn't work as well as snapping the fish off. Either way, the fish is tired and the shark is not and dinner is pretty much served. This doesn't happen every day, but every week or so I'd reel in half a fish. Bernard's Cay had a lot of sharks.

The first time I went out by myself bonefishing, I stepped out into a grassy flat with a large white sand area in the middle that was right next to shore. My plan was to eye the sand for fish coming in off the grass. I was only about ten feet from the beach—the water just topping my boots—scanning the sand, waiting. Out of the corner of my eye I saw movement—three bonefish had come around behind me about a foot from shore. The water was less than six inches deep—*that's* how shallow these fish can go. I froze. They swam by a couple feet from my legs, their eyes considering me, probably figuring I was an ugly piece of driftwood. They wandered away about thirty feet from me into the center of the white sand and began nosing the bottom. I flipped my fly next to them and one slammed it. That was the first fish I caught on my own.

By November, I used guides only a day or two a week. I'd gotten good enough to guide myself without letting the fish sneak up on me. I would bicycle to flats close to the island and wade them. Even with all the clothing and headgear, I was brown as a nut, and my feet were calloused and toes splayed. Full beard. Shaggy brown hair, with a gray streak. I'd gone native.

I had a lot of time by myself to reflect on everything that happened. In the evenings I would return to the lodge, where I had a room. Meals were served and there was a bar where the other anglers who came and went spent their evenings. I did too, sometimes.

A beer at my side, I was in the bar but at the fly-tying table off to one side. This is the setup for tying feathers, fake fur, and plastic fibers onto hooks to imitate the small shrimp and crab that the fish eat. I was working on a new pattern. There were four anglers at the bar swapping stories when the lodge owner came in. Her name was Tim, a handsome brunette with large blue eyes, business-like most of the time, but she knew how to swap stories and jokes with the men. And of course she could be seductive when she wanted to be. I first met her at Portsmouth Naval Medical Center. She was one of the counselors. I got to Portsmouth two months before Trudy was admitted, and Tim and I hit it off. I suppose it wasn't very professional, or discreet. No matter—I didn't really know

Trudy at the hospital, just knew who she was, so it wasn't until later that we bumped into each other in Edgewater and fell in love.

Tim and I were friends first, lovers second. So I thought. I was the one who broke it off when I learned she was also my handler, and that I had been handled. Didn't keep me from doing missions, though, once I got over it, once Phil Greene bought it. Or from coming in from the cold when things got too hot. She may have become a lodge owner and fly instructor, but she was also still a handler. I had no idea how many others she tended.

"Mike, you working on the permit fly again? I saw you wading Turtle Bight again."

"The crabs out there are different near the mangroves than they are out on the flat."

"You see your permit again?"

"I did."

"He refuse your fly again?"

"He did."

Unlike bonefish, a permit is a large, silver, disc-shaped fish with back, flowing fins top and bottom, a large eye, and a forked tail. They like to eat crabs and can be very hard to catch. When they feed on the flats their big forked tail waggles in the air as they nose the bottom.

I looked up from the fly I had just finished. "He showed up on the incoming tide and poked around those outer mangroves, the ones out by themselves. I cast a Merkin crab fly to him again and he turned and gave it a good look before wandering back to the deep water. So I went over to those outer mangroves and chased up some crabs with my foot. They're a little purple, I think as camouflage around the mangrove roots. Gum?"

"Thanks." Tim pulled a stick from the pack. "Give her a go. You might tie in some of that new synthetic material to the next one, the leggy stuff. Permit like that. I'll have the guides stay away from there on the incoming tide until you and that permit work things out."

"Thanks, Tim." Put another hook in the fly-tying vise, and began wrapping thread along the shank with the bobbin.

"So how does San Diego sound? There are lots of apartments and condos with decks there, lots of money and jewelry."

I paused. "West Coast, hm?"

"East Coast is done for you for a long while. We have people in San Diego who can set you up."

I looked over my shoulder at Tim. "Is momma bird kicking me out of the nest?"

She stuck out her lower lip and looked at the ceiling. "I wouldn't say that. But you can't stay indefinitely. You know you have to redeploy sometime."

And if I didn't?

"What's the fly fishing like there?"

"Just so-so. But you have the Pacific at your feet, plenty of places to travel pretty easily from there. Baja, Fiji, Vanuatu. There they go after other fish, bigger ones. And there are plenty of beautiful women there. I know Trudy was special, but you have to put that behind you at some juncture. I don't think you need me to suggest that the next gal in your life should not join you in your missions. You can't say we didn't warn you last time. It isn't in The Clause."

"When were you thinking I should go?"

"I've got your tickets for next week."

"I think I just fell out of the nest. Anything I should know?"

"About what?"

"This seems a little sudden."

"Sometimes the decisions come down that way. There may be a mission coming up there in San Diego, I don't know. Tie your flies, and go get that permit." Tim stroked my cheek and went to the bar to chat up her angler guests.

I finished the fly I was working on, bought a bourbon, and took it to my room. I was asleep a half-hour later.

FIFTY-ONE

THE MORNING BEFORE I was supposed to leave it was sunny with a light breeze. Good conditions. My bags were all packed, my flight left around noon.

One last time I saddled the bicycle and headed out to Turtle Bight—I hadn't seen a permit since tying my purple crab pattern. While wading out to that clump of mangroves, I was reminded of another Western. It was a funny one, about an ambitious, sarcastic gunslinger, played by James Garner, who was passing through a town. Of course, the townspeople hire him to be their sheriff to protect them from a local gang. He throws one of the gang in a jail—a jail with no bars around the holding cell—and manages to scare the inmate into staying put. The rest of the gang begin a series of attempts to break out their comrade but are undone by the gunslinger in inventive ways, like sticking his finger in the end of a pistol. Of course the gang is foiled, and the town is happy, but all along this gunslinger had been warning the townsfolk that he had only taken the sheriff job temporarily because—ultimately—

he was on his way to Australia. It's a better movie than it sounds. I liked that part, though, where he's always telling people that he's on his way to Australia. The commitment to a personal agenda over the expectations of others sat right with me.

Sure enough, as the flats at Turtle Bight flooded with the incoming tide, I saw the dorsal fin of that permit slice the water's surface as he came into the shallows, headed for that mangrove clump with the purple crabs. I put my new crab fly in the air, cast it next to the clump, and then waited for that permit to draw near enough to see it. I knew where he was headed, so why not get the crab cued up and in place before the permit got there? Less chance of spooking the fish.

The permit went to the far side of the clump first, and I lost sight of him. I thought maybe he'd eaten and left when that tail flopped into the air near my fly. I leaned forward and gave the line a small strip.

The tail turned, angled at my fly.

One Mississippi, two Mississippi…

Another small strip.

He followed.

Another small strip.

Tug.

Big strip.

That tail slammed the water and the shallows exploded. The permit shot out toward deep water, my reel screaming as the line peeled off.

On the second run the permit wrapped me on that mangrove and escaped.

I'd rather have landed the fish, but I'd fooled him. I'd figured it out and made it happen.

Reeling up, I headed to shore at the point. Crunching over the beach litter, I turned the corner of the brush.

There was a man in what looked like a mechanic's jumpsuit standing at the water's edge. His back was toward me.

Hair: short and gray.

Neck: pale, a white man.

He stood very straight looking out to sea.

I slowed. "Hello?"

He turned.

One half of his face was badly scarred, the ear gone. He held out his right hand and there was a piece of wrinkled paper in it.

I stopped a few paces away.

"Your gum wrapper." The accent was Eastern European.

It was Vugovic.

The first seconds I don't remember. I know I saw the flash of a knife but I can't picture it. I felt the icy slash across my chest.

My memory clicks in mid-dash down the beach toward the point. My eyes saw blood on my chest. My ears heard him behind me, grunting as he ran. My nose smelled my own perspiration. I veered into the skinny water hoping that would trip him up. He was just strides behind me.

I turned the corner of the point, around a clump of mangrove.

Tim was standing on the beach, in cutoffs and a black bikini top, wide-eyed when she saw me. In one hand she held a spear gun.

I vectored away from her out along a spit of sand into a little less skinny water.

To run in the water like that is hard and I didn't know how long I could keep it up. You have to lift your feet as high as possible to keep from tripping.

Shark: dead ahead, in slightly deeper water, the black form unmistakable.

I was bleeding.

I was splashing.

That dark shape with the fins out to either side changed course and vectored toward my path.

He smelled the blood.

He heard the thrashing.

I began to curve back toward shore but found the water getting deeper. Next to shore was a draw, like a trench with deeper, darker water created by the tides. I tumbled forward and plunged head-first into it. Now I was bleeding and swimming, with a shark nearby. The draw was only twenty feet across. The beach was five feet beyond that.

It was exactly like those dreams when you're being chased but struggle to move, the danger closing in, the desperation at the boiling point. This was a nightmare, but I was not asleep.

Water was up to my armpits, and the muddy bottom clung to my feet. I could only hear my own gasps and splash as I lunged through the draw for that shore.

Dragging myself into the shallow on the far side, I shot a look behind me, expecting to see the jaws of a shark or the flash of Vugovic's knife at my feet.

I didn't.

Vugovic was on the far edge of the draw, knee deep, knife in one hand, the other arm contorted, reaching for his back. He pivoted, and I saw the white shaft of the fish spear just below the shoulder blade where he couldn't quite reach it, his blood mingling in the water with mine.

In the distance beyond him was Tim watching from shore. Her spear gun: empty.

Between them, a dark shape angled through the water and shot toward Vugovic.

The first shark rolled and took Vugovic down by the one knee. He twisted and stabbed the shark in the head with his knife.

Now there was even more blood in the water. Dark shapes vectored in from all sides.

The second shark got him from the other side. It was only a three-footer, but with one swipe it ripped all the muscle from Vugovic's upper arm as he was trying to stand up. He fell back to his knees, head just above the water.

Those flat, depraved eyes locked on mine—not the shark's.

Vugovic's.

He grinned.

He grinned like what was happening to him was nothing.

He grinned like I was too weak to understand that being ripped apart by sharks didn't faze him.

Vugovic grinned because he was superior, and always would be.

The next shark was larger, maybe a five-footer, and it rolled up out of the water and clamped its vice of white teeth onto Vugovic's face with an audible crunch.

The water erupted in blood, arms, legs, and fins as Vugovic was pulled under. More dark shapes vectored in for their share. Vugovic was still fighting even though the big shark had him by the head, its tail whipping back and forth above the water. A large, dark shape approached the draw to my right, and I scrambled the rest of the way onto shore in time to watch the six-footer turn away from me and veer toward Vugovic.

Or what was left of him. Different sharks were fighting over different parts of the body by then, tails lashing the surface of the water.

That Vugovic had managed to find me, that he had escaped the FBI, that this shitbag had tracked me all the way to that cay, that he had been following me for days to know to find me on that remote beach … all just to kill me … it was beyond terrifying. Gum wrapper?

Tim approached.

"Nasty cut you got there, sport."

I just shot her a look of dismay, my breathing all gasps.

"You got sloppy, Gill. You dropped this back there on the beach." She sat next to me and held out the gum wrapper.

I managed to focus on it. My handwriting was on the wrapper, and it was the address of the fly shop in Manhattan. I didn't even remember writing it down. But Vugovic must have found it at the Plaza, in my saddle bag.

"Here, let me help you off with that shirt." Tim ripped the shirt open, backed it off my arms, soaked it in sea water, and rolled it. "Hold this against the cut."

I did as instructed, still trying to get my breath back. "How did you … what were you …"

"Gee, funny thing happened last week. We got word that Vugovic had been released. *By accident.*"

"By accident?"

"Yeah, pretty amazing. Somehow the ICE computers told them he was free to go."

Mouth open, my face contorted. "What?"

"Even stranger, his name didn't register on the No Fly List when he took the flight to Nassau."

"How is all this possible?"

"How is anything possible?" She shrugged. "Our guess is that the NSA subsystem profiled you when the FBI started looking into Gill Underwood and decided that you were a liability to the intelligence community."

"Why would it think that?"

"The odds. The odds were that coming to the notice of the FBI and making yourself a target threatened exposure."

Seemed to me it was the agency that put me in that situation.

"What would someone at the NSA care if a handyman for the CIA is exposed?"

"Not *someone*. The subsystem. It cares because it considers itself the guardian of all U.S. intelligence ops. Things have changed, Gill. Not like it used to be. Same as with us, there has to be a huge disconnect for X50 ops to continue undetected. That's why we don't even tell you what your mission is. We just put you in the situation and you figure it out. If the NSA subsystem operates on its own, there's no paper trail, it covers up for itself and deletes X50 ops as it goes, and what people at the NSA don't know can't hurt them. Plausible deniability inside and out."

"So it can arrange terminations."

"Some say the NSA subsystem can even use OnStar systems to cause fatal car crashes, make it look like people fell asleep at the wheel."

"Linked into every license plate reader, every face-recognition app, every credit card swipe, every phone call, every flight reservation, every Web purchase?"

"Like Google or Amazon, it profiles people on the grid, looks for patterns, then flags people of interest for deeper scrutiny in the subsystem. You're more or less off the grid here, but not enough that the subsystem couldn't track you using facial recognition cameras at the airport to link you to your new name and airline reservations. It probably knows where I am and that you'd come to me. So it eased Vugovic's way here. They have profiles on him, too, and played the odds. It knew the Kurac are relentless."

I removed the shirt and looked at the chest wound. The deepest part was about a quarter-inch deep. I'd need some stitches, butterfly bandages at the very least. The salt water had puckered the wound and made it stop bleeding, for the most part.

"Tim, does this mean the NSA subsystem will continue to hunt me down?"

She bit her lip and examined the horizon. "You'll have to keep an eye out. And so will we."

I studied the blue water, out where the sharks had taken the remainder of their meal, out to deeper water. You could see the flash and flicker of baitfish following the sharks, snapping up shreds of Vugovic.

"Question is: am I now a liability to you guys?"

"You've done good work, this time and before. You got Spikic. We're the good guys, Gill. Would I have saved you from Vugovic if you were a liability? Would we be flying you to San Diego and setting you up there?"

"That's hard to say." I reached into my pocket and came up with the bullet that killed Trudy. Tim looked at it in my outstretched palm. "You know where this came from, don't you?"

Her eyes examined the flat-nosed slug, then met mine. "And?"

"This didn't come from an M70, the kind of guns Serbs smuggle in through diplomatic pouches. Likewise, this is not the kind of ammo the Kurac throw. It's special-ops ammo, the kind for shooting through cars and windshields. While I suppose it could be .40 S&W or 10mm Auto, this seems more like a SIG .357, possibly fired from a P229, the kind of pistol a lot of ops use. To have hit Trudy at that distance the shooter had training, the kind only professionals get. Now, I can't see any reason why the NSA would kill her, or the FBI or even the Secret Service. But I can see why you would. Two reasons.

"First reason was to make sure Spikic was taken out. You knew if it looked like the Kurac killed Trudy I wouldn't stop until I got them. But you guys also live and die by redundancy. So I've also got to believe that once you guys set your sights on Spikic you wouldn't want to risk all your eggs in one basket by having just me chasing him down. You'd have had someone on the inside with the Kurac. Someone who just might have been on a detail with Vugovic's gang.

"Second reason was that next to operational redundancy you guys love economy, you love two birds to drop with one stone. Killing Trudy not only kept me motivated, but it also got her out of the picture. You people didn't like us hooking up to begin with, much less the way the heist of the Iraqi antiquities went down."

"You've been thinking about this the whole time you've been here?"

"The whole time since Trudy was murdered."

Tim sighed and squinted into the distance. "Gill, it wasn't up to me."

I unwrapped a piece of gum and put it in my mouth. "Then who was it up to?"

Tim shook her head at her feet. "You know The Clause, Gill. Trudy witnessed some things in Iraq she shouldn't have. They felt we had to close the door on that."

I held out the pack. "Gum?"

FIFTY-TWO

THERE WAS ONE WESTERN I saw at Portsmouth that had a bed-ridden old man who pays Lee Van Cleef to coerce information from a crook and then kill him. Van Cleef confronts the crook, and the crook hands him his life's savings to kill the old man instead of killing the crook. Lee gets the information, takes the crook's life savings, kills the crook anyway, and returns with the information to his client. The old man is very pleased to pay the balance of his fee for the information and murder. However, just as he told the crook, Van Cleef tells the old man—and for some reason I remember this word for word: "But you know, the pity is, that when I'm paid, I always follow the job through. You know that."

Lee picks up a pillow and uses it as a silencer to shoot the old man in the head.

Ten minutes after Tim took and chewed the end piece of gum, I dragged her body into the shallows and tossed my bloody shirt next to her. The sharks came back. Eagerly.

I went the long way around into the lodge and slipped into my room without anybody seeing my chest wound. I bandaged myself up and went to the airport, where I made my flight out. The little plane banked out over the ocean, the sun blinding me through the window.

Tim was right. It was time to redeploy, but not for anybody except myself. Aside from the fact that she had planted someone with the Kurac to kill Trudy, putting her down was the only way *for me* to close the door and get out. I had little doubt that despite what Tim said I was a liability to her, and thus my time was winding down. Who knows what was really waiting for me in San Diego? My next assignment might be as a decoy that gets caught in the crossfire. It happened before when I was set up in the Gulf. The point was that Tim and the agency had become a liability *to me*.

The Clause works *both* ways.

My ulterior motive to complete the mission was so that Tim would let me come in for a re-deploy. I needed to confirm why Trudy fell victim to The Clause, and to keep from being expendable myself.

Nobody would ever find Tim's body, nobody would know exactly what happened to her, but the organization would connect the dots. True, the NSA subsystem might still come after me, but maybe—just maybe—it would see that I had tidied up after myself and therefore wasn't worth coming after, so long as I went out and stayed out. After all—wasn't it Tim and the agency that created my situation? Weren't they the ones letting X50 ops rise too close to the surface? I had to believe that The Clause was part of the subsystem's logic algorithms.

Well, it didn't matter. You have to take it one adversary at a time. I really had little choice but to put Tim down. Just as with the Chinese friends, the Kurac, and the FBI, it was a matter of eliminating one enemy after the other, playing them at cross-purposes, taking advantage of their weaknesses, until there were none left. There's probably a Western like that. I haven't seen it. I guess I lived it.

I shielded my eyes with my hands. From the plane's window, I could see Turtle Bight a thousand feet below, and make out the sinister silhouettes of a few hopeful sharks gliding the flats.

NOBODY BENEFITS FROM PROLONGED WARFARE. ONLY THOSE THOROUGHLY ACQUAINTED WITH THE EVILS OF WAR CAN THOROUGHLY UNDERSTAND THE PROFITABLE WAY OF WINNING.

—*Sun Tzu,* The Art of War

© JOANNE MURDOCK

ABOUT THE AUTHOR

Originally from Washington D.C., Brian Wiprud is a New York City author of eight previous crime novels. Brian won the 2002 Lefty Award, has been nominated for Barry and Shamus Awards, and in 2011 was nominated for the RT Book Reviews Choice Award for Best Contemporary Mystery. Starred reviews have been bestowed on his novels by *Publishers Weekly*, *Library Journal*, and *Kirkus Reviews*. Brian is also an expert angler widely published in fly-fishing magazines.

His website is www.wiprud.com.